D1153280

This book is to be returned on or before
the last date stamped below.

MIDLOTHIAN DISTRICT LIBRARY

Renewal may be made by personal application, by post
or by telephone.
If this book is lost or damaged a charge will be made.

Midlothian Libraries

901066061 5

Reasonable
Doubts

Reasonable Doubts

JOAN LINGARD

059062

HAMISH HAMILTON
LONDON

First published in Great Britain 1986
by Hamish Hamilton Ltd
Garden House 57–59 Long Acre London WC2E 9JZ

British Library Cataloguing in Publication Data

Lingard, Joan
    Reasonable doubts.
    I. Title
    823'.914[F]   PR6062.I493

ISBN 0-241-11696-1

Phototypeset by *Sunrise Setting*, Torquay, Devon
Printed in Great Britain by
Billing & Sons Ltd., Worcester

For Martin

CONTENTS

PART ONE
Thomas and Claire

Had she ever felt that living was like walking on eggshells? Thomas asked, when he arrived, rucksack on back, breathing a little heavily from having carried his bicycle up three flights of stairs. He was bent over the back wheel trying to secure it with a padlock. 'One false move – Damn!' He had snagged his finger. 'See what I mean? One heavy step, and you're down there in amongst the slippery stuff struggling to try to keep your head in the air. Don't suppose you've ever been ankle-deep in albumen, have you, my lovely Claire?' No, he couldn't believe it. She was too sure-footed.

'You'd better come in,' she said, though she had not expected him and had been engrossed in the case of Millar v. Millar. One marital dispute would have been enough for one evening. For she had known, as soon as she had opened the door, that Thomas had left his wife.

She voiced surprise.

'But, Claire, I've often talked about leaving Sarah.'

'Talked, yes, but I didn't think you'd any intention of doing it.'

He must have had the intention, he maintained, since he had done it. Or could acts be totally unpremeditated? What did learned counsel have to say? 'What about impulse?' He denied that outright. His leaving was no impulse and he had no intention of going back, never, ever, for what was done was done, for better for worse, and he would almost certainly be poorer, if that were possible, which he doubted, but it would be until death did them part, and Claire should stop looking at him as if he were in the dock and she counsel for the prosecution.

'I never prosecute,' she said. 'I always defend.'

'That *is* reassuring.' He smiled. He waited until she said that

3

he had better come in to the warmth and not stand in the hall all night, then he let his pack slide down his body and bump from his hips on to the floor. Her eyes travelled downwards with the rucksack. It looked lumpy and hastily packed. He stripped off his wet anorak letting it lie where it fell and followed her in to the sitting room which glowed with burnished brass and polished wood and velvet-smooth fabrics in warm colours. The curtains were drawn across the long Georgian windows. She saw the room afresh, through his eyes, for he was looking around as if he were seeing it for the first time. He gave a little sigh, perhaps of pleasure, perhaps of relief. Then he went to the fire where he crouched with his chilled hands spread over the top of the flames. You'll burn yourself, Thomas, she almost said, but bit back the words. In her professional life she so often had to state, indeed stress, the evident, that in her private one she took care to try to avoid doing so. She moved the papers she'd been working on and poured him a drink.

But first, she must ask one or two further questions, and he must allow them. She stood by the fireplace looking down at his damp dishevelled head. He owned up at once and raised his eyes to look her straight in the face: yes, he and Sarah had had a row and it was after that that he had walked out, but it was only the last straw, there had to be one, or else the camel's back would bend so far its belly would touch the ground and eventually its entrails drag in the dust. His marriage had been virtually at ground level for years; she knew that herself. He'd only stayed because of his daughter. His beautiful Tasha. He spoke her name mournfully. He looked back into the orange heart of the fire. Claire saw the tightening of the muscles at the back of his neck. Then he struggled and got up, uncurling himself until he reached his full height and took the glass she held out.

'Cheers! It's all common enough isn't it? It's not as if I've done anything unusual.' She must know the statistics for this sort of thing? Whatever they were, they were bound to be bloody depressing and he didn't want to hear them. 'I suppose if I were a bishop or held high office in the land then I might stand out in a special column. But what am I after all? An axed university lecturer whose department no longer exists. Early retirement at forty-five. That was pushing the senior citizen

4

age down a bit far.'

'Now, Thomas!'

'Sorry, sorry!'

He hadn't meant to indulge in self-pity, that most despicable of sins. It was his own stupid fault anyway for having specialised in something no one wanted any more. At least not in Edinburgh. And he was only one of millions all over the world who'd been conned in their youth and who were now in their prime wondering what the hell to do with the rest of their lives.

'One's prime comes earlier these days. *You*, Claire, are in *your* prime.'

'Thomas, what was the row about?'

'You're not easily side-tracked are you? No wonder you shine in the High Court. Like a pure, white light.'

'Don't you remember?'

'It wasn't *that* trivial. It was over those bloody women, if you must know. You couldn't call them trivial, could you? They seem quite considerable when they're sprawled on your settee blocking the floor space with their legs, and their kids are playing druggies and San Francisco cops up and down the stairs and in and out of your bedroom, or what used to be your bedroom. She's got a new one in now, with four frightened children. The husband's an ex-con and prowls up and down the pavement outside with his eyes burning bright.' Thomas was sorry about the children, at least in a theoretical sort of way, but faced with them screeching like police cars on his stairway, his sympathy tended to weaken. But he wasn't a heel, unfeeling, a chauvinist pig, or anything of that nature. Claire would vouch for that wouldn't she? She did. And *she* smiled now. He was pleased to see her smile. He had been waiting for it. 'It's difficult when one's house is turned into a refuge. It doesn't really make for domestic bliss.'

'But you didn't have that anyway, did you? Did you?' she pressed.

'No.'

'What's everyone living on?'

'That's a good question. Hand-outs and hand-me downs.'

Claire sat down to make a note: ask Mr Millar about his drinking habits. Mrs Millar had one or two herself but those

5

Claire could not be expected to bring out. Thomas said she shouldn't let him keep her from her work.

'I'm in court in the morning.'

'I said don't let me keep you –'

'You know I often have to work in the evenings.'

She was so intelligent, so efficient, so successful, and so young, not to mention attractive: he loved her for all of that. He was not resentful. (He was intelligent enough, but he was not efficient, successful, nor young.) It was a combination of those attributes which had beguiled him in the beginning, when they had met on the Edinburgh to Inverness train. The train had broken down, they had been becalmed for nearly two hours in the middle of a moor while a snow blizzard had swept past the gunged-up windows and the temperature inside the carriage had plummeted, they had got into conversation and one thing had led to another – they had spent the night together in Inverness – which was the way, more or less, that most relationships started.

He came to squat in front of her. He examined her face.

'My nose is too long.'

'Nonsense.' He kissed the tip of it. He placed his hands on either side of her waist and she stirred, responding to their warmth. 'I don't *have* to stay.'

'Where else would you go?'

'There's always the down-and-outs hostel in the Grassmarket. It's recently been painted up, doesn't look half bad.'

She laughed again and laid aside her pen. All right, he could stay in the meantime and then they'd see how things went. He had not expected her to say stay for ever and ever even though he might have allowed himself to hope, just a little, that she would.

'We can't rush in, Thomas –'

'No indeed. We shall tread fearfully. Like the angels. Do you think that might put them on our side? Funny thing, though, the way people rush into matrimony, and not all of them are fools. They don't seem to have any fears about the shells cracking under their feet.'

She had never considered that he treaded particularly carefully, or fearfully. Before the train had started to lurch again across the white moor, he had said, 'Have dinner with me this evening!' She had been finding him entertaining and was not particularly looking forward to a solitary meal in her hotel with a book propped against the flower vase to discourage bored business men on the prowl. She had suspected that Thomas was married: he looked it, he was of an age, his sweater was hand-knitted (though, nowadays, these were easily obtainable at a price from boutiques), and earlier on he had taken from his brief case a package of sandwiches made with wholemeal bread. But what harm could it do to have a meal with him?

Before they had finished dinner, he had said, 'Stay with me tonight! The temperature's going to drop below zero.' She, being in Inverness when he made his second request, and half way across a moor when he made the first, had found it easy to fall in with both suggestions. Had she been in Edinburgh, she had told him, when they awakened in the morning to look out on the grey glint of the River Ness and the strange white-shrouded roofs, she would not have committed herself so quickly. Trains were lucky for him, he had said, and this confirmed it.

'Let's go on a long train journey – from Inverness to Samarkand. Let's not get off at Edinburgh Waverley!'

But they did, of course; and as they walked up the platform together they let the distance between them widen lest it be thought by anyone waiting at the barrier that they had done anything more than strike up a casual acquaintanceship on the train. A woman was waiting for Thomas. She waved with a hand from which the tag of a car key dangled. She wore a hand-knitted sweater. Claire glanced only briefly at her face.

'I'll phone you,' Thomas said and went surging ahead. Claire did not look to see if he and the woman met with an embrace and was irked that she was tempted to, or if they did, that it should matter to her.

She had known that Thomas would phone, but had not decided if she would see him again or not. On balance, she had thought not. Her life was balanced and she preferred to keep it that way. She had no desire to conduct an affair with a married man. Await his pleasure. His phone calls. From public call boxes. When he could sneak away. She had never experienced

7

such an affair but its drawbacks were well documented, in novels, plays, films, and court cases.

He had rung. He had said, 'Fancy a train ride to North Wales? To Llandudno? It'll be deserted, the rain'll be lashing the promenade, we'll get soaked to the skin, and there'll be no one in the boarding house but us.' It had been around that time that rumours had begun to circulate about the closing of Thomas's department. On the train to Llandudno, he had said, 'Don't mention the word *cuts* to me. It gives me a vision of my life blood ebbing away. I want to feel full-blooded this week-end.'

That was two years ago.

Claire put her hands over his where they rested on her waist. 'You don't worry about shells cracking under you do you, Thomas?'

'Oh I wouldn't say that! It might seem to the world that I carry on blithely but I still hear the cracking. Quite clearly at times. The thing is not to look down. And if you move quickly enough you can usually get to the next foothold before you fall through.'

Anyway, enough of this idle chat. He told her he loved her. And she told him she loved him, for she believed that she did. She had wanted no other man since she met him. But they both knew that two people loving one another was not necessarily a simple matter, especially if they were the kind of people who were not accustomed to making matters simple. Nor did it mean that because she loved him she necessarily wanted to live with him on a full-time basis. Yes, he understood all that, and accepted her terms. She drew back at his use of the word. He apologised. They kissed again, and went to bed.

Afterwards, when Thomas had turned over and gone to sleep, Claire got up and resumed work on her brief.

She crossed with her instructing solicitor on her way to work. He came galloping down the Playfair Steps, knees splayed outward, black-shod feet louping over every other step. It was all part of his fitness programme.

'Donald, you make me feel tired. I *am* tired.'

'What were you up to last night?'

'Working. Till the small hours.' She reached out and touched his waistcoat. 'You're squint again.'

'So I am.' He bent his head to rebutton it. His morning had been rushed, as usual. The children had been quite disgusting with their porridge. His wife had said it was all right for him going out to work every day. (She had studied Fine Art at university.) 'As if I was off to a picnic on Arthur's Seat! There!' He raised his flushed face.

'Does Amanda make porridge every morning?'

'Only when she wants to throw her housewifeliness in my face. Yes, most mornings. By the way, I've got a rape for you.'

'A rape?' She wrinkled her nose. 'I don't know that I fancy a rape.'

'This is not a particularly nasty one.'

'That is from *your* point of view. All rape is nasty.'

'You're assuming he's guilty!' cried Donald triumphantly. 'How's that for justice?' But he added that he did understand why she found rape offensive.

'I'm glad.'

'You find robberies with violence offensive too, don't you? Old women being mugged by heroin addicts? Arson? Murder? Yet you'd welcome the opportunity to take any of them on.'

'Not rape though.' She looked down through the shimmer of green and gold leaves at the frazzle of railway lines crossing and recrossing below. This bright morning, which she ought to be enjoying for the crispness of its air and the unexpected warmth of its sunshine, her nervous system felt as tangled as those lines, though when she let her eyes follow them through she saw that they emerged straight and sure to run into the station.

'You should welcome the chance to experience such a broad range of crime.'

'Don't start to lecture me, Donald. I haven't the time nor the inclination for that.'

She looked up at the hill which she must ascend to reach the High Street ridge where Parliament House was situated. Donald said he would walk with her before he turned and went back down to his office to check the mail; the exercise would do him good. They began to climb and Donald restrained himself from streaking ahead taking three steps at a time as he liked to

9

do when unaccompanied. Claire thought he must be fit enough without having to go berserk on his way to work: on Saturdays he gambolled on the rugby pitch and on Sundays played with his children in parks and on the seashore. That was Amanda's day of rest.

'Now, take this rape case,' said Donald.

'I would prefer not to. Especially since I am being asked to represent the rapist – *alleged* rapist.'

'You can't let being a woman stand in your way! Anyway, I don't see how you can say no to this one – he asked specifically for you.'

'For *me*? How would he know about me?'

'Your fame must be spread far and wide.'

'Ha, ha. And who is *he*?'

A Mr Laurence Ian Fyffe Finlay apparently, otherwise known as Liffey, though this was not a piece of information that Donald himself was aware of at that time; it came to Claire's attention later in the day from an unexpected source.

But she did not want to hear any more about Mr Finlay just now, she had other things on her mind. Not Millar v. Millar though, he'd be bound, said Donald. He loved such expressions, cosseted them and produced them like a conjuror bringing white rabbits out of hats. She *ought* to be thinking about Millar v. Millar, she conceded, but something more personal was troubling her. A domestic problem.

'Domestic problem – you, Claire? Never! You are your own woman.'

'Oh stuff it!'

Two bowler-hatted advocates overtook them, crying out something or other about the inclemency of the weather.

'I haven't had time to notice myself,' Donald called after them but they were gone, clinging to their headgear, their striped trouser legs billowing in a sudden upsurge of wind.

'It rained half the night,' said Claire absent-mindedly.

'What *were* you doing up half the night?'

'I was working on Millar. I couldn't get down to it earlier. Because of my domestic problem.'

'Could it be Thomas?'

'He's left his wife.'

'Good God!'

They stood now at the top of the steps looking down at the galleries of art and Princes Street below.

'This isn't going to suit your lifestyle at all,' said Donald; with some relish, she thought. And she hated the word lifestyle. This was definitely not going to be a good morning. She hoped she was not going to lose a perfectly straightforward case.

'No, it won't suit it at all!' repeated Donald. He had spells of yearning for a return to the state of bachelorhood himself – 'One doesn't foresee love and marriage being boiled down to broken dishwashers, chicken pox and coitus interrupted by the screams of one's offspring' – when he would sit in the pub and tell Claire how smart she was. He had always known she was smart, from the day he sat next to her in a jurisprudence lecture and admired the curve of her right calf. He had fancied her, but by then he was deeply embroiled in his affair with Amanda whom he married the day after receiving his LL B. Had he not married so young he would have been an advocate like Claire, he maintained, but with the need to support a family he had settled for going into Amanda's father's firm of solicitors as a junior partner. Amanda's father had no son. Donald still loved Amanda, in spite of the porridge and faulty dishwashers, and he still fancied Claire, in spite of the lack of encouragement on her part, or perhaps because of it. (This was what she told him.) He admired her right calf now as the wind swirled her black skirt round her knees.

She put her hand under his chin and lifted his head.

'How sleek you always look,' he said. 'Even when you have not slept particularly well. Like a black pussy cat with a white bib. *Beautifully* clean.'

'We ought to be talking about Millar. What do we know about his drinking habits?'

'Not much. Claire, what are you going to do about Thomas?'

'I've no idea. I hadn't exactly –'

'Bargained for this? No, I don't suppose you had. Most inconsiderate of Thomas, leaving his wife.'

'You're cutting it fine,' said Hetty. All the other women

11

advocates had gone from the robing room.

'I know, I know!' Claire began to rummage in her locker. Her wig was missing, and her gown.

'Terrible lot of breaking and entering going on these days,' said Hetty. 'Amazing what they'll lift.'

Claire remembered that she had been at the Sheriff Court the day before and had taken her wig and gown home. She had quite forgotten, until this moment.

'That's not like you,' said Hetty, who was stopping a run in her black tights with a bar of soap. This was quite like Hetty. 'Drat!' she cried. The run kept leaping ahead of the soap.

'You look as though you're after a flea. Hetty, you shall have to come to my rescue!'

In borrowed wig and gown, Claire went forth to do battle. By the time she had attended to the business of a client who was seeking interim damages, Donald had been down the Mound to his office and back up again and was looking even pinker in the face.

He eyed her scratching under her wig.

'Hetty's. We seem to have different shaped heads.'

'Lack of familiarity, that's what it is. Terrible thing, lack of familiarity. I don't go for it myself.'

They went in pursuit of their client, Mrs Millar, and found her, huddled, mouse-like, at the extreme end of a red leatherette bench. One tilt, and she'd be on the ground, like the occupant of an unbalanced see-saw. She pointed down the corridor. A man, presumably Mr Millar, frowning under monstrous eyebrows, faced up towards them. He, as pursuer, was claiming that she was a nymphomaniac, would open her legs to everyone who called at the house from the milkman to the school attendance officer, and that the children (both girls) were being brought up to think that the way to get free milk and not go to school was to lie on your back. Mrs Millar, as defender, was claiming that her husband was violent and dirty, and wanted her to do dirty things. The truth had been difficult to establish – in Claire's own mind – and the milkman and school attendance officer had naturally not been forthcoming.

Mrs Millar dragged her coat sleeve across her eyes and appealed to Donald to whom she addressed everything she had to say. 'It'll be all right, won't it? He willna get them from me?

12

For if he does there's no saying what he'll do to they bairns.' She lowered her voice and added, but not too quietly, 'I'd have been happier with a man.'

'You can have every confidence in Miss Armstrong,' said Donald, giving Mrs Millar his hand and raising her up. 'She is one of our rising young advocates. She has seldom been known to lose a case.'

'Liar,' said Claire. Only Donald heard, he turned his head to smile and acknowledge that he had; Mrs Millar was too intent on singing the litany of her husband's atrocities.

'I'm glad you had a good day,' said Thomas.

'It wasn't particularly good.'

'But you won.'

'Winning isn't everything. Oh no, nothing like everything. There's such a thing as winning in law, and another, winning morally.'

'Ah, winning morally! That is what we should all like to do.'

'And if the mother's had the children since the separation – which this one had – then there's little to commend the father.'

Claire kicked off her shoes and dropped into her favourite armchair. At the end of a day she liked to lie back and let her mind float free. This was the time at which she most valued her privacy. She enjoyed opening the door of her flat after work and walking into its silence.

Thomas put a glass of gin and tonic into her hand. The room had been tidied, vacuum cleaner tacks could be seen on the apricot-coloured carpet, and from the kitchen came the smell of cooking.

'Lasagne.'

'Marvellous.' She sipped her drink, still thinking of her day, not ready yet to switch over to the evening, and to him. 'The husband was stroppy afterwards,' she said. Mr Millar had shouted at the Bench and been warned that he was in danger of being in contempt of court. He had subsided without grace and although he was silent, as commanded, his lips had continued to mouth his protest. 'You'll rue the day,' he told the judge in his brief outburst. 'Those bairns'll be on the streets before they're fifteen.' At the time Claire had stirred a little with

13

unease, then quelled it, as she knew she must. It was not up to her to believe or disbelieve her clients but to put forward such defence as was available to her. She had done her job. She was not God. She could not be responsible for the afterlife of her clients and their dependants. 'No, it was not all *that* good a day.' She and Donald had gone for a drink after they had accepted thanks from the bottom of Mrs Millar's heart. Though goodness knows where that was, as Donald could not refrain from saying.

'You and Donald seem to do a lot of drinking together,' observed Thomas.

'Only when I'm acting for one of his clients.'

The first pub they'd gone into had had to be abandoned for, as they pushed open the swing door, they saw Mr Millar at the counter recounting his woes to the barman. *Hoor. Bloody lawyers.* Donald and Claire backed out but not before Mr Millar had seen them and come charging, beer running over from the pint glass in his hand. They had hastened, breaking not quite into a run, more of a jog, and made their escape down a close.

'A bit ridiculous, wasn't it?' said Thomas. 'You running away from him? You should have stood your ground.'

'It was ridiculous,' said Claire, smiling. In the next pub Donald had told her that excitement suited her: her cheeks, normally pale, had glowed with colour. 'But a confrontation would have been pointless. And we wanted a quiet drink.'

'Mm,' said Thomas.

'So how was your day?'

Less spectacular, he said: the drama content had been low. The electricity man had called to read the meter and been surprised to find someone at home; and he had gone after two jobs, one as a wholefood rep, the other as a charity organiser, but both had been filled before he got there, which probably just as well since he doubted his suitability for either.

'The lasagne's drying up.'

'Sorry,' said Claire.

Thomas went to the kitchen, she got up and, taking her glass, finished her drink by the window. Coming in earlier, she had noticed a young girl standing in front of the gardens across the street. She was still there.

14

The door re-opened and Thomas entered, his hands buried deep in oven gloves, carrying a steaming dish. The cheese topping crackled and ran over the sides of the dish.

'Looks fantastic,' said Claire. 'Far better than mine ever does.'

They had just begun to eat when the door bell rang. Thomas said he would get it, she could do with a bit of peace after a hard day. She heard Donald's voice in the hallway apologising for intruding. He hoped he wasn't disturbing them, he just wanted to give some papers to Claire? Not at all, Thomas was saying, overly polite. They came into the room together.

Donald waved a sheaf of papers in the air. The case he'd been talking about earlier. He just thought Claire would be interested to see them. Again he repeated that he had no wish to disturb them, he couldn't stop anyway, Amanda was going to an evening class on Gothic architecture and he was babysitting.

'Do carry on. Don't mind me.'

'A glass of wine?' asked Thomas.

'Oh well,' said Donald, who had been eyeing the label, 'if you insist.'

'I do.'

Donald would not sit down though; he drank the wine standing up, rocking gently from his heels on to his toes, watching them pretend to eat. He inquired after Thomas's job prospects.

'There doesn't seem to be much demand for Baltic studies at the moment.'

'Except in the Baltic, I suppose,' said Donald with a guffaw and quaffed the rest of his wine. 'Latvia, Lithuania and Estonia, isn't it?'

'Thomas's grandfather was Latvian,' said Claire.

'Was that the way of it? All part of the jolly old USSR now though eh? I don't suppose you'd fancy working there, Thomas?'

'I hardly think the question arises.'

'Ah well.' Donald looked into the bottom of his glass. 'I'd best be on my way then. See you tomorrow, Claire. No, it's all right, Thomas, no need to see me out. I know my own way. And thanks for the glass of the old grape. Jolly good wine.'

The lasagne was now almost cold. Claire apologised.

Thomas said it was not her fault. They heard Donald whistling as he emerged from the bottom door in to the street below.

'Pompous ass,' said Thomas. 'Acts more like forty-nine than twenty-nine.'

Claire had been glancing idly at the papers which Donald had brought. 'I see he's from your neck of the woods.'

'Who is?'

'Laurence Ian Fyffe Finlay,' she read out.

'Liffey! Good God! What's he been up to?'

'You know him?'

'We were at school together, he lived next door.'

'You didn't recommend me to him?'

'Of course not. Why would I do that? What's he charged with anyway?'

'Rape.'

'*What?*'

Thomas couldn't believe it. He didn't want to believe it, of course. Who would of a friend? Was she sure? He got up and came to read the name for himself, and the address.

'That's Liffey all right.' Thomas lit a cigarette although he was in the process of stopping smoking and had cut down to five a day. Claire hated the smell of cigarette smoke in the flat and he accepted that that was a perfectly reasonable thing to hate. Why should he poison her lungs?

'What's he like?' she asked.

Thomas went back to his seat. He leant back, looking away from her. Liffey? He shrugged. Bit of a rough diamond, restless type, always changing jobs, had been working on the oil off and on. Married? Yes, married. Did Thomas's voice tighten as he said yes, married? Was he thinking of himself as he said it? Claire knew that people seldom walked away from even the worst marriages without remorse. And she was not convinced that his marriage had come into the worst category. Her mind was fully alert now, after its pre-prandial slump, and she was listening intently, watching too, for clues. It was difficult for her to accept the coincidence, while knowing that coincidences did happen, all the time, yet in law they were always loth to accept them.

'Children?' she asked.

'Four. Eldest is twenty-six. Peter. He's a bright lad – well, no longer a lad really – but he's the best of the bunch. He'll do well.'

'Liffey must have married young then?'

'Yes, very young.' Again she heard that same tightening in Thomas's voice.

'Do you still see him?'

It seemed that they met up sometimes when Thomas went home to visit his mother, which he did at erratic intervals, either because his conscience nudged him or his sister Eunice rang up to harangue him. After a couple of hours with his mother and sister he needed a drink so he'd pop in to the local on his way home, and this was where he ran across Liffey. As a matter of fact he needed a drink now. The wine was finished. He got up and poured himself a whisky. Claire made a few notes on the margin of the papers.

'You know, I hardly think Liffey would need to go round raping women,' said Thomas.

'Because he's got a happy marriage?'

No, that was not what Thomas had meant. 'He's fairly popular with the women, that's all.'

'Is he what might be called a ladies' man?'

'I dare say.'

'Why not say?'

'You haven't got me in the dock, you know.'

His reprimand rankled. She was touchy when people teased her for being a cool-headed lawyer. It was not intended as a compliment. A woman should be warm and not ask penetrating questions.

'I didn't mean to snap,' said Thomas.

'That's all right.'

The telephone rang and she answered it. Call box bleeps sounded, money was inserted and a high voice said, 'May I speak to my father please?' Claire passed the receiver to Thomas.

She read Donald's notes. The only witness for the defence so far was the barman and his testimony might not be all that useful, especially if he were to turn out to be an old buddy of Liffey's. Thomas was talking on the telephone saying things like it's not like that, you don't understand, you've got to try to understand, you're old enough now. And then: 'Wait there,

Tasha. Wait and I'll come.' He replaced the receiver, looked at Claire. 'I've got to go to her.'

'I think you have. She sounded distraught. By the way, do you happen to know Alexander James McIlroy?'

'Alex? Yes. What's *he* done?'

'Nothing at all, as far as I am aware. Unless he's prepared to commit perjury. He's the barman at your pub hang-out?'

'We were all at school together, he and Liffey and I.'

'I was afraid of that. Not exactly an objective witness. According to McIlroy, the injured party, Janetta Beatrix Wilson Smith – you don't happen to know her too?'

'Jinty?'

'So you do?'

'Not well.' Thomas pulled on his jacket. 'I've seen her in the pub.'

'McIlroy says that the woman Smith bought a drink first for Finlay alias Liffey –'

'Claire, I don't think you should get mixed up in all that.'

All what? The case because it was sordid, as rape cases must be, or the group of people, because they belonged to his past? She did not ask.

She said, 'I'm not allowed to refuse. If I did I would be under pain of deprivation of my office. Unless I can advocate a good and sufficient reason why I should not. But I haven't got one, have I?'

'I suppose not.'

He went out to meet his daughter.

His footsteps rang on the stone stair as he went down. The bottom door clanged shut.

'Liffey,' said Claire aloud, lingering over the name.

She met him in Donald's office a few days later. There had been no need for her specifically to attend a meeting at this stage; in fact, it was quite unusual, but she had said that she might as well come.

Liffey was a big, well-built man, not bad looking, except for the evidence of hard drink in his eyes. She could see why some women might find him attractive. He had the look, in style and dress, of a man who believed that the main purpose of life was

18

enjoyment and who lived that life not within the four walls of a house but in public places. Pubs, restaurants, clubs; perhaps sauna parlours, if they could be called public. In these he would ask for 'extras' while telling the masseuse that he could have what he wanted any time he wanted, for nothing. But he would never pass up an opportunity. Claire knew about 'massage' parlours, having spent a week on a case involving one. She had lost it. Her client had lied to her, and she had believed him. Liffey had the look, too, of a man who was capable of the large gesture, which often appealed to women. The last ten pound note on a bottle of champagne. The unexpected sudden week-end in Amsterdam. But, no, perhaps his gestures could not go that far: he did have a wife and three children to support.

When he shook Claire's hand he looked into her face, appraisingly, noting her first as a woman and secondly as the advocate who would defend him. He smelled of cheap after-shave lotion and expensive cigars. 'I'm very pleased to meet you,' he said, keeping hold of her hand too long, letting his fingers curl up into her palm, and if he registered her disapproval he did not let it curtail the handshake. Or it might be that her disapproval encouraged him to prolong it.

'Please do sit down,' said Donald.

Liffey threw his camel-coloured coat over a chair and, asking if they would mind if he smoked, pulled out his cigars before they could either assent or object.

Donald, standing four-square with his back to the fire (his father-in-law was of the old school which considered central heating to be deleterious to the moral fibre and concentration), read aloud the statement of the complainer. Janetta Beatrix Wilson Smith, aged thirty-four, separated, with three children, stated that, on the night of September 13th, she and Laurence Ian Fyffe Finlay had had a drink or two together in the pub, and at closing time, when he had offered to walk her home, she had accepted since there had been a number of muggings in her housing scheme recently. At this point Liffey cut in.

'Don't make me laugh! More likely she'd be doing the mugging.'

'Unfortunately it's no laughing matter,' said Donald,

aiming a backward kick at a lighted coal which had descended on to the hearth. His trouser cuffs at the back were peppered with small singe marks. 'She's claiming you forced her to have sexual intercourse with her.'

'Forced? She's been screwed by half the men in the village.'

'Can you produce witnesses?'

'Who's going to stand up in court and say they've had it off with her to save my hide?'

Probably no one, Donald agreed, there was not a great deal of philanthropy about these days. Every man for himself and all that.

'She had injuries,' said Claire. 'Scratches, cuts . . .'

'Self-inflicted,' declared Liffey and relit his dead cigar.

'Why would she want to damage herself?'

'To make trouble for me. We knocked about together for a bit, you see, and when I dumped her she didn't like it.'

'People tend not to like being dumped,' said Claire, who was not by that remark censuring Liffey for ending the affair – she had ended many herself, before they tailed off, for she hated the last dregs, of anything – but was thinking rather of Thomas's wife, Sarah, whom she had seen, to her fairly certain knowledge, twice now. That morning, a woman loitering in Parliament Square had gazed after her with more than casual interest. At first, Claire had not been able to recall where she had seen her before; she saw so many people, one way or another, in the witness box, on jury benches, on the public benches. As she had been about to go into the Parliament House, the memory of the face waiting at the station barrier for Thomas two years before returned to her, but by the time she had looked back the woman had turned and was walking away across the square towards the High Street. A tall woman with brown hair and a long stride.

'Did your wife know about your relationship with Mrs Smith?' Claire asked Liffey.

'She asks no questions . . .'

'And you tell no lies,' said Donald. 'Quite so.'

'Look, I'm innocent,' said Liffey. 'I was set up, I tell you. But I realise it'll not be so easy to prove it.'

'Oh it won't be possible to prove it,' said Claire. 'The only way we could would be to find a witness who saw Mrs Smith inflicting the damage on herself, and that's highly improbable. But we don't have to prove it. We don't have to establish your innocence, Mr Finlay –'

'Call me Liffey.'

'We must be able to refute the charge of guilty and make it impossible for them to establish it.'

'You speak very well. You've got a lovely voice. I'm dead chuffed you're going to be handling the case.'

'Why did you ask for me?'

'I reckoned that a woman would have a better chance of getting me off a charge like this.'

'Who told you about me?'

'Why Tommy, of course.'

'Tommy?'

'Tommy Peterson.'

'I didn't lie to you. I didn't recommend you. I didn't even know he was in trouble. So I must have mentioned your name when we were having a drink. Is that a crime? Well, is it?' Thomas went on demanding until she had to concede that it was not, though she still did not like the idea of him sitting with Liffey in pubs talking about her.

Thomas came back quickly. She sat in pubs with Donald and talked about *him* didn't she? And what about Hetty? Had she never mentioned his name to Hetty in the robing room or wigging room or whatever it was called?

She could not deny it. But it was only natural to mention the name of one's lover to one's friends. But she never said anything – well, *revealing* – about him.

'Nor I of you. Only the bare details: female, advocate, unmarried.'

But she could trust Donald and Hetty. Could he trust his friend Liffey? She could see that Thomas did not want to answer that one. She went on, 'Do you think I can assume he is telling the truth?'

'Why don't you ask him?'

'One never asks a client that. It is not up to me to sit in judgment on him.'

'You are being inconsistent then, aren't you? Asking *me* if

21

Liffey is lying?'

Claire crossed to the window. On the other side of the road in front of the gardens which the square enfolded stood the same young girl. A street light shone on the tree overhanging her making the yellow leaves shimmer and the black trunk glisten. Her eyes and mouth were in shadow. Her long hair hung like a silvery curtain at the sides of her face. She looked as if she had not moved since Claire passed her earlier on her way home from work.

'I think your daughter is keeping us under surveillance.'

Thomas came and stood behind Claire, resting his hands on her hips. His sigh travelled from his body into hers and made her spine quiver. She put her hands over his. She wanted him to take her to bed but knew he would not, for although he registered her vibration and was rumpling the top of her head with his chin, his eyes were on the lit golden tree, and in a moment he would take the warmth away from her hips and back away from her and go down into the cool street to the shadowy, motionless girl.

Claire did not turn when he removed his hands. She remained by the window and when he appeared on the pavement below she watched him cross the street and take the girl's hand and ease her out from the shadows. Her pale hair swung back and her face showed under the street light, pale also, and high-browed. She embraced her father. He stroked her hair. Then they moved off together, hand in hand, keeping to the cobbled pavement under the trees. They walked slowly. They talked, turning to look at one another. Claire looked back at the golden tree and pulled the curtain across the window.

Tasha came nightly thereafter and took up her position under the overhanging tree. The leaves gradually drifted down until only a few remained like ragged banners above her head. On crisp clear nights and on muggy wet ones when the lamps were blurred, she stood, not moving, her face turned up towards the windows of Claire's flat.

Thomas knew that he should not go down to her and he tried not to, though usually in the end he went. They would draw

22

the curtains but after an hour, or less, he would lift a corner and when he saw that she was still there and the rain was heavier or the pavement sparkled with frost . . . Well, what else could he do? She was very young, and she had been thrown off balance.

Claire was annoyed to find that she felt unbalanced too. She rang Hetty whose husband was in London on business and who said why not come round for a drink? Why stay in an empty flat? The flat had never seemed empty before Thomas came to live in it but, since he had, Claire had found that when she was alone she was listening for the sound of his key in the lock.

It was ridiculous that she should feel jealous of a fifteen-year-old girl, she told Hetty, and she didn't really, at least she was pretty sure she did not. She was just exasperated by the girl's presence out there in the darkness, watching. 'I know I shouldn't bother, I have plenty of work to do, I don't mind being on my own. I didn't mind when I only saw Thomas three or four nights a week.'

'It suited you, didn't it? Having Thomas safely married unable to make too many demands?'

'You make me sound selfish. Is it selfish to want to keep space around oneself? If so, I shall have to plead quilty.'

'Of course it's not selfish. The kind of relationship you had with Thomas before was fair enough, as long as it satisfied both parties and injured no one. Which it didn't appear to do since the marriage had irretrievably broken down, had it not?'

'I believe so.'

'It may have been one of the reasons, though, that you were attracted to Thomas in the first place: the fact that he was not totally free. And not even all that suitable.'

Hetty warmed to her theme. Claire had always tended to get involved with unsuitable men. There was the oil man who worked in Venezuela where Claire would not have been able to practise law even if she would have wished to go there, the forester who was bent on living in a remote part of British Columbia, the solicitor who was old enough to be her father and the medical student who was not quite young enough to be her son.

'Oh come on now, Hetty,' said Claire, laughing. 'You exaggerate!'

23

Thomas blamed Claire's lack of desire for a committed relationship on Claire's parents. They were totally committed to one another – they were both architects, they had met as students, qualified at the same time, worked in the same firm for five years and then set up in practice together. They had never spent a night apart, except when Claire was born. They finished one another's sentences. Sometimes they had no need to articulate a sentence at all. A look, a nod, and they knew their minds were thinking alike. They were even beginning to look alike, which was not uncommon amongst older couples who were close.

'Parents are always useful to blame,' said Hetty. 'But surely yours are a good advertisement for marriage? They're so obviously happy together. I envy them. Oh, not that I am unhappy. Richard and I get along pretty well. But your parents are *so* devoted.'

Such devotion could be claustrophobic, Claire pointed out, especially if one was the child of such a marriage, the only child.

'But you had a happy childhood,' said Hetty. 'Your parents were so talented and intelligent and liberal.' Unlike hers . . .

All right, said Claire, feeling a little irritable; she knew she was lucky, her parents had been eminently reasonable and had treated her as a human being with rights of her own from an early age, though sometimes she resented – unreasonably, she considered – their very reasonableness and wished they would sharpen their response to her and say what they were actually thinking. *Thomas is not suitable for you: he is too old, too encumbered, too disorganised.* But she did love them and they loved her, which did not mean that she had to emulate them.

'My mother's never had a close woman friend for a start. There would be no room for one. I value my women friends, even when they are putting forth irritating theories!'

Hetty and Claire passed an agreeable evening drinking red wine and talking about love and friendship and sex and marriage and they even indulged in a bit of shop talk. And why not? Talking shop was one of the most enjoyable forms of conversation. It was midnight when Claire noticed the time. She'd better go, Thomas would wonder where on earth she'd got to. Hetty said that in spite of what she had said about

24

envying Claire's parents she was glad that Richard went away on business from time to time. It was bliss to come home and slop about in a housecoat and eat scrambled eggs for supper and rink red wine and have a friend round for a good gas.

'My mother never took off her corset until she went to bed and she sat upright in her own house as if she were sitting on a stage.'

Claire laughed, kissed Hetty goodnight. Walking home with warm cheeks through the cool night, untroubled by pools of darkness in the lit streets, feeling the world to be a harmonious, benevolent place, rather than the hostile, aggressive one that was often brought to her attention during the hours of daylight, she felt optimistic. Tasha would tire, Tasha would adjust, Tasha would find other interests.

The girl was not standing under the tree. She seldom was at this late hour but, even so, her very absence increased Claire's feeling of well-being.

Opening the door of her flat, she heard voices, male, Thomas's and one other. She went into the sitting room.

Sprawled in her favourite chair, laughing, gesticulating, spilling cigarette ash on her apricot-coloured carpet, was Liffey. She reproved herself for even noticing the ash. She must not become too houseproud. It narrowed the spirit, so her mother told her, though in the house that Claire's parents had built the furniture and furnishings had been brought together with considerable, if casual, care, and nothing in it jarred.

Something jarred in Claire's sitting room now. He said, 'Hi, Claire! Just thought I'd drop in and say hello to my old pal.'

His old pal, in an effort to cover his embarrassment, picked up the whisky bottle, there being not much else he could turn his attention to, and refilled their glasses, offering one to Claire who declined, saying she was tired and just off to bed.

'Ah come on, Claire,' said Liffey, 'give us the pleasure of your lovely company. I was just telling Tommy how bloody lucky he is. You always were a lucky son-of-a-bitch weren't you? How is it you're so good at landing on your feet? First you get Sarah – high class girl – and now a young chick like Claire here.'

25

'Claire doesn't like being called a chick,' said Thomas, trying to sound good-natured.

'Nor am I *that* young.'

'To my eyes you are. I like the way you lift your chin when you're annoyed. What would you like me to call you then? Bird? Hen?'

Might as well call me a laying-machine, like those ghastly Goncourt brothers, Claire was about to retort when she checked herself. That would be to leave herself much too open, to both of them.

'He has been lucky, you know, my old pal Tommy. He was the one who made good, went to university, married a surgeon's daughter –'

'He was a G.P.,' said Thomas. 'But I don't think we want to hear any more.'

Claire did, though did not say so. She accepted a drink and perched on the arm of a chair, neither in nor out of the group.

'He had a fancy wedding too, top hat and tails, would you believe it? The whole works, picture in the *Tatler*. His mother brought the pictures round for Jean and me – that's my wife – to see. Very proud she was. You met Tommy's mother yet? You should take her home to meet them, Tommy. Eunice – that's his sister, she keeps a wool shop in the village, never married has Eunice, pity about that really, she'd have made someone a good wife, course she's had to look after her mother, keep the home fire burning and all that – was asking about you only yesterday. Yes, your mother and Eunice enjoyed your wedding any road, Tommy. So did your grand-father. Died soon afterwards, didn't he? Still, he died happy. *I* wasn't invited to the wedding of course. Not that I hold any grudge –'

'I seem to remember you were away in Yorkshire at the time.'

'Messing up my hands.' Liffey displayed them. They did not look particularly messed up, thought Claire: they looked as if their owner gave them regular attention.

'Whereas mine are lily-white,' said Thomas. 'Oh belt up; Liffey!'

'I didn't mind not being asked to your wedding. I understood perfectly well. I mean, who wants their coat tails kept a hold of when they're on their way up in the world?'

'Christ!' said Thomas.

Liffey laughed and called for pax! 'I was just trying to get a rise out of you. Can't you even take a joke these days? Course you didn't come to my wedding either, did you?'

'I seem to remember I was in hospital.' Thomas fingered the white scar high up on his forehead.

'So you were! Fell off your bike didn't you? Nearly bought it.' Liffey smiled, though Claire could not see why that should be a smiling matter. Thomas had told her he had got the scar in a road accident. 'I was accident-prone at the time,' he had said, but would not be more specific. For a moment the two men stared at one another, with what looked, to Claire, like open hatred, then Liffey broke the spell and turning to her, said, 'Oh not that my wedding was anything like his.'

'Claire's tired,' said Thomas and got up to put the fireguard against the dying fire.

Liffey held out his glass. 'Small one for the road?'

An hour later, when they had managed to coax him down the stairs and into a taxi which Thomas had called, Claire suggested that it might be better not to let him in in future.

Thomas shrugged. That wouldn't be so easy. Well, Liffey *was* an old friend and how did you slam the door in the face of an old friend?

Claire realised they had been at school and gone fishing together and so forth but she could not understand why they were still friends. What did they have in common now? 'You don't even like him do you?'

'No, not a lot, I suppose.'

'Well then?'

Thomas shrugged. He said, 'All that about going up in the world and marrying Sarah – that wasn't why I married her at all.'

In the morning Claire let Thomas lie. He was still asleep when she walked up the hill to work and was glad not to meet Donald careering down the Playfair Steps and telling her she looked as if she must be burning the candle at both ends.

In the middle of a complicated reparation proof, when she was cross-examining a witness, the door at the back of the court opened and in came Thomas's daughter. Claire allowed her attention to be distracted for that split second and, by the time she had fully recovered it, her witness was rambling on about coming along the starboard side, going off for lunch, being on the early shift . . . A little late she cut in to ask him to make clear, for the sake of the court, which side of the ship starboard was. Thanking him and terminating his evidence, she took a quick glance at the public benches.

Tasha sat in a pew, her body inclined forward, her arms resting on the ledge in front. She was gazing at Claire with the full force of her dark blue eyes. Even at a distance, Claire knew their colour. They were eyes like Thomas's. But they did not look on her charitably, as Thomas's eyes did: they wished her ill.

Claire was glad when the case was adjourned for lunch and she could let off steam to Hetty.

'I feel as if she's trying to put the evil eye on me. Perhaps she sticks pins into my effigy! I woke up with a sharp pain in my left leg last night.'

'Thomas will have to do something about her,' said Hetty, 'sooner or later.'

The reparation proof trailed on. On Wednesday – Eunice's half-day – she and her mother arrived for the afternoon session. The noise halted the work of the court for a moment. Feet stumbled as they came into the room and two female voices, one low and quiet, the other higher, cursing, saying, 'Hush, Mother, for God's sake,' penetrated the quiet. The macer silenced them both and directed them into a bench. Claire, seated at the central table beside Donald, observed a small elderly woman in black, coat, hat, gloves, handbag, shopping bag, all to match, and a taller, bigger-boned, middle-aged one in a variety of knitted garments of many colours. She looked a bit like Thomas too, though much less handsome. Her nose was long and bulbous at the end, as if engorged with cold germs, and pinched between the eyes. The eyes were roving, and came now to rest upon Claire.

The judge also had his eye on Claire. She rose to cross-examine her witness. 'Mr Jackson, would you please tell the court exactly how you came to descend the ladder . . .' Even before she finished speaking she heard the whisper, 'It must be her!' followed by, 'Shush, Mother, for goodness sake!' Mr Jackson plodded through his evidence laboriously describing his movements taking so long even to reach the top of the ladder that Claire had to intercept several times to hurry him along. The judge looked drowsy. There was no one in the public benches except for Thomas's relatives. It took rapes and murders to bring the people out.

While the next witness was being sworn in, something dropped in the public benches. It had the unmistakable pinging sound of a knitting needle falling. Claire glanced sideways to see Eunice's head and shoulders disappearing below the yellow-varnished pew to re-emerge, face vermilion, blue and yellow hat askew. An arm came up performing an arc like that made by a bowler and she passed a long needle to her mother who nabbed it and removed it from sight. A second later the black shoulders began to move rhythmically.

Three witnesses later, a further kerfuffle ensued when Eunice and her mother rose to depart. The macer did his best to quieten them but Thomas's mother seemed to have trouble getting out of the pew; her shopping bag had lodged sideways, the knitting needles perhaps being the cause of the obstruction, and Eunice had to turn back to wrench it free. As they went down the steps, Eunice said, in a clear voice, 'God, that seat was hard on the bum.' 'I don't know what they have to keep going over and over the same thing for.' 'She wouldn't be bad looking, I suppose, if she wasn't wearing that funny wig . . .' 'Cold looking though . . .' The door closed on their voices.

Cold looking! Claire seethed inside. How dare the silly old fool sit in such facile judgment on her! In her eyes, *I* am the guilty one. Knowing nothing, understanding nothing, she sits and knits and condemns, in good traditional style. Stupid bitches, she would have liked to have shouted after them, but that would have been a contempt of court that really would have caused an uproar. 'Please conduct Miss Armstrong from the court!' She saw herself being hustled out, stiff-armed between two policemen, and suppressed a smile. She dabbed around the edges of her wig with a paper tissue, surprised by the strength of her response to Thomas's mother. She had never given her much thought before, had never thought she needed to.

There was only one other member of Thomas's family to come now.

'Ever felt you were being haunted?' Claire asked Hetty, as they came out of Parliament House together. Emerging from the lee of St. Giles' Cathedral was a woman whom she had no difficulty in recognising this time.

'I'll stick close by you.'

'No. I feel I should get this over.'

They parted and Claire went to meet Sarah. She was dressed in a long purple cardigan and a skirt of woven pink cloth. Her hands were pushed deep down into the pockets of the cardigan. A rubber band held her hair back at the nape of her neck.

When they came within speaking distance she said, 'I'm sorry to bother you – but I'm Tom's wife.' And she waited.

Claire waited too. Why should she help the woman out? Go half way. To what? A head-on collision? She had never had any intention of colliding with Thomas's wife although now that they were here, face to face, she did intend to stand her ground.

'Could we go somewhere?' asked Sarah. 'I haven't come to make a fuss or anything. I'd just like to talk to you.' She had a low, well-modulated voice, of the kind that was sometimes described as musical. In contrast, when she replied, Clarie was conscious of her own voice sounding cool and diffident, unreflective of how she felt. Her court voice, Thomas would have called it. When they had a disagreement he accused her of putting it on. An easy taunt of course.

'If you like,' said Claire. 'If you think it will do any good.'

They went to a coffee house where they chose a quiet corner.

'I haven't come to ask you to give Tom up,' said Sarah and smiled.

'I didn't ask him to leave you,' said Claire and did not smile. Poor Thomas, she thought, he is not coming out of this very well; we are not exactly fighting for possession. At least not on the surface.

30

'Yes, I know, he told me you hadn't. He said you had never made any unreasonable demands on him.' Sarah did not look as if she believed this and Claire did not blame her. Claire had nothing really to blame Sarah for, as far as she knew. 'No, it's Tasha I want to speak to you about.'

Oh God, Tasha, thought Claire, her spirit drooping. Could she not get away from the girl anywhere? 'She's playing truant and doing no work at school even when she does go,' said Sarah. Claire drank her coffee. She did not give a damn what Tasha did, in or out of school, as long as she was doing it out of her sightline. No, that was not strictly true. She cared if it made Thomas miserable. 'She's away from home for hours at a time,' said Sarah. Claire was able to tell her where her daughter spent much of that time. But what could *she* do about it? Tasha was perfectly entitled to prop up the railings across the road from her flat if she wanted to. And shouldn't it be Thomas to whom Sarah was talking?

'What I wanted to say to you was this: if you'd like to invite Tasha into your flat, I wouldn't object. She needs to feel a part of her father's life, you see. He always made such a fuss of her. So its understandable that the bottom should drop out of her world when he left. If we'd had another child it would have been better. But I wasn't able to. It was a big disappointment for Thomas.' Sarah paused. She looked at Claire. 'He's very fond of children, you know. He'd have loved half a dozen. So I wasn't surprised when I found out he'd taken up with a much younger woman. I do realise of course that you have your career to think of but you look smart enough to me to manage that *and* a family.'

'I "took up" with you because I was bowled over by your intelligence and beauty! And I could kill Sarah – '

She interrupted him. 'I'm glad you have no thoughts about having children.'

'Wouldn't you like to have a baby? Most women do want to at some time or other.'

She told him not to generalise though conceded that probably the majority of women did, sooner or later, either from the basic biological urge, or conditioning, or a feeling of

31

missing out on something.

'Sometimes a woman can wait too long.'

'Who's talking about *waiting*?'

'It's just that you're nearly thirty.'

'You're always telling me how young I am. Now suddenly I'm ageing!'

'Oh you've got plenty of time. But I suppose you must think about it occasionally?'

'I do. As you say, I'm at that age . . .'

'And when you *have* thought about it?'

'I've come to the conclusion that it wouldn't bother me greatly if I didn't have any.' She sat up, for they were lying in bed, side by side. 'You're surely not suggesting that we *have* a baby?'

'Is it such a monstrous suggestion?'

'Yes, I think it is. I've got my career –'

'Hetty's got two children.'

'So, okay, it can be done, but it makes life difficult. And Hetty's always having ghastly trouble with au pairs. I'd hate to have a stranger living in my house. And I don't like to remind you, but you don't have a job.'

But he didn't she see? asked Thomas, sitting up too now. That was what made it feasible.

She was beginning to see.

'You could look after it, you mean?'

'Well, why not? In these changing times . . .'

Times were changing in two ways, she reminded him: men could now stay at home and do the child-minding, if they were of a mind to, but women could accept or reject the idea of motherhood without being labelled abnormal or unfulfilled, or at least if they were labelled, which they might be by those who considered themselves to be 'normal' and 'fulfilled', they need not let it perturb them. They had chosen their condition. It was not a case of being left out.

'You are a marvellous orator,' said Thomas, 'even in bed.'

It was not a topic she had given much thought to, but now she found it occupying her thoughts. She tried to talk to her mother about it, obliquely, asking if she would have felt unfulfilled if she hadn't had a child? Her mother, predictably, had never thought about it.

'That's because you did have one.'

'Possibly. You came along before we got around to thinking about it.'

Claire had always known she could not have been planned but it bothered her to think her presence on the earth was so accidental.

'But we were delighted when you did come along.'

'Not so much that you wanted another?'

'Oh we did vaguely think. . . But we were busy. You must bring Thomas to lunch on Sunday.' They were not too keen on Thomas, for the obvious reasons, but they were prepared to try and get on with him for her sake. After all, the main thing was that she should be happy.

Claire kissed her mother goodnight. Her father was waiting to run her home. They had dined simply but elegantly, with candles shining on a glossy table and a posy of roses impeccably arranged in the centre. Her mother was also a splendid cook, but made no fuss about it.

In the car her father said, 'So Thomas has left his wife?' It was a question Claire was tired of. She did not answer and her father continued, 'There's a daughter too, isn't there?'

'I didn't break up the marriage, Dad. It had been in the doldrums for years. Don't you believe me?'

'I believe that you believe Thomas. And I'm sure he believes it himself. He struck me as a basically honest chap.'

'I thought you might have been pleased he had taken a definite decision? It's less messy this way isn't it? Surely you of all people would not expect people to stay in marriages that are unsatisfactory?'

'Depends on what satisfactory means. Your mother and I don't expect everyone else's marriage to be like ours.' Many husbands and wives of their acquaintance lived together in varying degrees of amity without being downright unhappy, and many people, anyway, they found, did not rate happiness a very high priority in their lives. Most put above it a comfortable home and enough money to enjoy themselves.

'Well, you can't accuse Thomas of that,' said Claire.

'I'm not accusing him of anything,' said her father mildly.

'We just want happiness to be a priority in your life.'

'I am happy.'

'Good.'

This talk of happiness on her visits home depressed her.

They turned into her street. Under the overhanging bare tree stood Thomas's daughter. Claire did not point her out to her father.

When he had driven off, she crossed the road to the gardens. Mist hung between the trees like skeins of pale fine wool, much too fine for Thomas's sister to knit with. She favoured chunky knits, nobbly knits and bouclés, in strong, primary colours. At Claire's approach, Tasha lifted her chin as if she expected a blow to be directed at it.

'Hello, you're Tasha, aren't you? I'm Claire, though I expect you already know that. You shouldn't be hanging around here at this time of night. Wouldn't you like to come up and have a cup of coffee?'

Suddenly, without a word, Tasha cut and ran. Claire watched her go.

This was the outcome she had expected, but at least she had tried, and she could tell Thomas that she had, though the telling made her feel hypocritical for he said that was good of her. She did not feel at all good where Tasha was concerned, or any of the other members of his family. They were getting under her skin, which was probably what they were trying to do. When they sat in court and knitted and dropped knitting needles and exchanged whispered asides, her head itched under its sheep's wool covering and she longed to tear the wig off and scratch until her scalp tingled.

After Eunice's next half-day, Thomas telephoned his sister. She was voluble and self-righteous in her defence, using phrases like 'a free world' and 'the right of citizens to see that justice was done.' Thomas became impatient. He knew what she was like. He knew that she and his mother were not going to the courts in the interests of either justice or enlightenment, but to gawk. At Claire. And embarrass her. And him. His temper erupted and while he spluttered Eunice took the opportunity to get another bit in. Claire detected the ebb and flow of quarrels brought forward from childhood. Thomas told Eunice to bloody well stay out of his affairs and banged down

34

the receiver. 'Damned bitch!'

'Have you always fought?'

Thomas knew that it was not very dignified for two middle-aged people to be scrapping as if they were still kids. Eunice bore him a grudge and he couldn't really blame her: he had got all the 'chances' going in the family, she had had to make the sacrifices. It was the old story: he was the boy.

'I always wanted a brother or sister,' said Claire. 'For company. Since my parents were so wrapped up in one another and their work.'

'A close relationship needn't be restrictive,' said Thomas.

'No?' If she went for a drink after work now she felt guilty. She didn't have to, Thomas said; really she didn't. But talking of pubs reminded him that he had found a job. 'We ought to have been celebrating,' said Claire. He was not so sure about that; it was just a stopgap, not the first step in a new and stimulating career.

He started work as a barman in a pub whose name changed every few months and was currently called 'Nippers'. The owner had his ear permanently cocked for rumours of new trends. Thomas had to work evenings which meant that he was gone by the time Claire came home from the court. The smell of lasagne no longer met her on the stairway. But she could now work peacefully on her briefs, Hetty pointed out. Often though she was restless, would go to the window and look out, to find the opposite pavement empty. Tasha only kept guard when her father was in the building.

One evening, answering the doorbell, Claire found Liffey standing on the mat. Thomas was not in, she informed him.

'I wouldn't call that a very warm welcome.'

'I wouldn't call it a welcome at all.'

He laughed, leaned his shoulder against the door post. He liked the way she'd said that, straight from the shoulder. She made to shut the door but it encountered an obstruction.

'I used to sell encyclopedias. I've done everything in my time.'

She said she doubted that, which seemed to amuse him. 'Your lines are too obvious,' she added, which amused him less. 'You'll find Thomas at the pub.'

'But it was you I wanted to have a word with.' While she was hesitating, he pushed the door open and walked past her into the hall. 'I've got us a new witness. Jinty Smith's neighbour saw her coming in that night.'

'You should talk to your solicitor. It's not usual –'

'Oh come on, you don't have to give me all that red tape stuff.' He went through to the sitting room. He took off his camel-coloured coat and threw it over the back of the settee.

'Look, Mr Finlay –'

'Liffey.'

'I am very busy and you have no right to walk into my flat uninvited.'

'I'm an old pal of Tommy's.'

'But you're not an old pal of mine.'

'So what are you going to do about it? Call the police? Tommy wouldn't like that. Relax! I haven't come to rape you.'

'I call that in very bad taste.'

'I thought you would.' He moved over to the sideboard. 'Mind if I help myself?' He picked up the whisky decanter. 'Tommy and I have always shared things from way back. Going to join me?'

'No thanks.'

'Cheers.' He raised his glass to her. 'Tommy and I have always liked the same women.'

'But have the same women always liked you?'

He laughed again. 'Some of them have.'

Donald interviewed Jinty Smith's neighbour, a Mrs MacAteer, and thought she might be useful. They badly needed another witness. Mrs MacAteer claimed to have seen Jinty enter her house at eleven-fifteen on the evening of the alleged rape and come out again fifteen minutes later, to go then into her neighbour's house on the other side. Mrs MacAteer had been aware of the intervals of time as she had been watching for her own daughter coming home.

'Sounds fair enough,' said Claire. 'So Jinty had time, if Mrs MacAteer is to be believed, to go into her house, tear her clothes and inflict scratches on her person. Though I still find it difficult to think she was prepared to go to such lengths.'

Donald found it more credible. Because he sympathised

with the man? He denied that. He did not find Liffey an easy man to sympathise with.

'Nor I,' said Claire gloomily. When he had called at her flat he had drunk two more whiskies before she managed to dislodge him. She had told him she was waiting for a friend.

'Your solicitor pal? Seems a nice enough bloke, none too sharp though, if you ask me. Strikes me as someone who wouldn't know his arse from the cooker, outside of all that legal guff, of course. You're pretty pally aren't you? Always got your heads together. Oh just business I'm sure. Except that any man who could get his head near yours and not think of something else must need it examining.'

'Mr Finlay, if you don't mind –' Claire looked at her watch. 'I *am* expecting a friend – a woman friend.' She was immediately annoyed with herself for saying too much.

'I don't mind a threesome. Adds a little spice. All sorts of interesting combinations.'

'Get lost!'

That made him laugh, but he did get to his feet. He took his time about putting on his coat. He hadn't meant to stay, he said, or rile her. He'd just wanted to have his little joke. 'Got to have a sense of humour in this life, otherwise you'd get buried under all the shit that flies about. Great brown dust storms.' He put up his arm as if to shield his face. And laughed. His laugh grated on her nerves like a finger nail squeaking on a blackboard. 'You don't think I was *seriously* suggesting that you and I –'

'If you come up here again uninvited I'll drop your case.'

He sent her a bunch of white carnations the next day with a note of apology. He'd had a drink or two, otherwise . . . Thomas was at home to receive the delivery. He was holding the flowers when Claire came in from work.

'You'll have to drop Liffey's case.'

'It's out of the question.' She read the florist's card. 'Why don't you drop Liffey as a friend?' When Thomas did not answer, she added, 'Or is that out of the question?'

She stuck the carnations in a wine carafe and next day found that they had been dumped in the refuse bucket under a heap of potato peelings and coffee grounds. She made no comment.

To Donald, she said, 'There's something in Liffey's case I

37

can't quite get to grips with. Perhaps we should take a run out and look at the locus? To see it in the flesh might just inspire me.'

'I'd do anything to help inspire you, dear Claire. And a jaunt into the hinterland will do us no harm.'

Claire wore sunglasses and tied a scarf over her hair. The day was dull. The mining village sprawled along the main road and half way up the hill. The lower part comprised pre-war council houses covered with greyish harling; the higher part, newer, but equally dreary modern ones which showed signs of half-hearted efforts to spice them up by colouring their doors and planting spindly trees in the areas of wasteland. They drove slowly past the old primary school with its barred railings and concrete yard where Thomas once must have played with Liffey and queued at the tolling of the bell to enter the squat stone building.

'No wonder Thomas wanted out,' said Donald.

They passed the wool shop.

'Perhaps you should nip in and buy a pattern. Can you knit, Claire?'

'Not terribly well.'

'I find that difficult to believe. I'm sure anything you can do, you can do well.'

They came to the pub.

'Shall we go in and fortify ourselves?' said Donald.

Alex, the barman, recognised him. He made a great fuss of wiping their table and when he spoke to them he lowered his voice. 'Come to see the scene of the crime?'

'Exactly so,' said Donald. He introduced Claire and Alex, and the barman looked at her with interest.

'How's Tommy these days? Haven't seen him for a while.'

'Very well.'

'I hear he's taken up my game?'

They did not tarry overlong in the pub. By the time they came out, the door of the wool shop, which was in the same block, stood ajar and there was Eunice on the step deep in conversation with another woman. Both women turned to examine them.

'Perhaps this was not such a good idea after all,' said Claire, unfurling her umbrella as the first spots of rain darkened the pavement.

They walked up through the housing scheme until open country yawned behind the houses. They managed to identify Mrs Smith's easily enough from their plan, and that of the two neighbours, Mrs MacAteer who would be testifying for the defence, and Mrs Black for the prosecution. Beyond Mrs Black's house was a narrow lane, rutted, edged with high weeds.

'That would appear to be the scene,' said Donald and tramped a little way into it dirtying his feet on mud and excrement which he hoped was merely dog's. Emerging, he wiped his shoes vigorously on the grass verge. 'I believe one can get eye disease from dog dirt. Strange how some people take their pleasures.'

'I suppose they were under the influence.' Claire gazed around, at the grey houses and the weeds in the lane and the balding gardens and the washing hanging limp in the wet air. Out of this dispirited landscape had sprung Thomas, full of life. And Liffey too.

'They would need to be under the influence of something.' Donald surveyed his shoes which despite his efforts remained streaked with substances of one sort or another.

A woman had come out of the Mrs Smith's house. She was wearing a dressing gown slackly tied about the waist. Aware that she was being observed, she stood on the front step and, seemingly oblivious of the rain, began with small slow movements of her wrist to shake out an oblong orange rug. She looked younger than Claire had expected, and more attractive.

'Mrs Smith I presume,' said Donald. 'She looks as if she –'
'No snap judgments please!'

She looks vulnerable, thought Claire, and was disturbed that she should find her so, but then she recognised that her own judgment must be called into doubt for there was no question but that between having to give sympathy to this woman or to Liffey she would certainly give it to the woman.

'I rather wish I didn't have to present this case.'

39

'Perhaps I could still replace you. Under the circumstances, your connection with Thomas and his with –'

'No, no, I want to see it through now.'

Donald admitted that he could see why she felt intrigued. He did himself. 'Odd though isn't it, this friendship between Thomas and Liffey? I don't know how Thomas can be bothered with him.'

'I rather think it's more a case of him being bothered *by* him.'

'Some sort of guilt thing? Over pulling up from his roots, leaving his old friends behind?'

'I have no theories about it,' said Claire, who was working on them.

Mrs Smith gave them a last look and, taking her time, turned and went back into her house. When she appeared on the witness stand she would not be clad in a dressing gown, they could count on that; she would look a model of propriety in a dark-coloured coat, with little make-up and eyes modestly lowered.

The rain swelled suddenly to a downpour. Huddling under the umbrella which afforded inadequate protection, Claire and Donald splashed their way back down through the estate to the main road where the woman whom they had seen earlier talking to Eunice accosted them. She was apologetic. She introduced herself as Liffey's wife. 'I just wanted to ask you what his chances were?'

'Pretty fair,' said Claire, raising her voice against the tattoo of the rain.

'We can't say better than that, Mrs Finlay,' said Donald. 'We'll do our best.'

She thanked them and hurried on dragging her shopping trolley behind her. The rain had plastered her headscarf to her head.

'I suppose you were all at school together?'

'I don't know what you had to gain from going out there.'

But Claire was interested in Liffey's wife.

Thomas said, in reply to her next question, that he thought Jean probably hadn't had much of a life with Liffey, she'd put up with his philandering by turning a blind eye to it, he

40

suspected, and getting on with her job of bringing up the children.

'Do you know her well?'

'We once went around together, as a matter of fact. Before she was married of course. A long time ago. When we were seventeen, eighteen.'

'Why didn't you tell me before?'

She hadn't told him about all her boyfriends, he countered, nor would he want to know about them. They were before his time, had nothing to do with him.

'But this seems different,' said Claire.

Thomas moved off to serve a customer. Claire was sitting on a bar stool in the pub where he worked. It was the only way she could see him in the evenings and sometimes, even then, Liffey would come in and drag up a stool and drive her out by singing annoying songs in her ear. '*I'm a rambler, I'm a gambler, I'm a long way from home . . .*' Even the pub owner pointing out the sign that said 'No Singing' did not deter him; he merely lowered his voice. '*And if you don't like me you can leave me alone.*' Claire said that she wished she could, but she didn't have much choice, in the meantime.

Scotty, the pub owner, was in the bar now, though Liffey was not. Scotty was looking at the door and frowning. He said to Thomas, 'That girl's under age, wouldn't you think?'

Thomas and Claire turned to look.

'Oh, God, Tasha! Sorry about this, Scotty – she's my daughter.'

'Better ask her to leave then, Thomas.' If there was one thing that Scotty didn't want it was trouble. And he didn't want school kids messing up his smart pub. 'You can't be too careful,' he said to Claire, taking the stool next to her. 'You'll appreciate that, being in the law yourself.'

Thomas had lifted the counter lid and had gone to speak to Tasha. He was talking so quietly they could not hear what it was he said.

'Yes, I like to keep a clean nose,' said Scotty. 'What are you drinking, Claire?'

She was just about to leave. She slid down from her perch.

'You'll have to go, Tasha, you can't stay here,' Thomas was saying less quietly now. 'So go home, please!'

41

'I've no home to go to.'

'Don't be so bloody childish!'

'It's full of women and screaming kids –'

'You have a room of your own, a large room –'

'So go ahead, tell me I'm lucky now, other girls sleep ten to a room, some don't have a room to sleep in at all.'

'Why doesn't he slap her?' Scotty asked Claire.

'My mother doesn't even notice if I'm in or out,' said Tasha.

'I'm sorry, love, but –'

'A mistake that,' said Scotty, 'to say he's sorry.'

'If you *were* sorry you wouldn't leave me in that house,' said Tasha. 'If you cared at all what happened to me –'

Scotty sighed.

'She's only fifteen,' said Claire.

'Please go now, Tasha!'

Scotty went to serve a customer who was rattling his money on the counter. Everyone in the pub was listening to the dialogue at the door.

'Go at once, please, Tasha! I have a job to do.'

Scotty strolled across to join Thomas and his daughter. 'Now then, young lady,' he began.

'*Tasha!*' said Thomas again, warningly.

The girl had picked up an empty glass from a table. She held it above her head for a moment and then dashed it to the ground. Splinters sprayed in all directions. A customer yelped. A slice of glass had landed on her knee, though not much harm was done, at least not to her knee, but the floor was in a mess and Scotty in a state. He danced up and down and waved his arms about. He roared at Thomas to get the fucking place cleaned up but Thomas was not paying any heed, he was running out of the pub in pursuit of his daughter. And he did not come back.

'Now what am I supposed to do?' demanded Scotty.

Claire shrugged. He could scarcely expect her to sweep the floor and serve the customers who, with the excitement, had downed their drinks and were seeking refills. Though perhaps he might. Since he'd purchased his Porsche he appeared to expect the world to turn on its axis about him.

'I'll sue the bastard.'

'For what? A broken glass? Breach of contract?'

'I've got a dinner date at eight-thirty. You should see her
. . .' He was moaning, as if in physical pain.

Walking home, Claire welcomed the cool night air on her
face. The windows of her flat were dark. She rang Hetty.

Hetty said, 'Perhaps Thomas should take her to a psychiat-
rist.'

'Take her? Would she go? Anyway, that's not what she
wants.'

Hetty sighed. 'Poor child, she's having to face the fact that
what she wants she cannot have.'

Cannot? Claire would not have said it was as final as that.

After she had spoken to Hetty, she stayed by the telephone
drawing idly on the message pad. She drew a house, a square
one with a door in the middle and four windows, two on either
side, one up, one down, such as she used to draw as a child,
when her parents would say that houses didn't look like that,
not really, not if one looked. They had insisted that she look,
gently insisted, never forcing the matter, aware that that
would only cause revulsion. But in spite of their sensitivity,
she had stubbornly gone on drawing her own house. You'll
never make an architect, they had said jokingly, though they
did not believe what they said, nor what she said when she
declared that she didn't want to be one.

The telephone pealed out, startling her, making her lift the
receiver on the first ring and startling the caller at the other end.

'That was quick,' said Sarah, in her low, musical voice and
gave a little laugh. 'You must have been waiting for a call.'

Claire drew curtains at the sides of the windows of her house
making them come into a loop in the middle the way curtains
do when they are held back by a sash. They had never had
curtains like that in their house and now that she could have
them she no longer wanted them.

Sarah asked if she might speak to Thomas and Claire was
obliged to say that he was not in. Sarah made an interested
noise at the other end of the line and Claire began to shade in the
curtains. She used to make them red and green and yellow and
blue, each set different, not caring whether the colours jarred
and did not blend. The graphite pencil strokes looked dull.

'Can I give him a message?' she asked coolly.

'It's about Tasha – she's been playing truant again. I had a

43

letter from her headmistress today asking me to come for an interview. I don't see why *I* should be the one to be put on the carpet. It was Thomas who upset Tasha, after all. What else did he expect when he ran off? When he'd spent all those years building her up. Spoiling her.'

After Tasha's birth, Sarah had ceased to be much interested in sex, Thomas claimed, and for a while had almost taken against him physically. He had been patient, he said, but their sex life had never returned to being what it was before. That was his story of course and Claire did not doubt that Sarah would have a different one to tell. She squiggled through the drawing of the house on the telephone pad.

She said, 'I think you had better speak to Thomas yourself.'

'I keep trying to but he's never in.'

Claire said she thought he would be in more often in the future since he'd lost his job.

'I don't know how we're all going to manage for money,' said Sarah.

'I shall cut down on my alcohol intake,' said Thomas. 'It'll be good for my waistline, anyway. And my liver. And I shall cycle everywhere, even out to my mother's, and save on bus fares. I am determined not to sponge off you.'

'Don't be silly. I don't see it as sponging. I'm earning quite a lot –'

She had depressed him. She tried not to rub in the fact that she was employed, well, most of the time, for she was a sort of freelance worker and it was always possible to have a quiet spell. But she was having a good run at the moment, and when the reparation proof finished she would move on to a fraud which would take her into the new year. And after that there would be the case of Laurence Ian Fyffe Finlay.

She had a clear ringing voice and an agreeable, non–bullying manner, so she was told; solicitors and their staff liked her, put work her way. She looked well too these days, in spite of the nervous friction: the regular meals agreed with her, the uphill walk to work through the crisp autumnal mornings freshened her cheeks and exercised her limbs, and having Thomas in bed pleased her.

'There is no doubt,' said Donald, 'but that you have it made.'

'The question of money, though, is a difficult one with Thomas.'

'Bound to be. Wasn't he given a golden handshake when he got the heave? Couldn't he do something with that?'

'They used it to pay off the mortgage and his wife refuses to sell the house so he can't get his half out.'

'He should take her to court, sue her. You could act for him.'

'Very funny. He'd quite like to open up an antiquarian bookshop.'

'Not another! Place is coming down with them.'

'He thought he could specialise in Baltic and Russian affairs. Well, it's an idea anyway.'

'But there's no money.'

Claire observed that Amanda didn't seem to mind not earning?

'She's looking after our children. Job in itself.'

'Thomas has offered to look after ours.'

'Good God you're not –'

No, she assured him, she was not.

She paid off her cleaning woman and Thomas spent his days housekeeping, doing it much more diligently than Claire ever would, cleaning the bathroom sink daily, vacuuming the carpets twice weekly, cycling from one district of the city to another to ferret our bargains, and cooking elaborate meals out of cookery books unearthed from the bottom of her kitchen drawers.

'What you seem to have got yourself is a jolly old case of role reversal,' said Donald. 'Amanda's always reading about it to me from magazines.' Claire hated the term, and Donald knew that she would, so had used it with relish.

'The trouble is that when I come home at night and see what Thomas has been doing I feel guilty. I know it's stupid.'

'It's not as if you spend your days eating cream cakes and doing the shops.' Donald admitted, however, that he did know what she meant. The admission depressed him momentarily then he brightened and suggested that perhaps Thomas enjoyed housework.

'Do you?'

45

'Not exactly enjoy, no.' At week-ends he made the beds though he was hopeless at tucking in the corners and they tended to come apart in the night and he loaded the dishwasher after the evening meal but not too expertly and Amanda usually had to re-shuttle the plates about. 'She says I am not a handy man.'

'How fortunate for you,' said Claire, who was handy enough herself in the house. Her parents had seen to it that she could mend fuses and put up shelves and things of that nature. So she didn't really *need* a man in the house, said Donald, not in that way at least. Cooking could be creative of course, mused Claire, who was still ruminating on the pleasures and pains of housework.

Not Amanda's cooking, said Donald. She was too exhausted by the time she finished with the children in the evening to do more than throw frozen beef-in-a-bag into boiling water. 'Sometimes I even have to snip off the end myself and let it ooze out.'

'Poor you. Whereas there am I feeding off lamb *pasanda* and *coq au vin*.'

Claire lost the reparation proof. It was only to be expected, said Donald, she hadn't really had a chance. But nevertheless she felt deflated. And the judge happened to give his decision on a Wednesday afternoon.

'I doubt if Eunice and her mother have actually been able to follow what's going on,' said Donald. 'I scarcely have myself. All that business of going up and down ladders interminably.'

Claire looked up at the public benches where Eunice and her mother were packing up their knitting. She was not so sure: there were no fleas on Eunice, as Thomas was so fond of saying. She was sharp enough and had she had his chances in life she might have gone far. When the judge had found in favour of the pursuer, Eunice had given Claire a triumphant look as if it were she herself who had presented the pursuer's case.

Claire stood up and eased her wig. Her head felt like a bird's nest.

'I think a drink is in order,' said Donald. 'We must drown

our sorrows and live to fight another day.'

'Just one then,' said Claire.

Two drinks later Donald said, 'Have another drink?'

'I said only one.'

'We all say things. If I go home now I'll get the baby to bath.'

All right, she agreed, but just one more, and she insisted on buying it, and going to the bar to do so encountered a fellow female advocate and two solicitors whom she knew. They got talking and the other three ended by joining Claire and Donald. It was a wet night out, as one of them said, coming down cats and dogs. Tasha would get soaked, thought Claire, and looked at her watch. She really should be getting home soon.

'In for a penny,' said Donald.

The rain had stopped by the time they emerged. A north-easterly wind had sprung up. Donald suggested a taxi but Claire preferred to walk, she always walked, and she was certainly capable of walking now, she had not had all *that* much to drink, though she did feel just a little light-headed, which was not surprising since she had eaten only a sandwich for lunch.

'Women can't take as much alcohol as men of course, can they?' said Donald. 'Rots the jolly old liver faster. Better hang on.' He presented her with the crook of his arm. 'I'll walk you home.'

They proceeded down the hill. Claire found the night wind freshening to the head.

'I do hope your *coq au vin* will not have become *coq brulée*,' said Donald.

'I hope your beef-in-the-bag will not have dried up.'

'Oh beef-in-the-bag can boil all night and its quality remains unimpaired. That is one of its virtues. In fact, there's nothing like bagged beef for tardy husbands.'

'As long as Amanda keeps topping up the water.'

Donald was philosophical: if the pot ran dry, so be it. Bread and dripping could always be eaten instead.

They reached the corner of Claire's street. There was no sign of Tasha under the tree.

47

'What about a cup of coffee before you go in and face Thomas?' said Donald.

'I don't have to *face* him.'

'Of course, I was forgetting – yours is a free relationship.'

Thomas was sitting on the settee, listening, or rather not listening, to Schubert's Trout quintet. His arms were folded in a set, unnatural way, too high up across his chest. She kissed the top of his head and said she was sorry.

'I had a dreadful day you see –'

'How awful for you.'

'I lost my case.'

'That's too bad.'

'So when I came out I felt like a drink.'

'There's plenty on the sideboard. Whisky, gin, sherry –'

'I wanted it then. And there. So I went for a quick one –'

'With Donald.'

'*And* a couple of other solicitors. And Angela Simpson. You remember Angela, don't you?'

'And the quick one turned into a slow one. Slow, slow, quick, quick, slow.'

'Well, you know how it is!'

'Have you *any* idea what the time is?'

And so the row developed in its inevitable way. He told her of the time spent shopping, cooking, even thinking about what to make, and she told him that she did appreciate his efforts and she had not intended to be so late. He said she could at least have rung, she said *he* had gone drinking many a time and forgotten the time. But not with other women! Ah, so that was it. He was jealous! And she was selfish. And self-centred. She put her career above people.

She paused to draw a long breath. She was sick of that damned stupid accusation. Just because she was a woman! If she were a man she wouldn't be accused of putting her career above people, no matter how ambitious she was. She would be praised for being hard-working. 'Anyway, you put your precious Tasha above me. She only has to whistle and you go to her.'

'She's disturbed.'

48

'So am I.'

'I left her for you, didn't I?'

'That in itself tells a tale. It wasn't Sarah you left, but Tasha. But I didn't ask you to leave anyone. I didn't ask you to come here – remember?'

How could he forget when she reminded him all the time? That was not true, she retorted. He was becoming so sensitive she couldn't let fall the slightest unconsidered remark.

'And you're so bloody insensitive!'

'I hate you!' she said.

She trembled. She felt the words quivering inside her head for although she had spoken them she had not rid herself of them. It was a long time since she had told anyone she hated them, not since childhood. She and Hetty used to fall out and scream I hate you hate you hate you. And walk away.

'In that case perhaps I should go?' said Thomas.

'If you find me so insensitive you will hardly want to stay.'

'Shall I go? Is that what you want?'

They were quiet now. She slumped into a chair. She did not know what she wanted. But she didn't hate him, not really, not absolutely, not for ever and ever, not any more than she had hated Hetty when they had fallen out, for the intensity was of the moment. But rancour would remain and was not so easily annihilated.

'Shall I go?'

She sighed.

He came to her, put his arms around her and she shed tears against his shoulder. Why did everything have to end in conflict? It didn't have to, he said. He told her he loved her, she told him she loved him. They kissed and went to bed.

As they came together, the telephone rang.

'Let it ring,' he said. 'Let it ring!'

She did not register when it stopped ringing. Nothing mattered but the fusion of their bodies, nothing would stop that, nothing could get between them now. Let it ring!

It rang again, as they collapsed, gasping, holding on tightly to one another. It rang and rang. Claire turned her head and looked at the cream-coloured instrument on the bedside table. It would not stop.

She stretched out her hand and lifted the receiver.

'I'm terribly sorry to bother you,' said Sarah in her low, musical voice, 'but it's Tasha. She's not with you is she? No, I didn't think so. Then – she's gone missing.'

PART TWO
Thomas and Sarah

'I'm sorry if I rang at an inconvenient moment,' said Sarah.

'Why didn't you phone earlier?'

'I did, but you weren't answering.'

'I meant earlier in the evening. It's eleven o'clock now.'

'I tried between six and seven, after I'd found her note. You didn't appear to be in.'

Thomas protested that he'd been in all evening, then remembered he'd slipped out to the Paki for some sunflower oil and fresh ginger, and on the way back had stopped off at the local for a quick beer. (He did not offer the second piece of information.) He said, 'You mean you didn't find her letter till six o'clock?'

'I wasn't looking for a letter before then. Why would I have been? She often doesn't come straight home from school. She's been doing all *sorts* of peculiar things recently.'

The policewoman, who had been finding the interchange interesting, coughed, with some reluctance, to interrupt them. But she and her male colleague had to get some facts into their notebooks. 'If we could just get back to the description, Mrs Peterson?'

'Five feet four –'

'Five,' said Thomas.

'Five feet four or five,' said the policeman, writing in his book. He stood in front of the gas fire, with his back to it, while his partner sat on a high chair, placed so that she could observe both Thomas and Sarah, though Thomas was not so easy to keep an eye on for he was roving around the room alighting on no one spot for more than a second or two. A restless type obviously. And an absentee husband too, so it would seem.

'Colour of hair?'

'She looks like her father,' said Sarah.

The policeman squinted at Thomas. 'Fair hair, blue eyes. Any distinguishing marks?'

'Scar on left forearm,' said Thomas. 'She cut herself going through a glass window –'

'I'm sure the constable doesn't need all those details,' said Sarah.

'We may do, for identification.'

'You're surely not suggesting – !'

There was a rush of feet in the corridor outside, then the door burst open and in came, treading close on one another's heels, Helen, Arlene and Marilyn. Sarah introduced them. 'These are my friends,' she said. The constables ran their eyes over them, mentally frisking them: Helen, in wool sweater and tweed skirt of good quality, though not new, Arlene, dazzling in tight trousers and top of electric blue with pencil-thin stiletto heels; and Marilyn, billowing in pregnancy and nearing her term. The women dropped down into the soft wide settee and Arlene immediately took a cigarette packet with some difficulty from the pocket of her trousers and offered one to Marilyn. Sarah shook her head at Marilyn who concentrated on lighting her cigarette from the flame of Arlene's lighter.

Thomas greeted the new arrivals perfunctorily before turning back to confront Sarah.

'But if you found her letter at six why did you wait all this time to phone the police?'

'I was hoping she might come back,' said Sarah coolly. She felt cool for the first time since finding Tasha's letter. At least Thomas's arrival had done that for her. And that terrible piercing anxiety had moved over to make room for indignation. What a nerve he had to come here reeking of that woman and upbraiding her for negligence! 'I thought she might even not have meant it. I thought she might just be trying to alarm us.'

'She still might of course,' said Arlene. 'Knowing Tasha.'

'I see,' said the policewoman.

'Have you tried my mother?' demanded Thomas. Tasha was fond of her grandmother, her paternal more than her maternal one who was prone to asking her what she *did* with herself. By doing, Sarah's mother meant belonging to the Junior Red Cross, which Sarah had belonged to when young,

54

or the Sea Scouts, or visiting the elderly. The family believed in public service, which Thomas thought a good thing, in theory, himself; he always denied, to Sarah, that he sneered at it. He agreed with her that the country probably would be in better shape if its citizens were to readopt the old ideas of duty and responsibility towards their neighbours. It took wars and disasters (but not the threat of them) to bring out the better sides of people's natures. Sarah's mother had run a contraceptive clinic in the days before contraception was much organised. Now ensconced in rural Perthshire in their retirement, she and her husband still did a great deal of good in the community.

'I have tried everybody's mother,' said Sarah. Tasha had not been seen at school, or anywhere in the neighbourhood, that day, though she had set off for school in the morning at the usual time.

'Set off for school as usual but did not arrive,' said the policeman, putting pen to paper once more.

'Christ!' Thomas strode up the middle of the floor, taking care to avoid banging into the legs of the women on the settee. 'I can't believe it. It sounds like an item you read in the newspaper.'

'That's how they often go,' said the policewoman. 'Walk out in the morning without a word. They don't all leave notes.'

'Not much the police can do, any road, is there?' said Arlene cheerfully. 'Wee lassie went missing at the back of us a year ago . . .'

Marilyn began to cough and wheeze and clutch her stomach as it if might come loose. Sarah, trying to control her irritability, said why didn't she go to bed? 'There's nothing you can do here, Marilyn, and you need your rest.'

'How could I go away to my bed when poor wee Tasha might be wandering God knows where?' Marilyn looked pained. And Sarah was always going on at them about involvement.

'Could she be on drugs?' asked the policewoman.

'No,' said Sarah and Thomas simultaneously.

The policeman looked at the three women on the settee.

'I wouldn't think so,' said Helen. 'We've never seen any signs of it.'

55

'Can't always tell, though, can you?' said Arlene. 'Wee laddie next door to us was sniffing glue and they hadn't a clue till he conked out.'

'Was she ever in any kind of trouble?'

'She was once arrested, with a friend,' said Sarah. 'After being shadowed by a police car for an hour. They were then held for a further hour and a half in a police box without being allowed to contact their parents.'

The constables exchanged looks.

'They were flyposting,' said Thomas. 'For Youth CND. They were advertising a jumble sale.'

'Oh she's like that, is she?'

'We are *all* like that,' said Sarah. 'We do not like being the premier nuclear target in the world. Do you know that we have over two hundred nuclear installations in Scotland?'

'Yes well, we'd better not get into that,' said the policewoman with a smile. 'We could be here all night. Did she have any money?'

'She took her Post Office savings book. There were about fifty pounds in it, as far as I know.' And Sarah thought that ten or fifteen pounds might be missing from her purse, but she was careless with money, even though she was short of it, so could not be certain and did not mention it. It scarcely mattered anyway, whether Tasha had fifty or sixty pounds. Where the hell was she?

'She's got her head screwed on, has Tasha,' said Arlene.

'But she *is* only fifteen.' Thomas appealed to the constables. 'Do you mean to say there's nothing you can do?'

Not a lot, they admitted. They wouldn't even know where to start though they'd certainly keep their eyes open.

'That's good. I am pleased to know that. Terribly pleased.'

'Between thirteen and fifteen thousand youngsters go missing in Britain every year, sir,' said the policeman.

'I heard something on the radio about that,' said Arlene. 'Lot of them go on the streets apparently. Imagine, twelve-year-old prostitutes! Some of them do it just to annoy their parents. Gloucester Road Tube Station in London's one of the places they hang out.'

'Did anything happen to upset her?' asked the policewoman. 'Would she want to annoy you?'

56

There was silence in the room. They listened to the burble of the gas fire. One of the pieces had fallen out. Sarah made a mental note yet again to get it replaced. It couldn't cost that much.

'Well, kids are easy annoyed, aren't they?' said Arlene.

'Do you all live here?' asked the policeman, looking round at the clothes horse covered with nappies, at the box in the corner overflowing with battle-scarred toys, at the women on the settee, and at Thomas.

'Except for me,' said Thomas.

The constable nodded. 'Have none of you any idea where she might have gone?'

'Suppose she could have gone off with a man,' said Arlene.

'That's highly unlikely, Arlene,' said Sarah. 'You know it is.'

'What makes you say that?' the policewoman asked Arlene.

'Well, at fifteen that's all you think about, isn't it? Sex.' She laughed and her electric blue ear-rings flashed.

'Do you know of any man she might have been involved with?' The policewoman searched their faces in turn.

'Only her father,' said Sarah.

The constables laughed. The man tucked his notebook into his top pocket and the woman got up easing her skirt over her hips. She put on her hat. They moved towards the door. They'd keep in touch and who knows but by morning Tasha might have returned of her own free will? A night out in the cold often brought these girls to their senses.

'*These* girls?' said Thomas.

They looked at him blankly.

He saw them out. He returned scratching the back of his head vigorously. 'They'll keep their eyes open!'

'She'll not do anything really daft, take it from me,' said Arlene. 'Like I said, she's got her head screwed on.'

'She has hasn't she?' Thomas looked at her gratefully.

Sarah began to tidy up, to gather newspapers and toys and bits and pieces of scattered clothing, to indicate that the day should be brought to an end. She had had enough of it. And she did not want Thomas here half the night pacing up and down the floor letting his imagination run riot. She could see it beginning to erupt. If he went she would have a better chance of staying calm, and she had no doubt that that was the best thing to do, for she thought that what the police had said was probably true and she did half expect Tasha to turn up the next day. Only half though. But she could not allow herself to dwell on where the other half of her expectations might lead.

'Sarah,' said Thomas, 'Do you know that there are two men standing on the opposite side of the street? They look as if they're keeping guard.'

'That's my man Gil,' said Arlene, 'and his brother. They cry him the Weasel. They were battering the door down earlier. They only stopped when the peelers arrived.'

As if on cue, the battering recommenced.

'He's gòt a right awful temper, has Gil. That's how he landed in the Nick. Assault and battery.'

'Theft too, though, wasn't it?' said Marilyn, heaving herself out of the depths of the settee.

'Aye, but if he'd not lost his temper and battered the man he'd have got away with it.'

'That can't go on,' said Thomas, making for the front door. Sarah called him back saying that on no account was he to open the door for if he did they'd have the two men in here and then where would they be? He could hardly take them both on. The police had already been called once and warned them off.

'It'd take a lot more than warning to keep them two away,' said Arlene.

'They'll give up eventually,' said Sarah. 'They usually do, don't they Marilyn?' Marilyn's husband had come only twice and stood on the doorstep saying stiffly, 'If you're not coming home that's it then. Please yourself.' 'That's what I am doing,' she had said. And Helen's husband had not come at all. When she had rung up to say she had left him he had told her that was okay by him. Turned out he had another woman. He'd been beating Helen up nightly. He taught English in a school in a deprived area and couldn't cope.

A child was crying somewhere overhead and soon was joined by another. The three women went up to bed leaving Sarah with Thomas. The crying and the battering went on.

'This is like a lunatic asylum,' said Thomas. 'No wonder –'

'That is not why Tasha left.'

They argued about that for a while and then Thomas

rummaged in the sideboard until he found a bottle of whisky. When the telephone rang in the hall Sarah ran to answer it.

But it was only a neighbour to ask what the hell was going on and to say that if the noise didn't stop at once he'd phone the police. Please do, said Sarah, feel free. She lifted the letter box flap and called, 'Go away!' The knocking ceased. She felt a man's breath coming through the slit and pulled her head back. 'You might as well go away for we are not going to let you in and the neighbours are calling the police.'

'I want my fucking wife and kids.'

'If you hadn't beaten up your wife –'

'I'll do what I bloody well like with her!'

'She's got other ideas about that.'

'Put into her fucking head by you. How did she get in with you anyway?'

'I found them in the St. James's Centre sitting on a seat. They were *all* crying. So goodnight!'

Sarah straightened herself and rubbed the hollow in her back to ease the crick in it.

'The police have arrived,' called Thomas.

Once that disturbance had died down, they had peace for a while. They sat on either side of the gas fire and drank whisky, too exhausted to harangue one another any more. Thomas read Tasha's letter for the tenth time.

I am going away. I realise that I shall have to start a new life on my own. Please don't worry about me. I shall write when I am settled. Love, Tasha.

Sarah slept no more than an hour or two and woke with a thick head. The house was quiet. She got up and dressed and went out. The street was shrouded in pale grey light, the sea a blur of darker grey at the foot of it. In the car across the road the two men were slumped, one with his head lolling back, like a straw doll, the other, the driver, over the steering wheel, his arms cradling it. She went past in her soft-soled shoes.

The promenade was deserted. No breath of wind disturbed it. Last night's chip wrappers lay immobile against walls or wrapped around railings, wherever the last gust had deposited them. The sea lapped gently on the sand making no more sound than a whisper. And into the Eastern sky the sun was nudging, etching a thin red line. Even as she watched the line expanded and the colour changed, from red to pink, and a hint of pale green appeared, and now a shaft of yellow. She might have let the sky detain her for another hour but she began to walk.

She moved rhythmically, letting her arms swing loosely. Her body felt strangely harmonious after such a discordant night. She usually walked on the promenade in the early morning, though not often as early as this. Thomas had stayed until late and they had talked and talked conjecturing where Tasha might have gone, how her mind might have worked. They thought in the end she might have gone to London: it was *the* anonymous place to go to, the place where young girls tended to go to, it was a city that Tasha knew moderately well and found exciting. They had sometimes gone on week-end breaks, taking in the zoo, a theatre, a gallery, Madame Tussauds, the usual things, something for everyone. Those times had been good times, Sarah remembered.

She became suddenly aware of footsteps at her back. She turned her head. Arlene's husband and his brother were only a few paces behind, and gaining, splitting now to fan out and come up one on each side of her. Their eyes were blood-shot, bristle sprouted on their chins. They said nothing for a moment though their jaws moved continuously. As Arlene's husband opened his mouth to speak she saw a wad of grey gum shift back on his tongue.

'Lovely morning.'

'It was.'

'Don't you like our company then?' said the Weasel. 'Hey, Gil, lady doesn't like our company. Can't understand it, can you?'

'Can't understand it at all. What have we ever done to you, hen?' Arlene's husband bumped into Sarah and said, 'Sorry, sorry, just an accident, didn't mean to lay hands on your lily-white body. You wouldn't fancy a man's hands on your lily-white body, would you? You don't fancy men, do you?'

'You a les?' asked the Weasel.

'I'm going to turn off here,' said Sarah. She indicated a side street.

'Oh let's walk a little further,' said Arlene's husband, putting his hand through her arm. 'Just to the end of the prom and back. "*Oh I do like to be beside the seaside*," he sang, very softly.

'Give me Blackpool any day. Or Torremolinos.' His brother gazed out to sea. 'Bloody Portobello! At six o'clock in the bleeding morning. Why don't you give him back his woman and then we can get home to our beds?'

'She's not mine to *give*. She's not a possession. She's got a mind of her own.'

'Don't make me laugh,' said her husband. 'Arlene?' He did laugh.

Sarah, forsaking coolness and pomposity (she felt annoyed at having been forced into both), decided to try the reasonable approach. 'Now look,' she began, 'Arlene was unhappy, you were maltreating her –'

'Maltreating?' Gil treated himself to another laugh. 'What else would a bloke do? She was screwing the television engineer.'

They reached the end of the promenade and turned, with the brother saying, 'Hup, two, three, four,' and keeping them in tight formation. Arlene had not mentioned the television engineer, not that that mattered, any more than it did whether she had been actually screwing him or not – her husband still had no right to beat her up.

He said, 'It fucks you up to come home and find your wife with another man.' Sarah said yes, it *was* wounding when a partner was unfaithful. But had *he* always been faithful to Arlene? The Weasel snickered.

'Well then, how can *you* expect –?'

'That's different innit?'

'How is it?'

'Stands to reason.'

'What reason?'

'I don't do it in my own house for one thing under the nose of my kids.'

She took the conversation no further, knowing it to be futile. Further along, a man who lived in her street was walking his dog. She waved to him and he looked surprised for they were not normally on waving terms. Hesitantly, he waved back. She said that she must go home now, she was *going* to go.

'That's all right,' said Gil, removing his hand from her arm. 'We're not holding you against your will nor nothing. We're not trying to kidnap you.'

'We've got enough trouble on our hands as it is,' said the Weasel.

'Just one thing though before you do go though,' said Gil. 'I want a word with Arlene. A quiet word. Can I come in and talk to her?'

'If you promise –'

'Anything, doll.' He raised his right hand.

She agreed, with reluctance, as she told the women later when they were having breakfast round the kitchen table, the four of them, in peace, with the children already fed and either taken to school or sent out to play in the walled back garden.

'He's got patter, has Gil,' said Arlene.

'Don't let him sweet-talk you then,' said Marilyn. 'You'll regret it three hours later. It's not so easy to walk out twice. I know – I did it.' She patted her stomach. 'And look what happened in between.'

'You've got to think of the children too,' said Helen, who thought of the children from morning till night and even right through it. She watched over them like a shepherd, rounding up any who strayed beyond the garden gate.

'Go back to him!' said Arlene. 'You must be joking. Who wants to get beat up every time their man goes out for a booze-up?'

Sarah had not mentioned the television engineer. But she did wonder what Arlene was going to do for sex. For it was clear that she would need to do something.

Arlene's husband arrived at the hour arranged. He had shaved and put on a clean shirt. Having made sure that he was alone, Sarah released the chain from the back of the door and allowed him to come in.

He stepped into the hall raising both hands above his head. 'I'm clean. What to frisk me?' He laughed. He looked up the staircase. 'Quite a big place you've got here. Funny set-up. You the Mother Superior?'

Sarah opened the sitting room door and asked him to wait in there. Then she called Arlene who had been listening at the back of the kitchen door.

'I'm not sure that I want to see him,' said Arlene. Rouge spots stood out on her pale cheeks. She lit a cigarette from the stub of the old one.

'You'll have to now.' Sarah gave her a little push.

Sarah joined Helen and Marilyn in the room across the passage which had once been the dining room and now served as playroom for the children. The children were not there: a friend of Sarah's had collected them in her estate wagon earlier and driven them off to her house for the afternoon. Helen was tidying the toys, Marilyn smoking a cigarette and rubbing her stomach. Sarah positioned herself by the window. She watched the empty car and the stretch of street that ran down to the promenade. There seemed to be no sign of the Weasel, though, as Marilyn pointed out, he could be hiding round the corner.

When the telephone rang Sarah went to the kitchen to answer it on the extension.

'Any news?' asked Thomas.

'Well, he's in with her at the moment –'

'Who's in with her? Is Tasha back?'

No, no, she was talking about Arlene, and went on to explain but Thomas cut her short saying, 'For Christ's sake, aren't you even concerned about your own daughter? Maybe you've forgotten you have a daughter?'

That was not true at all, she retaliated – and it was *not* true – but at this very moment . . . He would not let her complete any of her sentences; his voice managed to drown hers effectively.

'*Sarah*,' Helen was calling.

'Look, Tom –'

'Come quickly, Sarah!'

She dropped the receiver.

Arlene was in the hall with her husband. He had one hand on the front door handle and the other on her forearm which he had bent up behind her back so that her teeth were clenched in pain. Sarah had taught Arlene how to break a man's grip but she seemed to have forgotten. Her knees were buckled, one

63

ankle was twisted over and her long thin heel lay flat against the ground. Gil was telling her that she was nothing but a bitch and she had no right to keep his children away from him. He jerked the arm higher and she whimpered.

'Leave go of her!' said Sarah, moving towards them. 'You're hurting her arm.'

'I'll hurt more than her arm in a minute.'

'You promised –'

'And you were mug enough to believe me?'

'Yes, I was.'

'That's your problem then.'

Helen was in the playroom doorway with Marilyn behind her. 'His brother's out there,' she said.

'Phone the police, Marilyn,' said Sarah. 'Come on then, Helen!'

Helen came forward and together they tackled Gil. Their two terms of self-defence classes had made them ready for such an occasion. Gil winced and slackened his grip; Arlene wriggled free and fled up the stairs.

'Christ!' He reeled back against the door moaning. He nursed his genital area with his right hand. 'You won't get away with this.'

In the small of his back the letter box was being rattled. 'Are you there, Gil?'

'This is quite ridiculous,' said Thomas, who arrived just after the police. 'You can't go on like this.'

'We don't intend to,' said Sarah. 'We're charging him with intimidation and assault.' She pulled up the leg of her trousers to display a large bruise which was already flowering. 'There are four of us to give evidence. That should be enough to put him away, shouldn't it? With his record?'

'You can't tell,' said the policewoman, the same one who had been here the day before. 'Depends on the judge. Some of them would pat Jack the Ripper on the head and tell him to go and be a good boy.'

'The fact that he's Arlene's husband might be a mitigating circumstance,' said Thomas. 'He could plead emotional disturbance, unhinged by loss of wife and children . . .'

'Of course you'll know all about things like mitigating circumstances these days,' said Sarah. 'Perhaps we could ask your friend to act for us?'

'As far as I know, advocates don't act in such cases.'

'You *do* take an interest in her work.'

Arlene, who had been very quiet, said, 'I've changed my mind. I don't want to bring a charge against him.'

'You've got to, or he'll just go on harassing you,' said Sarah. She appealed to the constables. 'Isn't that right?'

'Very likely,' said the policewoman. 'Takes a lot to put a type like him off.'

'Behind bars is the only way,' said the policeman.

'I don't want to,' said Arlene.

'Well, we can't make you,' said the policewoman. 'It's up to you.' She got up. 'You can think it over.'

'Don't go on at me now,' said Arlene, when the constables had gone.

But Sarah did not have the energy to go on at her. The children had returned and she and Helen were cooking the evening meal and laying the table. Arlene was smoking restlessly, spilling ash around the draining board and asking if there was anything she could do? Thomas said he would hang on for a bit in case Gil and the Weasel came back. They had taken off before the police arrived.

Thomas followed Sarah into the larder.

'I don't know why the house has to be full of all these people.'

'You didn't mind when I brought Helen and Jamie home.' In fact, she thought he had been quite pleased, for he had just begun his affair with Claire and had taken to sleeping on the couch in his study saying he was having trouble with his insomnia again and didn't want to disturb Sarah. He would avoid her eye and give most of his attention when he was in the house to Tasha. On Sarah asking if there was anything wrong, he said he was worried about his job. Which he was. It was at the end of that academic year that his department closed down.

A piercing scream coming from some part of the house sent them dashing back into the kitchen and then, in Arlene's wake, to the hall.

Arlene's daughter, Marbella, lay on the bottom step

clutching her arm. Blood was trickling from it, just above the elbow. It was she who was screaming and the noise seemed out of proportion to the thin snake of blood. But perhaps not. For over her stood Arlene's son, Jason, holding a pink-tipped darning needle.

'He stabbed me,' Marbella was roaring. 'He stabbed me.'

'Did you?' Arlene cuffed Jason hard across the back of the head and he fell forward on to his knees, still clutching upright between two hands the darning needle as if it were a sword. She cuffed him again. 'If you've done that I'll bloody well kill you so I will.'

Jason, too, now began to roar. He lifted his head and looked with hatred at his mother. 'I was just giving her a fix,' he said between sobs. 'It was only a game. She done it to me yesterday.'

Eventually, the children went to bed, more or less. At least they had gone upstairs and the downstairs' rooms could be tidied and made habitable. Helen went up with the children, to remove all sewing needles, darts and other sharp-pointed instruments, and also, soft, rounded objects, like beads, for Arlene's other daughter, Melody, had stuffed some up her nose the evening before and had had to be taken to the Sick Children's hospital to have them brought down again. When all the offensive weapons had been gathered into a cardboard box and given for disposal to Helen's son Jamie who, although only nine, appreciated the dangers of sticking darning needles into people, Helen settled down to read to the two youngest children about the adventures of Jemima Puddle Duck.

'Go fuck that stupid duck,' said Jason, who was not one of the ones being read to.

'What did you say, Jason?'

'I never said nothing.'

'I *hope* you didn't say anything.'

'Fuck the duck,' said Damian, taking his thumb out of his mouth. Jason tittered and thus encouraged, Damian, with Melody joining in, screamed, 'Fuck the duck, fuck the duck!'

Helen rejected Jemima in favour of Tom Kitten.

'Tom titty Kitten,' said Jason.

'Titty Kitten,' cried Melody. 'Tom Titty.'

'Let's have *The Tale of Ginger and Pickles*,' said Helen – Jason was not quick enough or smart enough to think up something for this one – and quickly began to read. '"Once upon a time there was a village shop . . ."'

Arlene had remained downstairs. She had changed into leopard skin (mock) trousers and a blouse which could be seen through when she stood against the light. She was padding up and down. 'I feel like I'm behind bars. I could be doing with a drink. In a pub.'

'You can't go out, you know you can't,' said Sarah.

'Why shouldn't I? There's no sign of them out there.'

'But they could come back anytime.'

'I'll go stark staring bonkers if I don't get out of here for a while.'

'Oh all right, but I'll come with you.'

Thomas asked if he might join them so they went, all three, Arlene walking in the middle and holding on to their arms, to a pub on the promenade. A lively breeze was blowing off the sea. 'Fresh air!' cried Arlene, tossing her head. Thomas said he knew how she felt; he hated to be confined for too long himself. Sarah said that things would settle down eventually, the interim period was bound to be disturbing, but Arlene was only half listening, for Thomas was holding open the door of the pub and she could smell the beer and the tobacco smoke and see the bottles gleaming behind the bar. She went straight to the counter and leant her arms on the stained brown wood. 'What are you having?' she asked over her shoulder. 'I got my Social Security today.'

Sarah and Thomas took their drinks to a table but Arlene picked up her gin and tonic and went to play the one-armed bandit. The pub was quiet, it being early evening, and only one elderly man sat reading the evening paper.

'Do you know,' said Thomas, 'that Tasha's been gone more than twenty-four hours?'

'I expect she'll get in touch soon,' said Sarah and felt suddenly tired. Tired of reassuring other people. But she would rally, she knew. Knowing it made her sigh.

'You look all in.'

'I *am* all in.' It had only just occurred to her that she had been left now by both Thomas and Tasha. Was there something about her that invited rejection? She must talk to her Aunt

Edmée. God, she must. She needed to. Edmée, who had been in the North-West Frontier for some months, was due home soon. Her aunt, living in a state of perfect harmony with herself, was good on marriage and relationships; her non-involvement helped make her objective and being blessed with good common sense she could often see the problem in a clearer light than the person wrestling with it. And whereas she might not have answers, she usually had suggestions.

'Why did you go this time, Tom?' asked Sarah. 'You didn't for any of the others.'

'This time it's different. I am sorry, really I am.'

'I can see the attraction of course, especially for a man of your age.' (And for a man who had been made redundant in middle-life.) 'She's young, good-looking, on top of things. She is far from being all in.'

'It's got nothing to do with my age.'

'Do you expect me to believe that?'

He shrugged.

Arlene came over to their table. She fancied going along to the Amusement Arcade, she could be doing with a bit of fun.

'Fun?' said Thomas. 'In that place?'

'There's none going here is there?' She edged away. 'I'll see you later, Sarah.'

'Be careful!' called Sarah, but Arlene was gone, out through the swing door, heading for all the fun of the fair where the fairy lights glistened and show folk listened to the rattle of coins and the whir of fruit machines and the crack of long-nosed rifles.

'Roll up, roll up!' said Thomas. He frowned. 'Tasha's never hung about in those places has she?' Sarah thought not, though could not be sure. They had always warned her not to go to the arcades, and certainly not alone. Odd people went there, they had said, people who are up to no good. Saying that might have tempted her there. Whatever one said as a parent could turn out to be the wrong thing. Earlier in the day Sarah had gone up to Tasha's room to look for clues and had spent an hour or two guiltily reading old diaries, letters, poems on scraps of paper. The letters from friends were out of date, her current diary was missing, and the poems had been upsetting. They were all about loss.

'I must go,' said Thomas, looking at his watch. 'You'll ring me if –'

'Of course.'

They parted outside the pub. Mounting his bicycle, he turned inland; she went along the promenade in pursuit of Arlene.

The lights in the first arcade were dingy and made the people inside look seedier than they possibly were. A number of people were playing fruit machines with lip-biting concentration indifferent to the old man in a torn raincoat spitting on the floor or the two youths who were kicking a machine and screaming at the attendant. There was no sign of Arlene. Sarah moved on to the larger amusement park.

She circumvented a merry-go-round on which no one rode and thought she saw Tasha standing beside the rifle range. Her heart leapt and she began to run. *Thank you, God, thank you! I'll do anything. . .* She stopped dead. The girl did not look at all like Tasha. How could she have possibly thought that she did? When her heart beat had slowed down she resumed her patrol thinking now that it was Arlene whom she saw at every turn. And then she caught sight of her just as she was about to go into the Hall of Mirrors. She called her name.

Arlene waved back. 'Come on,' she cried and when Sarah reached her she took her by the hand and led her into the magic hall.

They stood side by side and watched themselves balloon into monstrous women. They laughed until they had to hold their sides together. Long and skinny, short and wide, pin heads, sawed-off legs . . . Their images were incredible. They pointed at one another. They doubled up. They couldn't stop laughing. They couldn't laugh any more. When they emerged their cheeks and stomachs ached. Perhaps laughter was the answer, thought Sarah; it submerged everything else, whilst it lasted.

'Let's go for a ride on the dodgems,' said Arlene.

Sarah sobered. 'I should go home. I can't leave Helen to cope with everything.'

'Helen loves coping. Come on!'

They clambered into a bright red car and Sarah took the wheel. Arlene covered her face with her hands and got ready to

69

scream. She kicked off her spiky shoes. Sarah drove with concentration, taking pride in her skill. She was not afraid to take risks. Arlene screamed loudly. There were only two other cars on the track, both driven by men, who pursued them relentlessly until one got them cornered and bumped them soundly, again and again, making Arlene renew her screaming. When they finally came to rest, she was laughing.

The man wore a navy-blue reefer jacket and had an air of belonging to the sea, or to the docks. He said, once they were hemmed in against the edge of the track, 'Reckon I owe you girls a drink for that.'

'You're on!' said Arlene, climbing out of the dodgem car, thrusting her feet back into their shoes and shaking out her earrings. 'A rum and coke would go down nicely.'

'You can make it a double,' said the man. He looked at Sarah. 'You're okay at the wheel, you know.'

She thanked him, feeling the madness seep out of her, the way a dream goes on waking, when one knows there is no way of holding it back. She looked at her watch.

'Oh who cares what time it is?' cried Arlene.

'I've got a mate,' said the man. 'He likes a good time and he's not short of a bob or two.'

'Sounds all right to me.' Arlene led the way forward.

Sarah said, 'We really ought to get home, Arlene. We can't leave the children.'

'It would do you good to let your hair down for once, Sarah. *Really* down. You spend far too much time looking after other folk. Think of yourself for a change! A few drinks with a couple of blokes won't do us any harm. We'll have a good laugh . . .'

'Yeah, come on, honey,' said the man, slipping his arm around Sarah's waist under her jacket. In the dodgem car her blouse had ridden up out of her skirt and she felt the man's hand against her skin. His warm fingers moved in a circle and the middle one suddenly found her naval. It plunged deep into the cavity making her feel giddy. She almost cried out, from pain, and surprise. He eased her back against his rough jacket and she did not resist. She liked the feel of the rough cloth and the smell of his maleness. She looked up. The sky was speckled with stars; below them glistened the fairground lights. They seemed to be intertwined, to be revolving. The man's finger was travelling downwards, searching for another space.

'No,' she cried and pulled away. She staggered, steadied herself and saw that the stars had steadied too. 'I'm going home, Arlene.'

'Suit yourself. But I'm not.'

Sarah had to let Arlene go. She couldn't be her keeper, as she said to Helen, when she got home, not day *and* night.

Arlene did not come back that night but Gil and the Weasel returned to take up their vigil. Before going to bed Sarah had a last look at the street and saw cigarette tips glowing inside the car. She climbed the stairs to Tasha's room and sat down on the bed. She stared at the four walls, at the anti-nuclear posters and pictures of pop singers, at the dolls of many countries collecting dust in the folds of their ethnic skirts and coiffed headdresses, at the stacks of records on the floor and the piles of books sprawled across the desk, and wondered what she knew about her daughter. Then she shook herself. She knew quite a lot in fact. And she knew that Tasha was almost certainly indulging in blackmail.

As she was about to get ready for bed, the telephone rang. Gil wanted to speak to his wife.

'She's asleep.'

'Waken her up then, there's a pal!'

Sarah replaced the receiver then took if off the hook but after five minutes put it back on again. She could not risk Tasha phoning and not getting through.

And then the door bell rang waking one of the children. Sarah went back to the window. The two men still seemed to be in the car and she could not see enough of the dark shape on the doorstep to identify the caller. The police perhaps, with news of Tasha?

'It's all right,' she called out to Helen, 'I'll see who it is.'

She opened the front door on the chain. 'Who is it?'

'Liffey.'

'Liffey! At this hour!'

'Let me in, Sarah, for goodness sake.'

He had been drinking of course, he nearly always had when he came, and would be looking for somewhere to sober up before he took a taxi home. She unhooked the chain and let him

71

come in. It was like getting into Fort Knox, he declared, holding aloft a bottle of red wine. He was in no mood yet to sober up. She took him through to the kitchen and as he poured her a glass of wine she realised that she felt like a drink herself.

'You've got troubles,' said Liffey, 'and so have I. Here's to us!' They drank. 'What are those two blokes doing out there in the car? They got out when I came up the path and shouted, ""You won't get any joy there, mate!"' When Sarah had finished her tale of Gil and the Weasel, Liffey said, 'I don't know what you have to take that lot on for. Except that you always did want to try to save the world. Taking petitions round doors, going on marches, collecting jumble for Oxfam.'

Sarah protested. The women had nothing to do with all of that; they had come accidentally, had not been part of a plan.

'I thought maybe with you having been a social worker and not able to get a job now –'

'That I was employing myself? That's what people who don't think would think. Sorry, Liffey – I didn't mean to be rude. No, I just responded to needs as they arose.'

'I'm all for that – responding to needs.'

'I think you should stay where you are.'

'Tommy's having a little adventure, there's no reason why you shouldn't have one too, is there? You know I've always fancied you? Tommy and I have had the same taste in women, right from the beginning. Funny thing. Ever since we were thirteen years old. When we used to get the girls up the back lane and give them a feel.'

'You passed them between you, did you?'

'I wouldn't put it as crudely as that.' He studied her face, then nodded. 'You still look bloody marvellous.'

'Still?'

'Well, I'm no spring chicken either.'

He had slid over on to the arm rest of her chair and was stroking her hair. Why didn't she repulse him, tell him to get lost? She was surprised at her passivity. Why hadn't she pushed away the man in the fairground either, until he had tried to go too far? She remembered the feel of his fingers exploring her stomach. His smell had not been unlike Liffey's. The two men were becoming confused in her mind. She closed her eyes.

Liffey was continuing to stroke her hair and tell her she was lovely. His touch was surprisingly gentle. Then he slipped his hand inside her blouse and took hold of her breast. She opened her eyes.

'No, Liffey.'

'Why not?' He whispered the words close to her ear making her shiver. He squeezed the nipple of her breast between two fingers. 'Why not eh? You're free.'

But she could not get used to that idea.

'Get used to it then! Think of yourself for a change. You want to have a bit of happiness, too, don't you? Why should Tommy lap up all the cream? First time I ever saw you I wanted to jump on you. Remember – you asked Jean and me to tea and you were wearing a long cotton dress with pink flowers on it and you had your hair tied back with a pink ribbon . . .'

'That's a long time ago.'

There was no time like the present, so Liffey said.

He turned her face up to his and she allowed him to kiss her and after a moment, feeling a quickening in her body, she responded. Then he eased her up out of the chair and keeping his arm tightly round her shoulders, led her upstairs, steadying her when she stumbled. I am crazy, she thought lucidly, quite mad – Liffey of all people! – and could already foresee the morning. (The fairground man would have been better for he would have disappeared with the night.) But the morning would have to take care of itself for it was the night and its needs that were consuming her now.

The first telephone caller in the morning was Arlene. Was it safe to come home? She was in a call box round the corner and she was freezing. Half the glass was missing. 'Wait there till we come,' said Sarah.

She prodded the man in her bed and he turned over muttering, scratching the stubble on his face. The underside of his chin looked purple, the pouches under his eyes yellowish. His breath smelt stale and heavy.

Sarah said, 'Come on, get up! We've got to go and rescue Arlene.'

He protested. What way was this to start the day? He didn't

give a damn about a scrubber like Arlene, especially when he had Sarah lying all warm and soft beside him. He had taken her arm and was holding it fast. He was always a step ahead of a woman, realised Sarah who, cursing herself for not having anticipated his moves, tried to pull away. He tightened his grip. He smiled. She tried to break his hold by jerking his hand up and back, but he was lying now half on top of her and he was heavy. And he had his other hand on her leg.

'I want to get up, Liffey.'

'No, you don't – you want what I want.' He was right on top now. 'And don't call this rape. For it isn't, is it? Is it? *Is it?*'

The door opened and Helen looked in. She paused, her eyes dilated and then she backed hastily away apologising. Liffey laughed, his pleasure increased. Sarah dug her nails into his shoulders, trying to push him away, trying to keep him there, hating him.

He collapsed on her chest, then rolled over onto his back and put his hands above his head on the pillow. He laughed again, a deep rollicking laugh. Sarah sprang up and seized her dressing gown.

'Any time, baby,' he said, 'any time!'

'There won't be another time.'

'No? You loved it. Sorry if I've sullied your reputation. But don't be cross. Helen's probably dead jealous.'

'You think you're the answer to any woman's prayer?'

'I was the answer to yours last night.'

'Get up and get dressed.'

'Okay, I'm coming, at the double, mam!'

Meeting up in the hall, Sarah and Helen did not look at one another. They spoke of Arlene. Sarah felt much in the way that she had as a child when she had fallen over and picked herself up and dusted off her knees and carried on as if nothing had happened. She had been brought up to make light of tumbles. That way the pain lessened more quickly: there was no question about it. She had seen it work with her own daughter. 'Mummy'll kiss it better!' Crying soon turned to laughter. Wherever Tasha was now, Sarah was confident she would not be crying; she would be trudging on with teeth set, stubbornly. Too stubbornly.

'Right, I'm ready,' said Liffey, saluting.

He accompanied them to the telephone box where Arlene was hunched up looking a bit tousled and blue under the eyes but otherwise cheerful. Under escort, she returned to the house. The men had left the car and were positioned on the pavement in front of the gate. Sarah asked them to step aside.

'Got a fella now have you?' The Weasel jerked his thumb at Liffey.

'You heard what the lady said,' said Liffey.

'I want my wife,' said Gil.

'He wants his wife,' said the Weasel.

'Away home to your beds,' said Arlene, yawning.

'You weren't in yours last night were you? Out on the streets eh? Abandoned your kids. Wait till the social worker gets to hear about this.'

'What social worker?'

'Gil's suing for custody,' said the Weasel.

'The children were not alone,' said Sarah. 'They were in our care.'

'Your care? How do we know you're not all on the game?'

Helen had edged round the back of the Weasel and opened the gate.

'I would go if I were you,' said Sarah. 'You're not going to get her away from the three of us. And two neighbours across the street are watching every move.'

As the two men turned to look Sarah pushed Arlene in through the gateway.

'Cheers,' said Liffey and followed the women, clicking the latch shut behind him.

'We'll be seeing you, mate,' said the Weasel.

The second telephone caller was Thomas. No, there was nothing in this morning's post, said Sarah, and no, she didn't know what she was going to do. What could she do? They'd been through all this before. Thomas said he'd be round in half an hour. Sarah asked Liffey, who had been finishing his breakfast and listening to the conversation, to leave.

'He can't object. You're not living together. He's got his bird –'

'I'd prefer him not to know.'

75

'We're not going to discuss your form or anything like that. Though it was pretty good if you want to know. I'd even say it was top class.' He seemed to find his remark amusing.

'Just drink up your coffee and go. *Please.*'

'Okay, okay,' he grumbled but he drained his cup and let her steer him towards the hall. He insisted on kissing her goodbye and it seemed to her that if she allowed him to she would get rid of him more quickly.

When she had locked the door behind him and secured the chain, she wiped her mouth with the back of her hand and then went upstairs to scrub her teeth. She made a face at herself in the bathroom mirror. Liffey had now become the only other man she had slept with apart from Tom. If Liffey were to know that it would please him. She suspected that he did know. She filled the bath, soaped herself all over and lay in the water until her skin began to crinkle.

When she was stripping her bed and putting on clean sheets and pillow cases, Helen came in to consult about shopping.

'Helen, about Liffey –'

'I'm sorry I barged in, Sarah.' Helen was blushing. 'I didn't think –'

'It's all right. But if Liffey comes back, don't let him in. I don't want to see him again!' Sarah flung the soiled sheets into a corner.

'You don't think there's anything in what Gil said do you? About Arlene? Being –'

'You wouldn't believe anything those two said would you?' Sarah plumped the quilt up vigorously.

'No, no of course not,' said Helen and left the room.

Thomas arrived on his bicycle.

'Keeps you young, I suppose,' said Sarah, watching him padlock the back wheel. 'You've got colour in your cheeks.'

'Don't let's start getting snarky with one another. Tasha's more important –'

She collapsed at once, like a pricked balloon, though she still felt full of wind. It was as if a tight ball of it had gathered behind her solar plexus. She turned and went into the kitchen where she filled the kettle so that she could make yet more instant

76

coffee. She and Thomas sat side by side at the kitchen table drinking it, waiting for something to happen.

It was another four days before anything did. They were in the same positions drinking coffee when the second post of the day arrived bringing a card from Tasha.

'Thank God!' Thomas's hand shook as he held the picture postcard of Trafalgar Square. On the back it bore the message: '*I am in London. I have found a room and a job. Don't worry. Love, Tasha.*'

'Not bad for fifteen is it?' said Thomas. 'A room *and* a job . . .'

'She's self-sufficient in many ways, I've always told you that.'

But what kind of job could she have found? Sarah shut out unpleasant thoughts from her mind. Arlene talked too much and read too many sensational newspapers. Whenever there was a silence in the house she filled it by recounting regurgitated news items. Rapes, murders, muggings. Tasha would probably be working in a shop, said Sarah, or as a waitress, possibly part-time, for she had no insurance card and should not be working at all.

'She should be at school,' said Thomas. 'She's still a child.'

Sarah scrutinised the postmark. It was blurred but looked like E8. Thomas thought Tasha might have gone out of her area to post the card in order to put them off the scent but Sarah doubted that, for she did not believe Tasha meant to be devious. Or too elusive. Though that point she did not make since it would only detonate Thomas and he would then accuse her of attributing to Tasha the basest of motives. It was essential that they did not waste their energies on arguing but united them to try and track down Tasha. They spread a map of London on the table and Thomas drew a circle round the E8 area. 'Hackney.' He got up. 'I'll go on the night train. I can stay with Jack Russell. I'll comb the area, street by street, shop by shop. I'll take a photograph of Tasha with me.'

And that was what he did. He phoned in every evening, late, around midnight, when there was no point in combing the streets any more that day, and made his report. As the days went by his voice became less bright. He had asked in Pakistani grocers, Indian restaurants, fish and chip shops, post offices, pubs. He had got several false leads and tracked down a number of adolescent girls, but not Tasha. He had even walked around Earls Court and hung about Gloucester Road Tube Station. And been accosted by two girls who looked no more than thirteen.

'Mind you, I don't think for a moment that Tasha would –'

'Of course not,' said Sarah.

She encouraged him, telling him to persist; Tasha *must* be there somewhere. Another card had come bearing the same postmark.

It had said only: '*Love, Tasha.*'

'If she was mine,' said Arlene, 'I'd kick her behind.'

'That wouldn't do any good. It hasn't done you any good, has it?'

'I dunno. Suppose not.' Arlene gazed out of the window. Gil and the Weasel were on watch again. When they were there, she was restless and wanted to go out; when they were not, she seemed not to be bothered and lolled about on the settee reading magazines. The men were there less often now than at the beginning. The boredom of sitting cramped up in a car must be immense, thought Sarah. But they could never be sure when they would come. And every now and then Gil would saunter down the street and stand by the gate for a while leaning his arms on it. Sometimes Sarah or Helen found him standing behind them in the supermarket check-out. He'd examine the contents of their trolleys, make some comment relating to his family. 'Damian likes Rice Crispies,' he'd say mournfully. Helen thought he was genuinely missing his children. Perhaps he was, Sarah agreed, but that did not mean he had reformed. And she was certainly not going to let him inside the house again. His word wasn't worth tuppence. Whenever he was unable to come to the street – probably out on a job, said Arlene – he'd telephone, usually at inconvenient hours.

Liffey called at the house at an inconvenient hour. Sarah told him so through the gap in the door which the chain allowed. 'Everyone's in bed.'

'That's where you and I should be.' He had his toe in the gap. He rattled the chain. 'Take this damned thing off for goodness sake!'

'I'm sorry, but you're not coming in.'

'Oh come on, love, you enjoyed it last time. Don't tell me you didn't.'

'Good night, Liffey.'

'So it was all right when you wanted it!'

'Yes, and it wouldn't be if I didn't. You must realise that.'

'I could make you change your mind, if you'd just give me five minutes . . .' His hand came through the gap now, the five fingers groping blindly.

'Good night, Liffey,' said Sarah again.

She had to resort to jabbing his foot with the point of an umbrella to get the door shut. He hopped about on the doorstep outside yelping and calling her a bloody bitch. He had obviously not been brought up to dust off his knees.

Undeterred, or perhaps because, as he claimed, he liked a woman to show fight, he returned a few nights later and they had a repeat performance. Helen thought it might be better, the next time he came, not to answer the door at all, but his persistent knocking and ringing of the bell wakened the children and Sarah did not trust Arlene to deal with him.

'Thinks will settle down,' she told Helen. 'At the moment everything has been disturbed. Like a dust storm. We must put on our goggles and remain calm until it's passed.' She was sure that was what her Aunt Edmée would do.

Edmée returned from the North-West Frontier. She had much to tell, but then so had Sarah. Sarah did her telling over lunch in a café off the Royal Mile, the house in Portobello lacking the privacy for intimate conversation.

'You thought she would tire of him since she's so much younger,' said Sarah. (Edmée had of course known about Claire before she set off for Pakistan.)

'She still might, of course. Things are far from settled.'

'He's in love with her,' said Sarah gloomily.

'Love does not always last,' said Edmée gently.

That was what she had said when Sarah and Thomas had met in their first year at university, at a Fresher's dance, and fallen in love. 'Young love is good love, but one should not expect it to last necessarily. It's something to be taken and enjoyed for the moment. At thirty-nine, or even twenty-nine, you may both be quite different from what you are now.' Sarah had not believed that, could not believe that she and Thomas could ever bear to be apart. And their love did last – well, for longer than Edmée had meant anyway.

'He never even thought he was in love with any of the women before this one,' said Sarah.

It had been when both she and Thomas were approaching forty that she first discovered he had transgressed. It had come about by one of those silly things like finding a long red hair on his corduroy jacket. She had said in jest, not expecting a confession, 'Who were *you* with last night?' And he had told her. In a state of shock, she had gone to Edmée. 'He says she means nothing to him. That it's not serious.'

'I daresay it isn't then. It's probably his age. He's restless. After all, you've known one another for twenty years. It must be difficult to sustain a sexual relationship from late teens into middle-age without feeling curious about other people.' Edmée herself liked variety, in all areas of life, and had a horror of boredom, so Thomas's unfaithfulness neither shocked nor surprised her. 'I would lie low if I were you.'

'Accept it you mean?'

The affair, if it deserved such a title, soon ended. 'It's you that I love, Sarah,' said Thomas. He was contrite. He bought her an amethyst ring, spending more than he – than they – could afford.

'You're bored with me, aren't you?' said Sarah.

He denied it. But their lovemaking *had* become a little boring.

'What else can he expect?' asked Edmée. 'After all this time.'

Sarah bought filmy nightdresses but felt rather a fool. It seemed so obvious. And Thomas did not even appear to notice. She went back to viyella. See-through nightwear was too cold for the house; they could not afford central heating. The house was really too large, had been bought for a big family, but both were loth to part with it.

For a year or two Sarah fancied that Thomas had the occasional fling but he never stayed away all night. There was a pattern: evasiveness combined with overhelpfulness when he was at home, followed by contrition. She accepted by trying to pretend it was not happening. She asked no questions. And then he met Claire and from the beginning Sarah sensed danger. Thomas bought new underwear and took baths before he went out in the evening. He phoned home late from call boxes and made ridiculous excuses about not being able to get back. The car had broken down. He had to look after a sick colleague. The bleeps would go in the middle of the explanation; he'd run out of coins.

Sarah kept having accidents: she trapped her hand in the car door, fell down the stairs, scalded her leg. Edmée told her she'd better voice her protests. To Thomas. But she had been afraid to, in case she forced the issue.

They walked up the High Street and Sarah led the way round the side of the cathedral.

'Where are we going?' asked Edmée and then, without waiting for an answer, 'Do you think this is a good idea?'

'Why should I care what *she* feels?'

Sarah pushed open the door of Parliament House. 'We're going to Court Nine,' she said to the security man. 'Yes, we know our way, thank you.'

The afternoon session was under way in the court. The side table was stacked high with documents tied with pink ribbon. A few men in business suits sat in the public benches. Another was on the witness stand being questioned. By Miss Armstrong.

'Fraud,' whispered Sarah, as she and Edmée slid into the back row. Claire had looked up as they came in and her eyes had met Sarah's, briefly, before turning back to her witness.

'Mr Bell, would you please look at the document in front of you? Is it dated the 4th of March of this year?'

'It is.'

'Have you seen this document before?'

'Yes.'

'Would you tell us when?'

'My secretary gave it to me with my other mail . . .'

Impeccably garbed in black and white, with slim back held straight, Miss Armstrong stood listening attentively.

Sarah released the buttons of her suit jacket. She had had this tweed suit for ten years so it wasn't surprising it was a little tight around the middle. It was seldom that she wore it these days, preferring less formal, looser fitting clothes. She supposed she and Helen ought to make an effort to get to some of the better jumble sales but they didn't really have time for all that that entailed, going by bus to the posher suburbs of Edinburgh on Saturday mornings, scrumming around with a mob of other frantic women and dealers. She supposed, too, that she ought to make an effort to lose a few pounds – though she was not fat exactly – and have her hair restyled. But she knew, even while she was making these semi-resolutions, that she would do none of them, for she did not care enough and had more urgent matters to attend to. But perhaps this was where she had gone wrong? Not that Thomas had ever bothered much about his clothes before he met Claire, and he had always had his hair cut by Sarah to save money.

Beside Sarah, Edmée, in her flamboyantly coloured clothes – for she loved exoticism – listened attentively, too, as if she found the details of the case absorbing. Claire was pursuing her witness tenaciously, not accepting any ambiguous or imprecise answers. She was not, for a second, impolite. Her very politeness and smoothness depressed Sarah. She had not been listening at all, could not even make out the nature of the fraud. Except that of course money was at the bottom of it. Money! There was a stack of crumpled bills behind the clock on the kitchen mantelpiece. She sighed, breaking Edmée's concentration.

'Want to go?' mouthed Edmée.

As they left, Claire turned her head again to look at them.

'Well?' demanded Sarah, as soon as they were out of the building and in Parliament Square.

'She's intelligent, very direct, not devious –'

'Yes, but can you see what she and Thomas have in common?' Sarah cut in impatiently.

'She's very attractive.'

'What does she see in Thomas then?'

'Well, he may be in his mid-forties but he has still an air of boyishness about him that is rather appealing.'

Sarah felt even more depressed, now. It was all right for a middle-aged man to look boyish but if a woman of the same

82

age were to be described as girlish it would not be regarded as a compliment.

'You're an attractive looking woman too, you know, Sarah, in your own quite distinctive way. Yes, I mean it, I'm not just trying to cheer you up.'

But Sarah was cheered. She said, 'Anyway, I don't know whether I'd have Thomas back now even if he wanted to come.'

She must start to think about what she did want, said Edmée.

They drove back to Portobello in Edmée's little canary-yellow sports car which attracted the attention of Gil and the Weasel when they drew up in the street. Edmée answered their questions pleasantly while Sarah went on in to the house to see what disasters had arisen in her absence. Mercifully, none had. And Jason and Marbella were sitting at the kitchen table actually doing homework, under Helen's supervision.

In the evening, Edmée showed coloured slides of her trip to the North-West Frontier. It was a treat, along with her commentary, which was light-hearted and amusing, and quite unlike the showing of most people's holiday slides. Aunt Edmée's Magic Lantern Show, Tasha used to call it and had said it made you want to travel yourself, but when she'd said that she'd been thinking in terms of Samarkand and Timbuctoo, not Hackney.

Half-way through the showing, Liffey turned up. Sarah allowed him to come in to the hall rather than stand outside arguing on the step.

'My Aunt Edmée's here.'

'I like your Aunt Edmée. She's a character. We get on great together. Anyway, she won't be staying the night, will she?'

'Nor will you.'

'Those two are waiting out there for me. They got out of their car when they saw me coming. Two to one isn't much cop, is it? You can't throw me into the lion's den now, can you?'

She had to admit that she couldn't quite see him as Daniel. All right, he could come in and have a drink and see Edmée's slides, but that was all. 'Understood?'

'Whatever you say, love.'

He told Edmée she was looking marvellous – which indeed she was, in her turquoise and plum-coloured jacket brought back from a previous journey to the East – and settled himself on the settee between Arlene and Marilyn, saying this was just like being at the pictures. He told Arlene and Marilyn they were looking marvellous, too, and put his arms round their shoulders. They shifted their positions to accommodate him. He was a definite asset to the evening, from their point of view. A fresh face. A man's face. And they liked men to have a bit of patter. What was wrong with it? Didn't mean you had to take everything they said for gospel. Be a fool if you did. But it added a bit of spice and God knows but you needed all the spice you could get in life.

Sarah doused the lights and a slide showing two fierce-looking tribesmen against a backdrop of mountains flickered into view. Arlene had a few comments to make about the physique of the men.

Edmée knew when to stop: she showed three boxfuls of slides and switched off while the audience was still enjoying itself.

'You've got plenty go in you, I must say,' said Arlene, when the lights went on again. 'You might have had your throat cut. Funny religion they've got there, isn't it?'

'They're Muslim. Very strict.'

'They cut off your hands for stealing, don't they?' Arlene shuddered, thinking perhaps of Gil handless.

'Rather you than me,' said Marilyn to Sarah's aunt. 'Billy and I went to Tenerife one year.'

'It was a good trip,' said Edmée, packing up her equipment.

'I envy you,' said Sarah.

'You too could –'

'Oh really?'

Edmée said she must go. Sarah suggested they all call it a day; the previous night had been disturbed by phone calls, so that everyone was tired, especially Marilyn who would not give in until the rest did. Arlene went reluctantly, with a backward glance at Liffey who although he had been squeezing her shoulder was showing no further interest. It was Sarah he had his eyes on. She felt them burning holes in her.

'Would you give Liffey a lift to the bus station, please,

Edmée?' she asked.

Edmée said she would be delighted and, asking Liffey if he would mind carrying the screen, placed it in his arms before he could object. She led the way out, telling him not to worry about Gil and the Weasel, she would soon tell them where they got off.

'By the way, Sarah, I've left a book for you on the sideboard, by Isabella Bird. Marvellous woman. Victorian. She's buried in Edinburgh, I must take you to see her grave sometime. Great traveller. She suffered from mysterious pains and the only medicine that would alleviate them was travel in remote parts.'

Sarah and her aunt kissed goodnight and Edmée went off down the path carrying her boxes.

Liffey hung back and said to Sarah, 'You sure gave me the bum's rush there, didn't you?'

'You asked for it.'

'No wonder Tommy walked out on you. You're as cold as that pavement out there. Now that new woman of his is *really* sexy.'

Sarah went to bed and read until she fell asleep and dreamt of camping out under the stars and getting up in the morning to roll her belongings in a blanket ready to set off for the far horizon. She was wakened from the dream, though she tried to hold on to it desperately, by the strident cry of a child and Arlene's voice shouting at Gil from an upstairs window, telling him to get lost.

'I don't know how you put up with it,' said Isabel Peterson. She looked about her as she knitted. 'It's a bit like a zoo.'

'There's plenty of room in the house for everyone,' said Sarah, scrabbling in the biscuit tin amongst broken biscuits. Her in-laws liked a good cup of tea and something to eat with it when they came.

'No news of Tasha, eh?' said Eunice. 'There's no saying what'll have happened to her, is there? Young girl in London.' She had never been there herself, she wouldn't go if you paid her, all that traffic, and crime; it wouldn't be safe to walk the streets by day let alone by night.

'Things can happen anywhere though, can't they?' said Sarah brightly, annoyed with herself for being led so inevitably into the making of trite statements. It was always the same when Eunice and her mother-in-law called, though she was fond of them and they were solidly behind her which she appreciated. She offered the biscuits. 'There was your neighbour round the corner. Mugged at midday, wasn't she?'

Isabel took half a digestive which crumbled in her hand. 'You used to make a lovely orange cake, Sarah. When you were first married.'

'Did I? I don't remember.' She vaguely did, but only vaguely. The young woman she had been then seemed to be some kind of distant relative, though she thought that sometime she must try to tie the two together. One must never forget the past, said Aunt Edmée, who, by means of her slides, carried through and wove together the threads of her life, whose fabric could then be seen in all the glory of its colour and varying textures. For she recorded not only the sunny hours but some of the more trying ones as well. She cherished light *and* shade. The slides and photographs which Sarah and Thomas had taken at irregular intervals throughout their married life were laying about higgledy-piggledy in boxes and drawers. She had always meant to sort them out.

'And what have you two been up to?' asked Sarah.

'We looked in at the court after lunch,' said Isabel.

'Makes a change,' said Eunice. 'Young fella was being tried for mugging an old woman of eighty-four. Turned out he was on heroin.'

'There were a couple of nasty types standing on the pavement looking at your house when we came in, Sarah,' said Isabel.

Sarah said that she knew all about them.

'You're running an awfy risk, you know.'

What kind of risk would Arlene run if Sarah were to put her and her children out in the street?

'But she's nothing to you, is she?' said Eunice, frowning over her knitting pattern.

'Of course she's something! She's a human being.'

'You can't take everybody in.'

'I'm not planning to.'

86

Sarah was too soft-hearted for her own good, they would agree going back on the bus, and for her family's good too. I mean to say, you must put your own family first, musn't you? It made you wonder about Tasha running away, didn't it? Sarah's good deeds were legends in Eunice's wool shop. And in fact that was how Marilyn had heard of her and come to her door seeking shelter.

Marilyn's time had now arrived. The waters had broken. She stood in the doorway trembling, appealing to Sarah, who got up and put her arms round her.

'Aye it's no a pleasant experience,' said Isabel. 'I mind when Eunice was coming –'

'You'll be just fine, Marilyn,' said Sarah, reminding her to do her deep breathing and not to panic. 'Helen will bring down your case and I'll call a taxi.'

'I don't know what you sold your car for,' said Isabel.

'We couldn't afford to run it.'

Her mother-in-law sighed. Sarah often used to take them for runs on Eunice's half-day, into the countryside or further down the coast. And when Thomas came out to visit them he came in the car and not on a bicycle. Isabel Peterson sighed again. Things changed too quickly and drastically for her liking. But all around you people said the same thing. *Nobody* seemed to like the changes. How then did they happen?

Sarah went with Marilyn to hospital and brought back her clothes. Her in-laws were still there when she returned; they were eating fish and chips out of newspapers and watching television with Arlene and her children. Marilyn was doing very well, she reported.

'Poor bitch,' said Eunice.

'Oh I dunno,' said Arlene. 'Mine were no bother at all. Popped out like shelled peas.'

'I mind when Tasha was born,' said Isabel Peterson.

'Yes, so do I,' said Sarah.

She had wanted Thomas to come to the birth, and indeed he had, initially, but half-way through had felt ill and fled, masked and gowned, along the hospital corridors looking for a men's lavatory. He had not made it. The recollection of his eyes above the mask came back sharply to her. Later, he had appeared in the ward, carrying a bunch of roses, looking sheepish. They held hands. The child seemed like a miracle as they gazed down at her in her crib. With his free hand Thomas counted her fingers and toes. Ten of each. 'Amazing!' They smiled at one another. Sarah had had three miscarriages before Tasha was conceived and brought to full term and the doctors had said she would not be able to have another. 'At least we have her,' said Sarah. 'And she's beautiful,' said Thomas. They agreed that they could always adopt another child but they never got around to it, partly because it was becoming more difficult to adopt children, and partly because Sarah intended, when Tasha went to school, to go back to work. But by the time she actively began to look for work again it was becoming more difficult to get that, too.

After they had seen the nine o'clock news, Isabel and Eunice rose to go. They wound up their knitting, speared the balls with the needles, and brushed the fish crumbs from their clothing. Eunice's bag was bulging with knitting and travel brochures.

'Got some new ones today. Morocco and Tunisia. What do you think Morocco'd be like?'

'Okay,' said Sarah. 'Exotic. Warm.' She went with Eunice and Isabel to the door. There was no sign of the two men in the street.

'By the way, we saw that woman of Tommy's today,' said Eunice. 'She was coming across the square behind St. Giles with another man.'

'Maybe she's getting tired of waiting for Tom,' said Sarah with a smile, not believing what she said.

Eunice snorted. 'She's just a flash in the pan, believe you me!'

'He's a middle-aged man.' His mother shook her head. 'It's ridiculous to see him making a fool of himself like that.'

It was not that unusual, Sarah pointed out.

'Well, she'll not be welcome in our house. You can count on that.'

Sarah thanked them.

'Maybe see you next week,' said Eunice. 'And mind and give us a ring about Marilyn.'

Marilyn gave birth to a healthy eight-pound boy just after midnight. She spoke to Sarah, Helen and Arlene in turn on the telephone. She sounded ecstatic.

'I quite envy her,' said Helen. 'I always wanted Jamie to have a brother or sister.'

'What's keeping you then?' asked Arlene.

'One or two things. Well, one in particular.'

'Easy enough to find a man to oblige. What about Liffey – good looking, well-built bloke?'

'I hardly think …'

Sarah visited Marilyn in the afternoon. Marilyn's mother was there and before the visiting hour was over so also was Marilyn's mother-in-law who had heard the news in Eunice's wool shop.

The grandmothers cooed and sparred across the cot and Sarah remembered her own mother and Thomas's behaving similarly, each claiming reproduction of their own family's features. Her mother-in-law had been undeniably right in that instance for Tasha turned out to be made very much in Thomas's likeness. At the thought of Tasha – Tasha sitting in a dingy room, Tasha walking the cold London streets alone – a physical pang stabbed her chest and she had to turn away and look out of the window. How could it happen that her daughter should *leave home*? Lying in this very hospital, looking at her newly born child, she had thought, we shall be close, for after all, she is flesh of my flesh. The thought of an estrangement coming at any point in the future would have seemed inconceivable to her then. But of course the child had been made of Thomas's flesh too. That other restless at odds-with-the-earth strain had also to be taken into account. The closeness between father and daughter had started as soon as Tasha could recognise him; her face would light up when he came in to the room, she'd smile, open her hand and extend her fingers to touch his face, and as he put out his hands to lift her she would laugh, deep inside her small fat belly. Daddy's girl, Isabel Peterson would say, with satisfaction, though she was quick to add that Sarah was a grand mother, there was none better.

Marilyn's mother-in-law was reminding them that the baby was the flesh of her son too. 'Billy'd love to see him so he would. He's daft about children.'

'First I heard of it,' said Marilyn, drawing her shawl (knitted by Eunice) across her chest. 'He always used to say it'd be better if we didn't have any so that we could go to Tenerife for our holidays every year.'

'He never would want to go to Tenerife *every* year. He went to Majorca in the summer. With four friends from work.'

'Oh he did, did he? And there he was crying hard up on the telephone telling me he couldn't spare anything!'

'Mind you, a man has a right to see his own son.'

His mother had a point and Sarah and Marilyn were forced to see it, though Marilyn's mother, scenting danger, could not, or would not. 'After what he done to her? Why should she let him within a mile of her and her baby?'

He was reformed, said his mother; he had promised he wouldn't lay a hand on Marilyn again, not in anger anyway. He'd talked to the doctor about it and got some pills.

'I don't want to see him,' said Marilyn, plucking at the fringes of her shawl.

'You see what you're doing,' said her mother to her mother-in-law, 'you're just upsetting her. You'll put her off her milk if you're not careful.'

Sarah took them both away.

Coming home, with the smell of babies in her nostrils and the cackle of grandmothers' voices in her ears, she was delighted to see Aunt Edmée's yellow car parked in the street.

'You need a break, Sarah,' said Edmée. 'I'll take you away. Up north for a few days.'

'I can't.'

Edmée insisted on taking her out for dinner and afterwards they dropped in to the hospital to see how Marilyn was doing. She was sitting bolt upright in bed looking very flushed. Billy had come in during the visiting hour and stayed for ten minutes. He'd plonked himself down on the upright chair beside the bed and wouldn't budge and she hadn't wanted to create a scene, not with all the other husbands in visiting ever so nicely with their bunches of flowers and clean nightdresses in plastic bags. Billy had brought her flowers, orange lilies, not her favourite, but, still, they were fresh, not about to droop or anything, and so it had meant that she had had a bunch just like the other mothers. He'd come in his best suit, the navy-blue one, with a pale blue shirt and red and white striped tie, and he'd had his hair cut. He'd behaved all right too, hadn't given her a red face. She put the back of her hand against her cheek. And he'd thought Gary – for that was to be the baby's name – was lovely.

'Marilyn,' said Sarah, 'watch it.'

'Oh don't worry, I've no intention of letting him worm his way in again.'

One Sunday morning in London, Thomas, wandering between the stalls in Brick Lane market, encountered a lost, lonely soul – his daughter Tasha. He looked at her for a moment almost not believing it, almost not recognising her, for she had cut her hair and she had looked, too, at first glance, when he had been about to apologise for coming face to face with her, like any other half-lost young girl hanging about with not much money and nowhere to go back to, except a chilly, drab room. For such in turned out to be, inevitably, with rotting linoleum, fungus growing on the damp walls, cockroaches bustling along the skirting boards, and a gas fire whose poisonous fumes might well, at some stage, have overcome her.

'Tasha!' he had cried. She had not recognised him in the first instance either.

She had collapsed into his arms. All her resistance was gone, had seeped away during the long, dreary, chilled hours. She wept against his shoulder, torrentially, until she shuddered and became quite still and dry, as if not another tear could be squeezed out of her.

Thomas wiped his eyes on his sleeve then touched the jagged hair that stood out in spikes about his daughter's head.

'Don't say anything!' she cried.

She was racked by cold and hunger. She had been fingering a rail of suede jackets when he stumbled over her. 'Would you like one?' he asked. 'Pick one.' She chose a jacket of emerald green which gladdened his heart. It was not expensive but if necessary he would have paid a hundred pounds (which he did not have) to see the glow come into her face as she fastened it across her chest. He bought her a hamburger from a stand and after that a jam doughnut and then they went back to her room to fetch her stuff. It went into her small rucksack.

She had been working in a corner grocer's, from midday till eight in the evening, with two half-hours off, six days a week. Understandably, she had hated it. The only job she had ever had was baby-sitting, if that could be called a job. Sitting in someone else's warm house with coffee left in a thermos and sandwiches on a plate. Thomas and Sarah used to argue about Tasha working. He thought she had enough to do with her school work, Sarah thought Tasha was inclined to be lazy and it wouldn't do her any harm to find out how the rest of the world lived. When he was at school Thomas had worked afternoons and Saturdays, not for the experience but because he needed the money; Sarah had not worked, there being no financial need. Thomas, therefore, had been in the stronger moral position to win the argument, and did. He had said there was plenty of time for Tasha to find out about 'the rest of the world'.

They went together, Thomas and Tasha, to the grocer's shop to tell the owner that she would not be coming back to work.

She said, 'This is my father, Mr Burt. I shall not be in tomorrow.' She enjoyed saying it, Thomas saw that. Her spirits were returning, she was holding her head up again.

He said, 'I called here, Mr Burt. To ask about my daughter.'

'I do not remember.' The man shrugged. He picked up a stack of wire baskets and took them behind the counter.

Thomas and Tasha left the shop.

Thomas borrowed money from his old friend Jack Russell and took Tasha to an Italian restaurant in Covent Garden for a slap-up dinner. They had a litre of red wine with it. He drank the greater share but she drank enough to get a little tipsy. They were happy. They walked around the streets afterwards, arm-in-arm, and Tasha said she wouldn't mind living in London when she was older.

Late in the evening they returned to Jack Russell's flat in Islington.

'We'll go home in the morning,' said Thomas.

'*Both* of us? *Home*?'

Well, he had not been talking literally – he had meant Edinburgh, rather than Portobello and the family house specifically. He was going back to Claire's flat. But he would see her every day.

'I won't go home unless you come too,' said Tasha.

'I would kick her behind if she was mine,' said Arlene.

'Yes, all right, Arlene!' said Sarah. 'But she's not yours, and as I've told you before, that never did solve anything.'

'But it's blackmail though, isn't it?'

'You don't have to spell *everything* out.'

'Call a spade a spade I always did say.'

'Sometimes that's not a good idea though, is it, Arlene?'

'So what's going to happen now?' asked Helen.

'For the moment, nothing, I imagine. It's stalemate. Until he loses his temper – which he will sooner or later – and calls her bluff. I'm sure she wouldn't want to be left behind in London. Starving in a cold room is all right for a little while.'

Sarah knew her husband and daughter well; her prediction proved accurate. The following day Thomas rang to say they'd be on the four o'clock train. 'I'm exhausted,' he said. 'And broke.' Sarah said she would have a meal ready.

They arrived about half-past nine. Both looked weary. Thomas thought he would not stay to eat, but Tasha pleaded and he said oh all right, and went in to the hall to make a phone call, keeping his voice so low they only heard it as a murmur. He talked for some time and when he returned he looked even more tired.

Tasha dragged out the meal until it looked as if she would fall asleep over it. At eleven Thomas rose saying that he *must* go. He kissed Tasha and said, 'Now remember your promise to me, won't you, love? I'll see you tomorrow.'

He left quickly.

'I think you should go to bed now, Tasha,' said Sarah. 'It's been a long day for you.' She put her arms around her daughter and felt the girl's shoulders squaring up to resist her. 'You could at least kiss me goodnight.'

'I don't feel like it.' Tasha turned her head away.

Sarah dropped her arms. 'Don't take it out on me please,

Tasha. It's not my fault.'

'Oh you say that, don't you?' Tasha's head swung round and she looked Sarah in the face. 'But if you'd made him happy he wouldn't have gone.'

'And what about if he'd made *me* happy?'

'He'd make anyone happy,' said Tasha and went upstairs.

Sarah sat down at the kitchen table. She stared at the old clock on the wall which they – she and Thomas – had bought in an old dusty junk shop. They had been happy that day: they had laughed as they lugged the clock home and spent a good hour or more cleaning and polishing it. They were pleased because it was *theirs*. Everything had been theirs then, not his or hers. She watched the long thin spidery second hand moving steadily round the parchment-coloured clock face and when it came up to the top the big hand moved over, just a fraction, to record the passing of that minute. It was a long time ago of course, that day, and yet not, for staring at the clock, watching the movement of the hands, she could remember clearly, as if frozen on a picture frame, the look on Thomas's face, and she could still feel the excitement they had shared. But now she sat alone with the clock, and between that other moment and this, many things had happened and many emotions had been lived through; there had been acts of love and of tenderness, of anger and even of violence, there had been misunderstandings, pain, joy, indifference, tolerance, disillusionment. To try to sort them all out would be like trying to unravel a half-dozen badly tangled skeins of wool. Best not to attempt it: there would be no one single revelation that would show what it was that had brought them from that moment to this one now. The clock ticked on.

If you'd made him happy he wouldn't have gone.

After he'd met Claire she had felt he was drifting further and further away from her like a ship bobbing out to sea and that if she were to call, 'Come back, Tom!' he would probably not even hear. His gaze was fixed on the horizon. He was unhappy about her, she knew that, but when he was not unhappy he was very happy. Thinking himself unobserved, he would remember something and smile, and when she saw the delight in his eyes pain burned in her making her physically ill. She went to bed with a high fever.

94

'Are you trying to kill yourself?' asked Edmée.

Tom was attentive. He made hot lemon drinks, changed the sheets, put flowers by her bedside.

'Tom?' She caught hold of his hand and he sat down on the edge of the bed. 'Talk to me.' He said.

'I'm sorry, Sarah.' He sounded miserable. 'I don't know what else to say.'

'Is an exciting sex-life so all-important? What about love – just plain love, caring for someone, feeling affection for them, feeling upset when they're upset?'

'Calm down, dear, you'll put up your temperature.'

'I don't care about that.' She flung aside the bedclothes and got up, pulling on her dressing gown. 'It's sky-high anyway.' She stood in front of him. 'I'm waiting for an answer.'

'Sarah, we haven't been getting on all that well in recent years have we? We seem to irritate one another easily, more than we used to.'

'You're still not answering.'

'I know it sounds selfish – and I suppose it is – it's just that if one *can* have everything . . .'

In the morning Sarah went in to her daughter's room and told her she would not be spoken to as she had been last night, that it was time Tasha grew up and realised that not all was black and white or could be neatly classified as right and wrong.

'You're always telling me it was time I grew up. What does it mean? That I should see things your way?'

'I think you'd like me to slug you one, wouldn't you? But I am not going to.'

Sarah left before she yielded to the temptation. *For yielding is sin . . . Each victory will help us some other to win . . .* The words of the old hymn came back to her. Regardless of whether she yielded or not, she was clearly not on a winning streak. Victory was not even a meaningful concept. Tasha's words of last night still stung in spite of being able to reject them intellectually.

Thomas turned up on his bicycle the next day. He had something on his mind and came to the point at once.

'I don't like raising this, Sarah,' he began, putting her on the alert, 'but I must. I've got to make a fresh start. I'm too young to be retired.'

'I feel the same way.'

'Yes, but you weren't made redundant.'

'No?' she said, unable to resist it. 'Anyway, like you, I'm jobless.'

'I want to open up an antiquarian bookshop.'

'So?'

'I need money.'

'I'm afraid I can't help you there.'

'This house belongs to both of us. I'd like my share out of it.'

'I can't afford to buy you out, you know that.'

'I want to put it on the market.'

'You'd evict us? You can't though, can you? I have to agree to the sale.'

'With your half you could buy a flat big enough for yourself and Tasha, and probably Helen and Jamie as well.'

'And what about Arlene and her children and Marilyn and her baby?'

'You can't afford to house that tribe forever.'

Never mind the tribe, as he referred to them, what about his own daughter? Tasha had lived in this house since she was born. Was he prepared to put her out when she was just beginning to settle down again at school? Tasha would adjust, he said; she'd be going away to university in a couple of years time, and he thought she should go away, and not stay in Edinburgh.

'What about me?' said Sarah. 'This is my home. I love this house. I suppose I would adjust, too? What if I don't feel like making the adjustment?'

The row developed and after further hot words Thomas cycled off.

Sarah sought out Helen. 'Why should *I* lose everything?' She intended to dig in her heels. By fair means or foul.

At suppertime she said to Tasha, 'Your father's trying to get us to move. He wants to sell the house. Put us out. Evict us.'

Tasha lifted one shoulder in the way that Sarah found so infuriating. 'I don't mind.' She went on eating.

'I suppose everything he does is okay with you? What about going off to live with this other woman? Is that all right too?'

Tasha got up. 'I'm going out now.'

'I thought you were going to do the dishes?'

'I'll do them when I come in.'

'They'll be done by then.'

Tasha put on her jacket.

'Where are you going?'

'Into town. I won't be late.' She went.

'If she was mine . . .' began Arlene.

'Oh shut up, Arlene!' cried Sarah.

'I know you're going to be cross with me,' said Marilyn. She was sitting on the upright chair beside her bed. She bent her head to examine her finger nails. 'I'm going home with Billy tomorrow.'

'I see.'

They sat in silence. Billy had been a regular visitor in his navy-blue suit with a fresh bunch of flowers daily. Marilyn had had to stay on in hospital for an extra few days, due to a minor complication. That had given Billy his opportunity, thought Sarah.

'He's reformed, you know, really he is,' said Marilyn. 'He's dead sorry for what he did.' (He'd beaten her when she was pregnant, with a leather belt.) 'Becoming a father's changed him.'

'Gary's only five days old.'

'But he was starting to change before that, Sarah. It's all in the past. It's at the back of us.'

It was difficult, said Sarah, ever to put the past quite at the back of us; it had a habit, if not of keeping pace with the present, then of dogging its footsteps. But as long as Marilyn was sure . . . Sarah sighed. What was the use of talking about being sure?

'I'd still like to be friends with you, Sarah. You've been awful good to me and I'm ever so grateful –'

Of course they would remain friends, said Sarah, while knowing that Billy would do everything he could to discourage it; he would not want to be reminded of that part of his past. 'And I'm certainly not cross with you! Why on earth should I be? It's your life.'

'I'll miss Marilyn so I will,' said Arlene. 'We used to have a good laugh together. Will you be getting somebody in her place?'

'Not necessarily. I'm not going to look for anyone – it's not like that.'

'Don't take anyone in in her place, Sarah,' said Edmée. 'You need some time and space for yourself. You need to find a new direction. You, too, have to make a fresh start.'

Of course they never knew when Marilyn might come back, said Arlene. Sarah had told Marilyn not to hesitate if things did not work out, to jump in a taxi and come. Marilyn had said thanks very much but she didn't think that would be necessary. She rang when she'd been home for three days to tell them that Billy adored Gary and was dead gentle with him and was giving him his bottle at his late night feed.

'You don't like that, do you?' said Tasha. 'You'd rather he turned out to be rotten? You hate men!'

'That's not true,' said Sarah. 'Just because I'm at odds with your father over selling the house doesn't mean I'm at odds with all men.'

'What about Liffey? You used to like Liffey, you said he made you laugh. He used to come here all the time. Why didn't you let him in last night?'

'I was tired.'

'It was only half-past nine.'

'I'm tired now and it's only half-past four in the afternoon.'

Arlene had not come home last night and Sarah had lain awake until late listening for the sound of the front door opening. She had phoned at breakfast-time to say she'd be in shortly. Helen had gone to town to shop.

'You don't have to look after all those children,' said Tasha. 'Why doesn't Arlene look after them herself? Where was she last night? Where is she now?'

'Perhaps you should join the police force when you leave school?'

Tasha got up and went to the window putting her back to the room and to Sarah. She peered through the glass.

'Who's that out there?'

'The children?' said Sarah, jumping up to look herself.

They had been playing outside and she had just been about to call them in, would have called them in earlier if she had not been arguing with Tasha. Vague shapes were moving about the garden, some too tall to be children.

'There are two men out there, they look like Gil and the Weasel,' said Tasha. 'They're taking away the children!'

They ran out through the back door into the garden in time to see the Weasel's back disappearing round the side of the house. He had Melody over his shoulder. She was laughing as she was joggled up and down. Jamie stood in the middle of the garden, alone, holding a football. 'I didn't know what to do,' he said. Sarah and Tasha went after the men.

'Stop!' cried Sarah.

The Weasel was fastening up the back of an old blue van. The number plates were spattered with mud. The engine roared, the passenger door was flung open and the Weasel leapt inside. He waved. With the exhaust gushing smoke the van swerved round the corner, and was gone.

'You do seem to have an eventful time in this house,' said the constable, writing down the particulars.

'The events are all inter-related,' said Sarah.

'A new chapter, you might say?'

'I suppose you might.'

'And where is the mother?' He looked about, but only Helen and Tasha were present.

'She's not actually here at the moment, she's gone into town . . .'

'Does she normally reside here?'

'You know she does. On your last visit –'

'That was two or three weeks ago. So she's out –' He began to write again.

'On the tiles,' said Tasha softly but not so softly that he did not hear clearly.

'Tasha!' said Sarah.

The constable looked at Tasha. 'Do you know where she is?'

'No, I don't, honestly I don't.'

'What did you mean when you said *on the tiles*? That has a fairly definite meaning, does it not? What do you understand by it?' The constable had clearly sat in court. He had his witness floundering. 'Does she go out with other men?'

'I – I think so,' hiccuped Tasha. 'Well, I mean I don't really know –'

'Does she stay out all night? Does she, Mrs Peterson?'

Sarah attempted to sidestep the question by saying that she thought Tasha had just been trying to make a smart remark but was forced to admit that once or twice Arlene had missed the last bus and stayed with a friend in Edinburgh. But no, she could not say who that friend was, what her name was, or where she lived.

'Or if she exists?' said the constable, writing again. 'Ask her to come down to the station when she comes in, will you? There's a few questions we'd like to put to her.'

When he had gone Sarah took Arlene's advice concerning Tasha.

'God,' said Arlene, 'can a woman not have a good time sometime?'

'It's because of the children,' said Helen.

'Oh I know that! But they can't expect you to be a saint just because you're a mother, can they? Maybe they do,' said Arlene gloomily, taking a long drag on her cigarette. 'It's all right for *him* isn't it – nobody expects him to sit in the house and do his knitting.'

'I don't think anyone's taking his side,' said Sarah.

'Don't you believe it. You should have heard the police. Trying to suggest that I was neglecting the children and that might be why he took them.'

'They've no right to *suggest* anything.'

'The next thing'll be the bleeding social workers. Oh sorry, Sarah, I was forgetting –'

'That's all right. I don't mind. It's so long since I've been employed as one that I scarcely think I deserve the title.'

Arlene blew smoke angrily towards the ceiling. 'I want my kids back.' Anger rather than anxiety dominated her mood. She said she knew he wouldn't harm them, it wasn't like he was an ordinary kidnapper keeping them in a hole in the ground and demanding ransom.

'But think of the trauma for *them*,' said Helen.

'Oh they're used to the ups-and-downs of life,' said Arlene.

'Don't say that to the social workers,' said Sarah, 'or you might never get them back. You will have to appear distressed and worried.'

The police had gone to Arlene's husband's house but nobody had been at home, nor at the brother's house either. 'What did they expect?' said Arlene. 'They'll have gone to ground.' But where that might be she had no idea. They had their places, which they kept secret even from their wives. 'Best you shouldn't know too much,' Gil had said. When the police had come she had always been able to say with truth that she hadn't a clue.

'We will have to apply for a court order,' said Sarah.

'Oh God, not more of all that court and lawyer stuff,' said Arlene wearily.

In the evening, her husband rang from a call box.

'Where are the children?' demanded Sarah. 'The police are looking for you.'

'Tell Arlene I'm keeping the kids till she comes back.'

The house was quiet with Arlene's children gone and the street seemed deserted without the two men patrolling. The women kept going to the window to look out, even though they knew there would be nobody there. Liffey, too, had given up calling.

'All quiet on the Western Front then?' said the constable, when he looked in.

'He fancies his repartee does that one,' said Sarah, wishing that he might actually *do* something instead of writing in his notebook. She suspected he did not take them seriously. Houseful of batty women, he probably said down at the station.

Tasha, too, was in a quiet spell, spending much of the time in her room – working, she said – behaving with unnatural docility when she was with her mother and the other two women. Sarah watched her uneasily. She did not believe that a kick in the behind had worked miracles. (Arlene had not been able to resist saying I told you so, nor had she tried to.) Tasha had fled outraged to her father who had supported Sarah. He rang to say that he'd told Tasha she'd behaved abominably.

101

'She's biding her time,' said Sarah to Helen. 'Aren't we all – in our own ways?'

Walking on the promenade, enjoying a rough buffeting wind, Sarah realised that for years she had just been letting things happen. She had been bent on survival. Now she *would* have to ask herself what she did want. Her mothering was almost at an end and then she would be free. For what? There was the rub, by no means unique, faced by millions of women whose families have gone and who cannot get their jobs back. Edmée had had a suggestion. She was thinking of making another long journey in the spring, travelling eastward, and wanted Sarah to come with her. She planned to be away for a year. How could she come? Sarah had asked. Think about it, said Edmée.

She was thinking now when she caught sight of Liffey up ahead. He was emerging from the amusement arcade in his camel-coloured coat. On seeing her, he broke into a run, which he could not sustain. He arrived beside her, wheezing.

'Sarah! What've you been avoiding your old friend Liffey for?' He linked his arm through hers. She smelt drink on his breath. 'You're breaking my heart, darling.'

'I doubt it. Taking me to bed had as much to do with Tom as with me, didn't it? More.'

'How can you say that?'

'You must have wanted to do it for years. To have Tom's wife.'

'It added spice to our little tumble, I won't deny that.'

'I doubt if you'll get anywhere with his new woman though – not unless you rape her.'

'No need to turn bitter.' He allowed her to free her arm. 'Just because *you*'ve been dumped.'

She removed her arm and walked briskly away from him. Dumped, she said to herself, and the word fell inside her head like a sackful of potatoes. One can only dump passive objects.

On arriving home, she found that Arlene had flown, back to Gil's nest.

Thomas, informed of the latest turn in events by Tasha, returned.

102

'There are only you and Tasha now,' he said, 'and Helen and Jamie. So it would no longer be a case of putting Arlene and her children out on the streets to be gobbled up by the big bad wolves. We must talk about the house, Sarah, and we must do it calmly and sensibly.'

Sensibly meant one thing, as far as he was concerned, said Sarah: that she should give in to his demands.

PART THREE

Thomas and Eunice

The Orient Express is rolling on through the night, flashing across the plains, plunging into tunnels, streaking over viaducts. Behind drawn blinds, the passengers are sleeping and intriguing and making love. He's coming towards her, the swinging, shaded pink light sending a warm glow across his bare chest. She feels the tremor of the train run through her body –

The door pinged open letting in a swirl of damp air and Eunice's eyelids flew upward. Swimming into focus came Jinty Smith.

Eunice steadied herself and got to her feet.

'Having a wee nap, were you?' said Jinty in that soft slow way of hers. 'Don't blame you. Day like this.' She dropped her grubby shopping bag on top of the clean counter.

Eunice had to lock her fingers across her stomach to calm herself. She said icily, when she was able to unlock her tongue, 'What can I do for you?'

'I'm looking for a hat pattern. For the bairns. Something easy like. I'm not a great knitter.'

Eunice placed the hat pattern box on the counter and let Jinty rummage through. Though rummage was too strong a word, for her fingers moved like her tongue, as if they could not be bothered. You'd think butter wouldn't melt in your mouth, you silly bitch, said Eunice inside her head, and had a sickening image of a great blob of yellow butter melting inside that soft moist mouth and oozing out over the plump pink lips.

After a few minutes, when she couldn't stand there watching any longer, she intercepted the lazy fingers and took out a pattern, saying, 'This one's dead simple,' with emphasis on the 'dead' but she might as well have saved herself the effort for Jinty just smiled and said that would do her then. She could obviously stir herself when she wanted to, as on the night of

107

her so-called rape: she must have worked frantically, ripping her clothes apart and tearing at her skin with her nails. Eunice barely repressed a shudder. She would not have liked to have seen the look on Jinty's face then.

'Were you wanting any wool?' she asked.

'I've got bits and pieces in the house.'

Bits and pieces just about described Jinty's house, from what Eunice heard. She had never set foot in it herself, wouldn't if you paid her.

She popped the pattern into a paper bag and stated the price. Her customer looked as if she might have stood there all day staring at the picture of the woollen hat with the tassel on top. 'This is a very popular pattern,' said Eunice automatically and could have immediately cut out her tongue. She did not want to say one word more than was necessary to the woman. She waited for Jinty to count the coins in her purse. They came out in five and ten and two pence pieces. Jinty laughed, said anyone would think she'd been singing.

'Cheers then, Eunice.'

Eunice tidied up the hat patterns. Bugger her, bugger her, she said inside her head.

Jinty crossed with Jean Finlay on her way out. Jean, looking more embarrassed than Jinty, stood to one side in the porch and let the other woman meander past her. 'Ta,' said Jinty and paused to look up at the sky. 'Still spitting, I see.'

Jean came in and closed the door behind her. Eunice exploded.

'What a nerve! Fancy coming in here like that!'

'Why shouldn't she? She's got to get her shopping like everybody else. After all, it's not her that's on trial.' Eunice stared at Liffey's wife. Jean went to the shelves to look for some sock wool for her eldest son Peter. Her pride and joy. She made no secret of it. Eunice did not like Peter, she thought he was too cocksure of himself; he worked as a computer scientist in London and drove a brand new car with a smile on his face. He was good to his mother though, Eunice had to admit that. But no wonder Liffey didn't go home very often. Some life he'd had, knowing his wife thought more of her son than of him.

Jean pointed to some wool and Eunice pulled it from the shelf toppling the package beside it which Jean immediately bent to retrieve. She placed it neatly on the shelf, increasing Eunice's irritation. She seemed to have an extra thumb on each hand as she opened up the wool and took out the number of balls required, and all the while Jean stood patiently waiting. Patience was Jean's speciality. It was not a virtue Eunice thought particularly highly of.

'*To Russia, With Love.*' Jean eyed the book spreadeagled on the counter. 'I thought I'd seen you reading that before?'

'Oh I read it over and over. I do with all the James Bonds. Your Liffey looks a bit like James Bond, don't you think?'

'Liffey?'

'Sean Connery. He's the same build –'

'Oh I don't know.' Of course Jean wouldn't be able to handle a man like 007.

'I wouldn't mind a trip to Russia on the Orient Express. With James Bond, of course.' Eunice laughed and then Jean laughed, uncertainly. 'She didn't look as if she'd been through a terrible experience,' said Eunice. Jean stared blankly back. 'Jinty Smith. *You* don't think that Liffey –?'

'No, of course not,' said Jean and pulled on her gloves and retied the knot of her headscarf beneath her chin. Before she left she asked after Thomas. She usually did.

'I'm expecting my son for his tea the day,' said Isabel Peterson, as she eyed the cream cookies and jam doughnuts and vanilla slices and smoothly-iced French cakes and the trifles. Oh the trifles! They oozed with fresh cream and were decked with glistening red cherries.

'That's nice,' said the bakery assistant, putting a loaf on the counter. She yawned and asked if there would be anything else?

Isabel still hesitated in front of the glass cake counter. She reasoned with herself. Such items were luxuries, things she could do without, and usually did, for she only had her pension and Eunice was paid a pittance for minding the wool shop, but they tempted her though, that she could not deny. She felt a watering of the mouth and sucked her bottom lip in sharply.

'Rotten day,' said the bakery assistant with a glance towards the door at the grey drizzle which was seeping into every crack of the village and blurring the landscape surrounding it, the low moorland hills and the pit slags.

Isabel felt suddenly tired. Her system cried out for sweetness, for something extra to stabilise it. She pointed with her black-gloved hand. 'I think I'll take a trifle today.'

A little of what you fancied did you good, said the assistant, reaching into the glass case with her floury hands. Isabel watched carefully as the woman put the fluffy trifle into a white paper bag. 'You'll need to mind you don't tip it now.'

They fussed a little over the repacking of Isabel's shopping bag and placed the trifle on top of a box of eggs.

'Enjoy yourself – it's later than you think!' The woman had a braying kind of laugh which was not much to Isabel's liking. She bid her good morning and, holding her head erect, stepped out into the wet street.

Hearing the shrill of a bicycle bell, not imagining it could be connected with her, she did not look round, but then she heard a familiar voice. 'Hi, Ma!' Again, came the ringing of the bell. She turned her head now, as did the few other people who were about, and there coming towards her, mounted on a bicycle as he used to be when he was a schoolboy, his hair plastered to his head with rain, his face brick red, was her middle-aged son Thomas. She let go of her shopping bag and it plopped on to the pavement in front of her feet.

Thomas swooshed into the kerb spraying her legs with water, and flinging the machine aside, seized her bag. The movement ejected the trifle which skidded across the pavement releasing itself from its white bag and came to rest, inevitably, cream side down. Isabel gazed at it mournfully. Damn and blast, Thomas was declaring, and she did wish he would not swear. Both he and Eunice could be foul-mouthed at times. She was inclined to blame their grandfather. He used to teach Thomas to swear in Russian and when the boy came out with a string of oaths he would laugh until his belly shook and the watch dangling from its chain swung to and fro like a pendulum. The children's father, in contrast to his own father, had been clean-living and clean-talking, but then he had died too young to influence them. Carcinoma of the lung. When she thought of him she still felt a pang at the base of her throat, though could no longer clearly remember what he looked like.

110

The picture on the sideboad was a poor likeness. Grandfather Peterson, when he moved in with them, had said there was one thing for sure, Thomas was not going down any filthy pit and end by coughing his lungs up too.

'I'll get you another trifle, Mother,' said Thomas and made for the shop still holding her shopping bag.

'No,' she cried after him. 'I don't want one now.' And she did not. The mouth watering moment had passed and she knew that she should have known better than to yield to the temptation. That was a sin, after all, it had been dinned into her in her childhood, and the good Lord whom she often spoke of though no longer believed in was punishing her. 'Come back, Tommy!' He came.

He was apologetic. He peered into the bag holding the top wide open and letting the rain lay waste to its contents. He might have a university degree but there were times when he was lacking in plain common sense. Like his sister.

Isabel held out her hand. 'Now give me my bag please, Tommy.'

'I can carry it.' He slung it over the handlebars of the bicycle.

'*Please!*' She flapped her black-gloved hands and he put the bag into them. She looked inside. 'The egg box has burst.' Sticky yellow fluid had slid everywhere in the bag, over packets of tea and sugar, round the newspaper parcel which shrouded the haddock bought for their tea, inside a brown-paper parcel containing mince for the next day's dinner.

'Don't fret, Mother. It's not the end of the world. I'll get you some more eggs.' And away he dashed into the grocer's shop next to the baker's leaving her standing there with the sprawling bicycle and the devastated shopping bag.

The end of the world might have been on its way, to judge by the suddenness with which darkness had descended cutting off the last of the grey daylight. She shivered.

Thomas reappeared waving two egg boxes in his hands. He tucked them under one arm and picked up the bicycle with his other hand. They proceeded homewards, she walking with quick little steps, her eyes averted from the eggs clamped into his armpit, he keeping close to the kerb, pushing the bicycle through the gutter. They did not speak until they reached the shelter of her kitchen.

Then she said, 'You didn't have to buy a *dozen* eggs. You were aye extravagant.'

He wanted to clean the bag for her but she would not have it, she must do it herself, and that she did before removing her hat and coat though she did take off her gloves. She tetched and clucked over the cleaning of it, soaping and rinsing and wiping until not a speck of egg slime remained.

A knock on the back door sent Thomas flying into the living room. The caller was Mrs Finlay from next door – Liffey's mother – on the scrounge again for sugar. Pity it hadn't been for eggs.

She took the opportunity to ask after Thomas. 'I thought I saw him coming in with you, Isabel? On a bicycle? What's happened to yon big car he had?'

'Sarah was needing it the day – she's aye gadding about, she's got that many friends – and Tommy likes the bicycle for the exercise. Keep fit you ken. At his age he's got to watch himself . . .'

They had a discussion then about sudden death, heart attacks and strokes, and about lingering illnesses such as ulcers and hardening of the arteries. They recalled friends and neighbours who had succumbed.

Then Mrs Finlay said, 'I thought Tommy and Sarah weren't living together any more?'

'Where did you hear that, Effie?'

'Laurence tellt me.'

'Your Liffey has got a fine imagination if you ask me. Sarah and Tommy are as happy as a couple of sandboys together, just as they always have been.'

Isabel handed Mrs Finlay her sugar and showed her out. Mouth like a letter box on her that one had. Then Isabel went through to the sitting room where Thomas was squatting in front of the fire drying himself off. Steam rose like mist from his arms and legs and for a moment she thought he was on fire.

'What on earth do you have to go riding a bicycle round the place for at your age, Tommy?'

Because he was short of cash, that was why, he said. Skint. She protested that he couldn't be that hard up surely to goodness, didn't he get that big handshake when he left his job?

'It went into the house, to pay off the mortgage, you know

112

that. And I didn't *leave* my job – I was made redundant.'

'And when do you think you'll be getting another one?'

'You know jobs are hard to come by.'

'But with your qualifications –'

She sighed, took off her hat. She thought of the flattened trifle lying in the rain, its cream dribbling away across the pavement. She could have done with some of that sweetness.

'I might start up an antiquarian bookshop. Old books.'

Old books. She didn't much like the sound of that, at the very least couldn't he set up a shop that sold new books, although she didn't want him to be a shopkeeper at all. That's what Eunice was after all. And Eunice had had no chances in life.

'Anyone in?' sang out Eunice as she always did on her return from work.

'Tommy's in the sitting room,' her mother called back, from the kitchen, where she was frying the haddock coated in orange crumbs for their tea.

Eunice's woollen hat was rimmed with raindrops. She took it off and shook it. A few of the drops landed on Thomas. He dried his face without comment.

'Bloody awful night out,' said Eunice.

'Anything to drink in the house?'

'Bit of Cyprus sherry. Sweet. Not what your fancy palate's used to.'

He made a face but said that would be better than nothing. She joined him in a glass. They sat with their feet on the fender and their knees reaching out for the heat. The air at their backs was cold.

'What's new with you, then?' asked Eunice.

'Sarah and I are putting the house up for sale.'

'So you're shoving her out in the street, are you?'

'She has agreed to the sale.'

'Mother,' said Eunice, as their mother edged into the room carrying the haddock on a tray, 'Tommy's putting Sarah out.'

'I told you, Eunice – she's agreed.' He got up to try to take the tray but did not succeed in breaking his mother's grip.

'Last time she talked to us she said she'd no intention of

leaving the place,' said Eunice.

'You're not going to sell that lovely house?' Isabel faced her son across the trayful of fish. 'Put your wife and child out in the street?'

'It's not all that lovely, the roans are leaking and the back wall needs repointing and we can't afford –'

'I'd never have thought a son of mine could be so hard.'

'Hard? I feel like a marshmallow that's been trampled on!'

'Come on, Mr Innocent,' said Eunice, '*you* were the one that did the walking out.'

'Let's drop the subject, shall we? I came for my tea not a lecture.'

'Oh aye drop anything that doesn't please you. That's you all over, always has been. Turn your back and walk away. Way you did with us here.'

'That's not true. I've always been back to see you both. You couldn't expect me to live here for the rest of my life.'

'Oh no we certainly didn't expect that. You always made it perfectly obvious that you couldn't wait to get the hell out of here.'

'Eunice!' said her mother.

Eunice lit a cigarette and pulled her skirt up so that her knees could get a bit more heat. She loved blasts of direct heat. She thought longingly of the North African sun. She fancied the desert in an odd sort of way though she couldn't have said why. It was not the sand that appealed, she hated getting it in her shoes at the seaside, or the Arabs themselves, for they had some funny ways that she didn't think she could be doing with, or the food, which might give you dysentery and that wouldn't be much fun. It was more a feeling of some sort of mystery. She gazed into the leaping flames.

They were about to eat, said Isabel, who wished that Eunice would not smoke either. Her husband – she glanced at him where he sat on the sideboard frowning over his tooth-brush moustache with no hope of ever smiling again – had been a heavy smoker. That was the only vice he had had and in those days it was not even considered one, or particularly unclean. She invoked their father now reminding Eunice of the number of cigarettes he had smoked a day and of his untimely death.

'It was the coal dust,' said Eunice.

'Let's eat,' said Thomas wearily.

'So that you can get away?'

'Oh shut up, Eunice.'

'Yes, that's enough now, Eunice,' said their mother.

They ate at a card table pulled up to the fire. The fish was almost cold though only Isabel remarked on it. 'If you two hadn't started your arguing . . .'

Thomas glanced at his watch and Eunice said, 'Got a date?' He denied it and she went on, 'She's not a bad looker – if you like those sort of looks – but she's far too young for you.'

'She's not *that* young.'

'Fish didn't seem too fresh to me, what did you think, Eunice?' Isabel scraped the remains on to one plate.

'Can't be much more than thirty, is she?'

'That's enough, Eunice. I'll just wet the tea.'

When their mother had gone to the kitchen Eunice said, 'I suppose she makes you feel young again? Like having a second childhood?'

'Shut your mouth.'

'Charming. Wonder what *she*'d say if she could hear you talking like that?'

'If she knew what I'd to put up with she'd wonder my language wasn't worse.'

'What *you*'d to put up with?' Eunice relit the cigarette end which she had squashed earlier. It tasted foul but beggars couldn't be choosers. Thomas sniffed as if he didn't much like the smell. Pity for him. He had given up smoking, since going to live with his fancy woman. 'What about me and what I've had to put up with, all these years *for you*?' she demanded, thumping herself in the chest with two fingers of her right hand and singeing her fluffy jumper. She rubbed the mark. 'You used to stand there like little Boy Blue all sweet and lovely as if you hadn't a nasty thought in your head and everybody said, what a lovely laddie, what a smart laddie, he'll go far: that's what they said. As far as the buroo's where you've got yourself now.'

'That appears to please you.'

'Oh it doesn't please me one little bit. What was the point in *my* sacrifice can you tell me if you haven't even got a job and won't be able to help us out when I retire? I was thinking of taking early retirement. Everybody else is. I've worked enough in my life.'

'Come off it, Eunice, what would you do if you didn't have the shop?'

He got up and went to the kitchen to ask if he could help his mother carry the tea through. He could not of course and he would not have expected to, Eunice knew. Turned his back and walked away, that was what he had done: he had proved her point.

Thomas stood about in the kitchen looking as if he didn't know where to put himself. Isabel infused the tea and reset the tray.

'I don't think I can stay too long,' said Thomas, when there came another knock on the door. His mother opened it.

'Jean! Come away in.'

Liffey's wife hesitated. She would come back later, she hadn't realised they had anyone in.

'Thomas isn't anyone,' said Isabel, drawing her into the kitchen.

'I just came to show you the jumper I was knitting.' Jean held it up diffidently.

Isabel insisted she come through to the fire to show it properly and that she sat down and had a cup of tea. Jean protested saying that she really shouldn't, she'd left her dishes and the younger children should be doing their homework.

'Expect you need to keep them up to the mark,' said Eunice. 'Not like our Thomas here. Do you remember him with his head in his books like a horse with its head stuck in a trough?'

'Your wit slays me,' said Thomas.

Isabel gave them both a warning look. She turned the attention to Jean's jumper.

It was examined and admired. Eunice's praises were exceptionally loud and she called on Thomas who sat on the edge of the circle to admire it too. 'Jean's a grand knitter, isn't she, Tommy?'

'Looks like it,' he said and swallowed his tea in a gulp.

'And how's Peter doing then, Jean?' Eunice had brightened up since Jean had come in.

'Very well thanks.'

'Coming home for Christmas?'

'Yes.'

'That's nice isn't it, Tommy?' said Eunice. 'Peter coming home for Christmas?'

'Very nice.' He poured himself another cup of tea and sneaked a look at his watch though not without Eunice noticing it.

Noticing it too perhaps, Jean got to her feet saying that she must go. Isabel saw her out even though Jean did know the way perfectly well.

'Nice girl, Jean,' said Eunice.

Thomas assented.

Eunice glanced at the sideboard where the family photographs were displayed. She nodded at the one of Thomas as Gala King and Jean as Gala Queen at a miner's Gala Day when they were twelve years old. They had velvet cloaks round their shoulders and cardboard crowns on their heads.

'Course she was your first sweetheart, wasn't she?'

'That was a long time ago.'

'Your cloak cost a week of my wages. I was only earning fifteen shillings –'

'Change the record for God's sake, Eunice! I'm sick of hearing about your sacrifice for me. Every year it gets bigger.'

'Well, why couldn't you have done something useful – like trained for a doctor or a dentist? But Baltic studies! You had to be different, didn't you?'

He stood up, putting his back to her, and lifted his jacket. She saw that he was staring at the photograph of their grandfather. Toms Petersons. It had been his fault, so their mother said. Full of tales he'd been, tall ones for all they knew, about his adventures on the high seas and his Latvian childhood on the borders of Russia. He had claimed to have been brought up in a country house with a swarm of servants and parents who travelled regularly to Moscow, St. Petersburgh, Vienna and Paris. (They'd been inclined to believe the bit about the servants as he'd expected to be waited on hand and feet, by the women in the house at any rate.) His family had suffered some kind of financial setback and young Toms had had to go out into the world to seek his fortune. Eunice had always imagined him with a bundle on the end of a stick, in the manner of Dick

117

Whittington. To her it seemed like a fairy tale. She loved fairy tales.

Thomas turned away from the photograph.

'You don't really need a job though now, do you? Your woman must earn plenty money to keep you.'

'Eunice, if you were a man –'

'Okay, so you'd punch me in the mouth. But if you're really wanting a job why don't you ask Liffey if there's anything going alongside him at the warehouse? You probably wouldn't go for that would you – unskilled work, dirtying your hands? He – ' she nodded at their grandfather ' – had to dirty his hands. He didn't like doing it but he had to.'

He had come over to Leith as a deckhand on a timber boat, met their grandmother who, in blue and white striped skirt, frequented the docks selling fish from nearby Newhaven, and, against the wishes of her family who did not like foreigners (that meant anyone from outside Newhaven), had married her. They'd settled in the village here and he'd got a job down the pit. Some fortune that was! He'd exchanged the light of sea and sky for darkness. Eunice felt for him there. She hated darkness herself and as a child would have slept with the light on, if her mother had let her. In his last years, when his fisher lassie lay long buried underground, Grandfather Peterson would sit by the fire staring back into his unseen – as far as they were concerned – past. Thomas was the one he'd tried to take with him, though Eunice had gone uninvited. He had taught Thomas Latvian and they'd talk together for hours and laugh. When she had pleaded to be let into their secrets, her grandfather had said that it was men's talk, but on November 18th, Latvian Independence Day, she'd been allowed to have a glass of wine and celebrate with them.

'I hardly think there are any openings in the mining business these days,' said Thomas and went through to the kitchen where his mother was bent over the sink. Could he dry the dishes for her before he went?

Don't be so daft, she told him, that was women's work. He said that he often dried dishes, washed them too, cooked as well. He was quite a good cook.

'You never used to cook in Sarah's house.'

'Mother, I'm no longer living with Sarah.'

'Aye and now you have to do women's chores and all. That's what you get with women like yon other one. Career women. They're no use to a man. And don't bother telling me I'm out of date, I know that human nature doesn't change. I know what men are like. Those women libbers need their heads examined. No wonder they hang about together – they couldn't get a man if they had all the tea in China.'

'That was quite a speech, Mother.'

'What's all this about?' asked Eunice, joining them.

'Women's lib.'

'Oh that.'

Thomas took his rain cape from the peg.

'You didn't stay long,' said his mother.

'Only came for the grub, didn't you?' said Eunice. 'Probably don't get properly fed at your fancy woman's. She's too busy trying to get criminals off the hook. I wouldn't have her job if you paid me. Downright immoral if you ask me.'

'She's going to be defending Liffey.'

Eunice sniffed. Why did he have to bring Liffey into this? Everybody knew *he* was no criminal. 'That bitch Jinty Smith should be the one that gets locked up. She's been bad news since the day she was born. She'd lie in her teeth as soon as look at you. She's out to get Liffey. But she won't, for he's innocent.'

'I'll be seeing you,' said Thomas, and opening the back door plunged into the night.

'In all the old familiar places,' said Eunice.

'What do you have to keep going on at him for? You drive him away.'

'I was only teasing him. Doesn't even seem to be able to take a joke these days.'

Eunice went back into the sitting room and took another look at her grandfather. When she stood face to face like this with him, she felt he was staring straight into her eyes. In many ways she was closer to him now than when he'd been alive. She liked talking to him, knew he understood her better than her mother did.

'I know you always wanted to go back to Latvia,' she said softly. 'Just once. Just to see it. Maybe I'll go for you.' She

119

wondered if she went on one of those holiday packages to Russia whether she could take a side trip to Riga. She would go and look for his family's country house – *her* family's country house. It was part of the Soviet Union now, Latvia; at other times, it had been under German rule. It had only been free for twenty-five years. 'Shame, isn't it?'

'What's that you're saying, Eunice?' asked her mother, coming into the room.

'Just that I'm out of cigarettes. I'll nip down to the pub. I won't be long.'

Without waiting to hear her mother's protests, she went into her bedroom to get ready. The chill of the room made her blench every time she opened the door but her mother didn't hold with heating bedrooms. Eunice thought again of North Africa.

She sat down at the dressing table, gave her hair a quick comb and put on some lipstick. Pressing her lips together, she leant forward to look into the mirror. The glass was slightly pocked and the light poor; she had to peer to see her face at all clearly. Might have been as well not to see it but, still, you couldn't run away from your own face could you? You had to face up to it. Ha, ha. It wasn't as if it was *that* bad. It wasn't ugly or deformed or anything. Okay so maybe there were a few creases across the forehead and the sides of her mouth were streaked with faint lines but you couldn't expect anything else when you were almost fifty. She'd worn pretty well, all things considered. The thing was not to give up. You could see what happened to the women who did. Look at Jean. She'd let herself go. It was no wonder Liffey was always roaming. Now if he could only have a woman who appreciated him. Who would satisfy him . . .

For a moment she screwed her face up, making it worse, then smoothed it out with her fingertips. She stretched the skin up and back from her mouth and saw the lines almost disappear. She looked years younger. Perhaps she should get her face lifted. Become a new woman. Put the clock back. She turned this way and that to see herself from all angles. Then she dropped her hands and her face sagged into place again. Oh well. What the hell. Never say die.

Plunging her hands into the drawer where she kept her

make-up, she scavenged amongst bottles of half-used lotions and potions and spiky rollers entwined with strands of old hair and plastic cases all silvered over with spilt talcum powder, and finally extracted the rouge stick which would bring a glow into her face and thereby transform it. Golden amber. It carried a hint of the East, of warm days and sultry nights. She smeared the rouge over the top of her cheeks and spread it out to the hairline. She had high cheekbones. That was meant to be good, according to the magazines, though she couldn't remember why. All she retained from her magazine reading was a string of half-remembered hints on How To. How To Make Yourself More Glamorous. Have Glossy Hair. Make Your Eyes More Alluring. Your Spine More Supple. The magazines were supposed to have changed their tune in recent years, according to Sarah, but she couldn't see it herself, except for one or two that were a bit off (her dentist always had those) and went on about women and their bodies until it got embarrassing. (She'd look round the dentist's waiting room hoping no one had noticed that her face had gone all hot.) Sarah said that women's sexual expectations had changed; at least those of women under a certain age had. What that age was, was not clear to Eunice. She didn't like to ask Sarah questions directly; she'd just sit and get on with her knitting and let Sarah talk. She relied on Sarah for a lot of information about other ways of life.

Thinking of Sarah, she sighed. She wished she and Thomas hadn't split up. She liked her sister-in-law even though she disapproved of her filling her place with all those loopy women. But at least there was always something going on in the house in Portobello. And now it was to be sold. What a silly fool Thomas was. He had never been good at counting his blessings, he had always thought there must be something else going. And for him, there usually was. Still, she was sorry she'd been a bit sharp with him, she hadn't meant to be, her tongue seemed to run away with her when he was around, she was fond enough of him when all was said and done, for he was her brother wasn't he, and when you came right down to it blood was thicker than water. Or at least you had to think that way.

'Eunice? What are you doing in there?'
'Talking to Sean Connery.'

121

'I thought you were going to the pub?'
'I am. I am.'

Thomas was sitting with Liffey in a corner and they had both
had a few drinks, to judge from the empty glasses on the table.
Liffey waved her over. 'Hi, Eunice. You're looking great the
night. What'll you have? Your usual?'

'Thanks, Liffey.'

She arranged herself on the bench so that it would be Liffey
she would be sitting beside when he came back from the bar.
Her cheeks, which in the bedroom had felt glacial to the touch,
were warm now. She hoped she had not overdone the amber
glow; it was difficult to be sure in that bedroom, with the light
being so bad. Her mother always bought the weakest light
bulbs available in order to keep the electricity bill down.
Eunice changed them for brighter ones – she would have had
them brighter than a thousand suns if she could, even though
they would show up the lines on her face – but when she'd get
home from work she'd find that her mother had changed them
back again.

She lit a cigarette and crossed her legs, letting her skirt ride
up to her knee. She had good legs, Sarah said. Thomas was
staring across the pub as if he had never set eyes on her.

'I didn't mean to get at you,' said Eunice. 'My tongue just
seems to run away from me at times.'

'That's all right.'

Liffey brought their drinks. Vodka and orange for her and
drams for the men with pints of beer as chasers. Thomas said he
shouldn't really drink any more, but he did.

'Bottoms up!' said Liffey. 'Let's see you put yours down in a
oner then, Eunie.'

'Oh no, I couldn't do that. I'd choke.' She giggled. Liffey
always managed to cheer her up. You never saw him right
down in the dumps staring moodily in front of him even when
he did have problems.

'Here's to victory in the courts!' said Liffey and drank.

'So Tommy's fancy woman's going to be defending you?'

'You're quite wrong,' said Thomas, coming alive. 'A fancy
woman is a *kept* woman.'

122

'In that case I should've called you the fancy man.'

'In that case I should've called you a bloody bitch.'

'Now, now,' said Liffey, laughing, 'that's enough from the two of you.' He put a hand on their knees, keeping the one on Eunice's longer than the one on Thomas's. 'You can still scrap like a couple of kids, can't you? Fancy is as fancy does – that's one of my old ma's sayings. What about tickling your fancy?' He squeezed Eunice's knee and made her giggle again. Then he removed his hand. But she felt the heat of it for a long time afterwards.

'If you'd like to know,' said Thomas, looking at Eunice across Liffey, 'a fancy man is someone who lives on the immoral earnings of a prostitute.'

'All right, genius, you can have the last word on the subject.' Eunice took out her purse. 'It's my round. What are you both having? Same again?'

Thomas declined, saying he was about to go. He had to cycle back to Edinburgh.

'Better watch you don't get lifted for drunken cycling,' said Eunice. 'Then she'd have to defend you and all.'

He went without answering.

Rather Tommy than him, said Liffey. Imagine, all the way to Edinburgh on a bike! He'd collapse before he got out of the village, and to think he'd once been a junior boxing champion!

'No, you wouldn't. You look pretty fit to me. You're still a fine looking man for your age, you know. Mother was just saying that last night,' Eunice added quickly to shift the weight of the compliment. Liffey looked pleased though, so she ventured, 'You remind me a bit of Sean Connery.' 'Oh aye, on a dark night?' 'No, you do.' She thought it was something to do with the eyes and the build. And of course they *were* both Scottish so it was not that surprising. 'They say everyone's got a double going about somewhere.' Liffey pulled his shoulders up. He'd need to take up cycling again then, keep in trim. Sean Connery played a lot of golf, Eunice had heard, but Liffey didn't think he could be bothered whacking a wee white ball round a field with a stick. Now if it was football! But he was long past that. He sighed and patted his paunch and his shoulders slumped again. Eunice said, 'Of course it's all right for Tommy – he's got nothing else to do all day but jog and cycle and look after himself.'

After Isabel had watched Eunice go along the street with that peculiar sloping walk of hers – she looked as if she were walking the deck of a ship – she went into the kitchen where, first, she drew the curtains. You could never be too sure round here that somebody wouldn't be peering in your back window, especially that Effie Finlay wouldn't be peering in, and when it was pitch black outside you couldn't see their faces from inside. When Isabel had made sure that not a chink was left between the curtains, she pulled a stool from under the table and placed it in front of the built-in cupboard that went right up to the ceiling. Carefully, she climbed on to the stool holding on to the handles of the cupboard, taking no more chances than she need, for her knees were not what they used to be, nor her ankles either. She straightened herself up, shifted her feet to get a better balance and, thus poised, eased open the top part of the cupboard and from the shelf uplifted a packet of porridge oats.

With as much prudence as she had made the ascent, she descended. She laid the packet of oats on the draining board and from a lower cupboard took a chunky drinking glass. She polished the glass with a clean cloth and held it to the light to see that it sparkled. Then sinking her fingers into the porridge oats she slowly brought upwards, glinting like the amber old Grandfather Peterson had brought from Latvia, a half bottle of whisky. She poured a dram into the glass, added the same amount of water and, before taking it to the sitting room fire, replaced the bottle in the packet, swept up the few scattered oats, returned the packet to the top shelf and put away the stool. Eunice would never even think of looking in the top cupboard; she hadn't the slightest interest in anything domestic.

In her high-backed armchair by the fire, Isabel sipped her whisky, enjoying each warm droplet as it slid down her thirsting throat. It was her only vice, unless one counted the occasional cream cake or trifle, and she liked to enjoy it in private. When she drank with other people the pleasure was never the same. And she never overdid it, kept always to the one drink. That was where other folk – her son and daughter amongst them – went wrong: they overdid things. Her children had got that from their Grandfather Peterson. He had had no sense of proportion either: he was over the moon one minute, full of wild schemes; the next, was down in the depths, bemoaning the fate of the world, his family, himself. Just as well he hadn't lived to see Eunice making an exhibition of herself drinking far too much and Tommy losing his job *and* deserting his wife for another woman. She must be a wicked one, that lawyer, say what you like, for she must have known when she took up with Tommy that he was a married man. And Sarah was such a good person too. But it seemed that being good got you nowhere.

Isabel drained the last drop of her dram letting it rest a moment on her tongue until it went over, then she washed up the glass and put it away. After that she did her knitting and watched a bit of television but switched the set off at ten o'clock, when the news came on: the sight of all the dead bodies put her off her sleep, and whether it was Lebanon, or a football match, that was all you seemed to see. At eleven she changed into her nightdress and dressing gown and filled her hot water bottle. Nursing the bottle on her knee and a cup of Ovaltine between her hands, she sat close to the dying fire and awaited the return of her daughter.

'Time!' called Alex.

'Are you right?' said Liffey.

Eunice did not feel totally right as she got to her feet, but she took a deep breath (Sarah had been telling her about the value of deep breathing) and steadied herself.

The rain had stopped but a wind had sprung up, a playful wind, which was whirling a few papers and packets about. Eunice wound her scarf of many colours about her neck.

'Hang on,' said Liffey, pushing out his elbow. 'If we stick together we'll not get blown over.' He laughed.

Nothing would blow him over, he was so tall and broad. She took his arm and hugged herself in close to him, seeking warmth.

'Where are you thinking of going for your holidays this year, Eunie?'

'I'm considering Morocco. It's only a short boat ride from Southern Spain but it's enough to take you into a different world.'

'Is that right?'

'The mysterious and exotic world of the Orient.'

'I fancy beaches and warm sea.'

'Tangier has a splendid beach, long and broad and golden. And the nightlife's varied and cosmopolitan. There's belly dancing and folklore shows.'

'Sounds like just the ticket.'

'Slender minarets . . . swaying camels . . . the scent of spices.'

'I can't wait.'

'Mosques and bazaars and cool courtyards . . .'

'When do we go?'

'Easter would be a good time for Morocco.'

'Well, if I win the pools . . .'

Eunice smiled in the darkness. She saw them lying on the beach under a coloured umbrella sipping iced drinks from tall glasses. Blue sky, blue sea . . . She would have to wear a bathing costume though, she could hardly lie there clothed from head to foot. The thought dimmed her pleasure a little but perhaps she could go and get that electrical treatment which tightened up flabby muscles. And she could have a few sunbed sessions so that she would have a beautiful golden tan. To match the beach.

'Wouldn't it be lovely, Liffey, to be on a beach right now? In the sun?'

He squeezed her arm. 'Sure would, Eunie.'

Funnily enough, in spite of the dampness and coolness of the night, she felt perfectly warm, right through, as if she were wandering through a Moroccan bazaar. She unwound the scarf with her free hand and let it hang loose and opened the top button of her coat. As she undid the button she had an image, a physical sensation more, of Liffey undoing the next button, and a hot flush swept through her body. She was relieved that it *was* dark and Liffey wouldn't be able to see the angry red skin of her throat. During the last couple of months these flushes had been coming over her at unexpected moments. Embarrassing it was. Sarah said not to be embarrassed, it was just another part of a woman's life and the more embarrassed you got the worse it would be. It was all right for Sarah, she could carry anything off, she had that easy way about her. The violent heat passed and Eunice breathed again more freely.

They had reached the end of the street at which they would separate, round the corner from both their houses. There was a high wall here and often they stood for a moment in the lee of it finishing off their conversation. Usually, too, Liffey gave her a goodnight kiss. She lifted her face to his expectantly and his mouth came down heavy with whisky fumes, which she did not mind. She liked his smell. A man's smell. Their lips met and she put her arms up and around his shoulders. He put his hands in the small of her back pulling her in to him. She felt the line of his body against hers. His tongue was moving against her mouth, she let her lips part. It was the first time they had ever kissed like this. Her body was on fire again, not from a hot flush this time, but for wanting him. She wanted him to lay her on the ground and come down on top of her and crush her until she screamed. The blood sang in her head. When he lifted his mouth she gasped for air.

He pushed her slightly away from him. 'God, Eunie, I was forgetting it was you there.'

She said his name, softly, pleadingly.

'It's all right now, Eunie.' He patted her shoulder. 'You'll be okay.'

'But I want you to – Liffey, I want you –' She fumbled for the zip of his trousers and he laughed and caught hold of her hand.

'It's all that vodka talking, Eunie. Come on now, we're old pals, aren't we, just like brother and sister? We don't want to go messing one another around.'

Hearing the sound of feet running outside, Isabel left the dead fire and went to the window to pull back the curtain. Eunice was coming along the pavement as if someone was after her. Yet the street was empty as far as the eye could see. Isabel craned her neck to look a little further but the only thing that seemed to be moving was the old black and white dog from

127

next door which was nosing round the garbage bags. Not noticing her mother's face at the window, Eunice opened the gate and lunged up the path towards the front door. Isabel shook her head. Both of her children could be quite violent in their movement at times: when they were worked up about something they seemed almost to fall headlong through open doors as if their bodies were propelled by some outside force, whereas she was particular as to how she moved, placing her feet carefully, watching where she was going and keeping strict control over her body.

She went into the hall. Eunice's hair stood on end like a burst mattress and her eyes were wild.

'Has anything happened, Eunice?'

Her daughter swept past her like a rush of wind and went hurtling into the bathroom. The lock was snapped shut. Then there was silence.

Frowning, hugging the hot water bottle which was no longer hot, only vaguely warm, to her chest, Isabel waited (she had spent much of her life waiting), and when five minutes had passed during which she heard no sound of water running or of the cistern flushing, she edged closer to the bathroom door and asked, 'Are you all right, Eunice?'

'I'm great. Just great.' Eunice's voice rang out surprisingly loud and clear and made Isabel take a step back.

'What are you doing in there then?'

'Nothing. Sweet f.a.'

It was raining again. Eunice opened up the shop and as she stepped inside, closing the door behind her, she took a deep breath and felt her rib cage expand. She always felt better as soon as she was across the threshold. She switched on the electric fire and all the lights, filled the kettle and plugged in the radio. In spite of what she had said to Tommy about wanting to take early retirement (as if that was even a possibility!), she loved the shop and had no intention of giving up until she had to. This was the only place she could call her own. This was the only place where she could suit herself. Except for once a month when the area supervisor came round, but she usually only stayed half an hour or so, had a cup of coffee and smoked a cigarette and told Eunice about the problems of being an area supervisor. A quick look at the books and the shelves was enough to reassure her that Eunice had everything in order. 'If only they were all like you!' said the supervisor.

Humming to the music, Eunice made a cup of instant coffee and set out a chocolate caramel wafer biscuit on a plate. She had her little treats lined up at intervals throughout the day. It was the little treats that kept you going in life. Then she opened the full-length cupboard and selected her day's reading material from the piled-high stacks of brochures, magazines and paperback books. She didn't go in for romances where you could see what was coming a mile off, like Mills and Boon, preferring novels with a bit more meat to them. Her favourite authors were Catherine Cookson and Frances Parkinson Keyes, apart from Ian Fleming, but then he came into a different category altogether. Quite different. She also took out her big atlas, which Thomas had given to her last Christmas, and three brochures featuring the Caribbean, Morocco and Florida. There were lots of good bargains going for Florida and you could fly direct from Prestwick which would be very handy, though, mind you, the pound was low against the dollar, and from what one heard, there might be too many muggings in Miami for comfort. There were all sorts of things to take into consideration when you were planning a foreign holiday. After a bit of rummaging she found a summer edition of a woman's magazine carrying an article on How To Make Yourself Beautiful For The Beach.

She laid the magazines and her knitting bag beside her chair which was placed strategically in the back shop so that, with a sideways glance, she could keep an eye on the door. Then she fetched her coffee and chocolate biscuit.

You can enjoy dancing every night to live music and have all the fun of the pool or beach for your daytime pleasure . . .

Eunice read on about nightlife that was vibrant, views which were magnificent, beaches which were sandy and secluded, service which was attentive. Shows, night clubs, concerts, bars with music, cabarets, cinemas, casinos, and a host of other glittering entertainments to keep you happy night and day.

Night and day, you are the one, she hummed.

She took up her knitting and thought now about last night.

Liffey might come in at any moment, he might take the morning off work, to come and see her.

About last night, Eunie – I want to explain.

It's all right, Liffey, you don't have to.

But I do. It wasn't that I didn't want you, you know that. (He puts his arms round her.) I did, very much, but I couldn't make love to you on the corner like that. If we make love together I want it to be properly. I respect you too much –

The shop door jangled open. Looking round, Eunice saw Marilyn coming in. She got up and went to the counter. Outside was parked a high cream-coloured pram decked with baubles that hung limply in the air.

'I'd like another of my balls of wool, Eunice, please.'

Eunice reached up to the shelf where she laid wool aside for some of her steady customers who could not afford to buy the whole lot at once. That was most of them. From the cellophane packet she took a ball of blue Double Knitting. She asked how things were with Marilyn.

'All right.' Marilyn bent her head to take the money from her purse but not before Eunice saw the purplish-yellow mark under her left eye.

'Billy behaving himself?'

'Oh he wouldne lift a hand to me now. He's daft about the bairn.'

'Aye, but is he daft about you?'

Marilyn laughed.

'A man should respect a woman,' said Eunice. 'If he doesn't the relationship'll never be any good.'

She could see Marilyn looking at her with a little smile and thinking what does *she* know about a man and his respect? She knew plenty, more than Marilyn could ever dream of, but she was not going to waste her breath telling her for the girl wouldn't listen.

On the other side of the window Gary began to protest at being abandoned and the baubles swung to and fro. Marilyn said she'd better be getting along.

'Tell Sarah I was asking after her.'

Eunice went back to her seat by the fire, and to Liffey. *He* was daft about *her*.

I've always been crazy about you, Eunice. When we were kids I

130

used to look up to you – you being that year or two older. But at our time of life age doesn't matter any more. I've never been able to tell you how I felt about you before, I was afraid you'd laugh.

Laugh, Liffey? I'd never laugh at you.

The door opened again and in came a woman looking for a pair of number four knitting needles. Controlling her irritation, Eunice went to serve her. The woman then thought that since she was here she might as well take a look at what Eunice had in Chunky Knits. Normally Eunice loved taking down the wool, showing off the colours, inviting customers to feel the quality, but right now she had not the patience for it.

After she had got every packet of Chunky Knit on the counter the woman said she'd think about it and also she'd need to check if it was number four needles she wanted after all. She thought it might be five. After she had gone Eunice considered turning the open sign to closed so that she could get a few minutes' peace, but decided better not, for you never knew who would report you for what round here, some of them had nothing else to do but make trouble.

She sat down again. Where were they now? Oh yes. . .

I love you, Eunie.

I love you, Liffey.

We'll go away somewhere, just you and I. We could have a villa in Tenerife or an apartment in Corfu. . .

Or we could take a slow boat to China.

(They kiss. They cling to one another.)

I don't want to make you lie down on the floor, Eunie.

I'd lie down anywhere with you, Liffey.

(They lie down.)

The merciless jangle of the doorbell cut across their passion. 'Eunice? Are you there, Eunice?'

'What?' Eunice came to to find she was lying on the floor, between the electric fire and her chair. How had she got there? The fire was scorching her leg. She struggled up into a sitting position.

'That's where you are,' said Mrs Finlay, appearing round the corner. She stared down at Eunice. 'Are you all right?'

'I was just doing my exercises. For flattening the stomach.' With the help of the chair, Eunice made it up on to her feet. 'What is it, Mrs Finlay? Is it Liffey?' she asked with alarm.

'What would it be Laurence for? No, your mother's fallen off a stool. She was spring cleaning yon high cupboard in the kitchen. There was an awfy mess of porridge oats and broken glass all over the place, and a smell of whisky.' Mrs Finlay eyed Eunice with suspicion. 'What she had to be doing her spring cleaning in December for I don't know. The doctor's sent for an ambulance to take her to the hospital to get her ankle x-rayed.'

Thomas came out the next day to help take care of his mother. Eunice just told him straight: it was time he did his bit, she was expected to look after their mother year in year out and she had her work to go to, whereas he – He cut her off there saying all right, all right, she needn't go on, he'd be out in the morning.

Their mother had sprained her ankle and pulled a ligament in her right leg and been told to keep her foot off the ground for several days. After that she could go about on crutches. She lay on the settee moaning about being idle and watched Thomas performing her tasks. She had a sharp eye for fluff under chairs and dirty specks on cutlery.

'Now you know what I've to put up with,' said Eunice when Thomas grumbled to her in the kitchen.

'I don't think it's necessary for me to stay the night though, Eunice.'

She knew what he wanted of course: to get back to the bed of his fancy woman. She restrained herself from saying so since Thomas was in a foul enough mood as it was and she knew that if she pushed him too far he was liable to jump on his bike and pedal off. She said in a more persuasive voice, 'I really could do with you here, Tommy. Mother usually has to get up a couple of times in the night –'

All right, all right, he said, he'd stay for a night or two until they saw how things worked out.

'I was thinking I might go away for New Year,' said Eunice, drying the dishes which Thomas had washed.

'Where to?'

'Lanzarote. I got this new brochure today.' She nodded at it lying open on the table. They stared at white-washed walls and blue sea and exotic flowers in bloom. 'They tell me it's warm there at this time of year.'

How does that feel, Liffey? (She smoothes more oil into his shoulders and back, feels the muscles rippling beneath her supple fingers.)

Fantastic. Don't stop, Eunie, don't stop, please . . .

'Eunice!'

'What is it, Mother?'

'You're taking an awful long time with that tea. I'll be dead from thirst before you get it here.'

'I'm just coming.'

Spooning tea into the pot, waiting for the kettle to re-boil, Eunice thought of the night before when she had stood with Liffey on the corner in the shelter of the wall. She kept going over the things that he had said and she had said. After he had said, 'I don't want to mess you around, Eunie,' she had asked him if he thought she was – well, that she had never –? He had shrugged, said he hadn't thought about it, but of course he hadn't wanted to say one way or the other. She had told him straight out that she wasn't a virgin, but not that the only men she'd ever been with were ones she'd picked up in the pub. Strangers who'd wandered in and who wouldn't have known her face in the street next day. She had never been with a man she loved, or even liked particularly.

'*Eunice!*'

She carried the tea through on a tray and poured a cup for her mother.

'I'm just going to pop down to the pub for a minute.'

'And what if I need the bathroom while you're gone?'

'You've just been,' said Eunice firmly. 'And Tommy'll be back from Edinburgh any minute.'

She wasted no time on trying to transform herself tonight but pulled on her coat and put the Lanzarote brochure in her bag.

'Eunice!' Her mother called her back when she got as far as the front door.

'What is it now?'

'Maybe you'd get me a wee bottle of whisky? Just a quarter.'

'But you don't drink whisky.'

'It's for the pain. I was thinking it might help dull it a bit.'

Eunice hurried out before her mother could think of anything else.

The pub was quiet, or would have been if Jinty Smith had not been sitting there, at a table near the door. Not that Jinty was actually making a noise; she was not talking, or banging her glass on the table, or even moving at all, but her very presence seemed to create a jangle in the quietness. The only other customers were two men playing draughts in a corner. Alex was reading the evening paper behind the counter. Eunice walked straight past Jinty as if she hadn't seen her and went to the bar to buy a drink. She and Alex had a little chat about Lanzarote – he had once been to Tenerife – and then she took her vodka over to another corner where she studied the brochure, marking the particular holiday and the kind of accommodation she wanted.

A studio apartment for two with sliding doors opening directly on to the beach . . .

She knew that Liffey was coming by the way the door blew open. He was very physical was Liffey: that was how he always struck her. He saw Jinty first, he could not help seeing her the way she was placed, deliberately, Eunice was sure, and after a moment's hesitation, when he rested on the balls of his feet, he walked past her without a word. Jinty turned her neck to look after him.

'Hi, Eunice!' he called, lifting his arm up high, a bit like a Hitler salute, not that one would ever think of Hitler and Liffey in the same breath. She waved back.

He took a stool at the bar. Eunice waited. He would buy her a drink, he didn't even have to ask what she wanted, he'd bring it over to her table, she'd show him the page in the brochure. And Jinty Smith could turn her soft thick neck to gawk all she wanted to.

Looks rather nice don't you think, Liffey, the apartment with the white walls and the purple flowers growing all over it . . .

Liffey was leaning on the counter with his back to the room. Alex drew him a pint and a half for himself. They raised their glasses. Liffey drank about a third of his straight off, wiped his mouth with the back of his hand and resettled his elbows on the counter. Eunice sipped her vodka. Liffey and Alex were talking about football. Men's talk. All men liked to talk about football. (Except their Tommy of course but you couldn't count him amongst normal men when he'd spent his life trying to prove he wasn't.) She didn't mind Liffey talking to Alex about football. Why should she? It was like when she had a good blether with her customers about knitting patterns or Princess Diana. Eunice finished her drink. She was thirsty, could have drunk three in a row, one after the other.

Liffey drained his glass too and set it on the counter. 'I'll need to be off, Alex.' He slipped off the stool. On his way out he turned towards Eunice. 'Be seeing you, Eunice,' he said. He did not look anywhere near Jinty. The door swung to behind him and then was still.

Eunice's shoulders slumped for a moment. But he'd said he'd be seeing her. He had: those had been his words. Perhaps he had meant her to follow him? Perhaps he had thought they should be careful and not start any gossip going in the pub, especially when his case was coming up and Jinty Smith was sitting there watching with her Miss Innocent stare. That must be it. He couldn't be too careful. Eunice lifted the brochure and forgetting to say goodnight to Alex hastened towards the door.

'Hey,' said Jinty softly.

Eunice stopped.

'What's the matter? Don't you think I've as much right to be here as you?'

Eunice could not get a word out, she felt she might gag at the back of her throat if she were to try to. She swept on and out, slightly staving her thumb as she thrust the swinging door back.

She looked up the street and down the street. The pavements, wet and shiny under the overhead lights, were deserted. A crumpled paper bag was bowling along, resting for a moment and then, with a sudden lift, moving off skittishly again. It looked so free and light that she almost envied it. What a silly thing to envy! But where was Liffey? It was as if he had vanished in an upsurge of wind. She imagined him flying over the rooftops on a magic carpet.

Her mother was watching a juggler on television.

'Anyone been in?' asked Eunice.

'Not a soul. Did you mind my whisky?'

'What whisky?'

'Honestly, Eunice, I don't know! It's not as if I ask you to do much for me. And there's been no sign of that brother of yours either, and here have I been needing the bathroom right badly for the last half-hour.'

Jean came into the shop the next day to buy wool for a sweater for Peter's Christmas. Eunice put the Male Chunky Knits box on the counter and together they leafed through the patterns.

'He's a good looking lad your Peter, not unlike some of the men in the knitting patterns. He could be a model if he wanted. Still, I don't suppose he'd want would he? Not when he's got computers at his finger tips, ha, ha! He doesn't look at all like Liffey, does he? Oh not that I'm suggesting that Liffey isn't good looking –' Eunice laughed again but Jean did not join in. It took a lot to make her laugh. 'It's just that you'd never know they were father and son.'

'All the children are different. I'll take this one thanks, Eunice.' Jean turned her attention to the wool which she chose just as quickly as the pattern.

Eunice took her time arranging the wool in a bag and sellotaping it up; she liked to do things properly and not be rushed. She said that it must be a worry for Jean with Liffey's case hanging over their heads? Jean admitted that it was, but nothing more. She was a close one was Jean. Never gave anything away. Never said more than she had to.

'Peter must be upset about his dad, too?'

'He doesn't know yet.'

'You'll have to tell him, won't you?'

That would do fine, said Jean, nodding at the parcel, and put out her hands to take it. Eunice watched her leave the shop and go along the pavement in her coat with its drooping hemline and a woollen scarf tied over her head. She looked a bit like those women you see waiting in queues outside shops in Moscow. Eunice had a couple of brochures in the cupboard about holidays in the Soviet Union (not that they showed the dreary-looking women), but she didn't really think she'd fancy it much, in spite of the possibility of a side trip to Riga, not with all those queues and Big Brothers watching you, and never knowing if the two men on the corner were from the KGB and might lug you off to the salt mines if you as much as looked sideways at them. Not unless she was to go with 007 of course. On the Orient Express. That would be a different story entirely.

Tasha was learning Russian. (Eunice couldn't see the point in it, hoped it wasn't going to be another case like Tommy all over again. Still, she supposed there'd be more demand for Russian than Latvian, especially when, according to Tommy, Latvia didn't exist as a country any more, at least as far as the West was concerned.) Tasha was doing her Russian homework at the kitchen table when Eunice called at the Portobello house on her next half-day. Sarah was showing a man and woman round the house.

'Quite a nice sized kitchen,' said the man, standing in the doorway.

'Needs a lot doing to it though,' said the woman. 'It's not got many units.'

Sarah took them off to the dining room which for some months had been used as a playroom.

'What a nerve!' said Eunice. 'It's a lovely kitchen.'

Sarah showed the man and woman out and the bell rang again and this time it was a property developer who had been before. He thought the place might have potential for division into two flats.

'Can I have a look up the stairs again?'

Sarah accompanied him.

'Flats!' said Eunice. 'It'd be a sin. Your mother's making a big mistake if you ask me. Your father might be back any time.'

Tasha lifted her head from her books. 'I hate that black and white woman of his. Shall I tell you something, Aunt Eunice?' she asked softly. 'Sometimes when I've been sitting in the court I've tried to put the evil eye on her. Do you think that's dreadful of me?'

'I don't know as I'd say that exactly. I mean, I can understand your feelings.'

137

Sarah showed the developer out and when Helen and Jamie came in they all had tea. Then Tasha rose saying she was going into town so Eunice decided she might as well go with her for company on the bus.

'What about coming out for the week-end?' she suggested. 'That way you could see your dad, and your granny'd be pleased and all.'

'Okay,' said Tasha, who was squinting into a small mirror, putting on puce eyeshadow whenever the bus halted at a stop.

When they got off in Princes Street, Tasha said it was too early for her to meet her friends and why didn't Eunice take her for a drink?

'In a pub you mean? But you're under age.'

'I don't look it though, do I?' Her aunt was dubious but Tasha took her arm and said, 'Oh come on, Aunt Eunice, I get away with it all the time and I'll only have a lager and lime.'

'I don't know what your mother would say.'

'Oh, Mother! She's so *middle-class*.'

Eunice didn't know what to say to that. Tasha was already towing her along the pavement towards Rose Street. 'Just one quick one then, Tasha,' she said, with a feeling of helplessness, as they turned into the narrow street. She was amazed at her niece's knowledge of its many pubs. There were thirteen in all, said Tasha, who had comments to make on quite a few as they passed.

'I like this place,' she said, pushing open the heavy mahogany door of the Abbotsford.

'I thought you'd have liked something smart and modern?' said Eunice, who was beginning to enjoy herself. What the hell anyway! You only live twice. One lager and lime couldn't do anyone any harm. And it *was* rather nice to have a niece to go about with. She saw herself, in the years to come, having evenings out with Tasha.

'Oh no! Old pubs are much nicer.'

The first two people they saw sitting on a bench near the door were Tasha's father and his woman.

'Why are you not with Mother?' demanded Eunice, striding forward to confront Thomas.

'And what are you doing bringing Tasha in here?' he retorted, getting to his feet.

'Perhaps it would be better if everyone sat down?' said Claire, moving over to make room.

Tasha sat down at once and Eunice, less eagerly, followed her example. She and Thomas continued to glare at one another.

'I hope you've not left Mother on her own?'

'Of course I haven't. Do you think she'd let me? Mrs Finlay's in with her. But you haven't answered *my* question yet.'

'It's my fault, Dad. I bullied Aunt Eunice, you musn't blame her.'

'Aren't you going to introduce us?' asked Claire, who was smiling. It would take a lot to put her out, thought Eunice, as she took the cool slim hand she was being offered and said how do you do? 'And shouldn't you get them something to drink, Thomas?'

'I'll have a lager and lime, Dad.'

Still looking disgruntled, Thomas went to the bar.

'You and I have met briefly before, Tasha,' said Claire, 'if you remember? And I believe I've seen you, Miss Peterson, in court?'

Miss Peterson indeed! Made her feel she was eighty years old. Nobody called her that but she didn't like to say to the bitch, 'Call me Eunice.' She didn't want to have to say anything to her. She mumbled something and bent her head to look for the squashed cigarette packet in her bag. Miss Madam Armstrong had turned her attention back to Tasha and was asking her about O levels and what subjects she particularly enjoyed.

'Russian and history,' said Tasha. 'Marxist history.'

'Interesting.'

'You don't really think it's interesting, do you?'

'Indeed I do.'

'You probably think the capitalist interpretation of history is the only valid one?'

'I'd be stupid if I did.'

Eunice was glad to see Thomas returning with the drinks. She didn't know where the conversation was going to go next. Tasha had the smile of a little devil on her lips. Both she and Claire seemed to be enjoying themselves but Eunice knew that Thomas was not at all amused. He looked as though he'd like to clout her one. She would have to get Tasha out of here as fast as she could. But how? Tasha was not the easiest thing in town to handle.

'Could I have a cigarette please, Aunt Eunice?' Before Eunice could stop her, she had leant over and taken one. She knew how to light it too and how to inhale. She blew out a long stream of smoke. 'I'm not a baby any more, Dad, so stop fussing!'

He put his whisky over in one gulp.

'I'm coming out to Granny's for the week-end,' said Tasha. 'So I'll be seeing you then. I'll bring my bike, shall I, and we can go for a run?'

Claire looked questioningly at Thomas.

'Well, we had actually got plans for the week-end,' he began.

'But I haven't seen you for ages!' cried Tasha. 'And I wanted you to help me with my history. You promised you would if I'd come out for a week-end.'

Tasha, as a house guest, was helpful and obliging. She waited on her grandmother, plumped the cushions at her back, cooked breakfast and washed the dishes, without being asked to. Eunice couldn't get over the change in her. You'd think she was a totally different girl from the one who'd sat in the pub that night driving them all up the wall. In the end Thomas had lost his temper and sent her packing.

'It just shows you what she could be like if she lived in a proper home,' said Eunice.

'She had a proper home before,' said Thomas irritably. 'And she didn't wash the dishes then. She likes rôle playing.'

But he helped Tasha with her history and on Saturday morning they went for a long cycle ride across the moors and came back in a good mood with one another.

In the afternoon, Tasha came to help her aunt out in the shop. Not that Eunice was run off her feet exactly – trade, in fact, had been dropping over the past year and the area supervisor, when visiting two or three months ago, had pursed her lips and said they'd need to see what they could do to pep it up. Business was business after all, and you couldn't expect the

140

company to keep shops open if they weren't paying their way. They weren't a charity organisation. The supervisor didn't tell Eunice anything she didn't know. At first Eunice had been alarmed and scurried about trying to give the place a new look and put on cheap offers but then things had settled down again and on her last visit the supervisor hadn't even mentioned it. With Christmas coming, trade had picked up a bit anyway. And in the New Year Eunice planned to have a sale.

'I do like your shop, Aunt Eunice,' said Tasha. 'I love all the colours. They make me wish I could knit properly.'

Eunice said there was nothing to it and helped her cast on a thick knit sweater in scarlet wool. She could do bands of green and white round the cuffs and neck, suggested Eunice; then she'd have the Italian colours. She had always liked the Italian colours: they were bright and cheerful, like the Italians themselves. And Italian men were so romantic.

'I'll take you to Venice one day, Tasha. We could go on one of those gondolas and have a gondolier to pole us along. They sing too, so I believe.'

'You'd need to win the pools, Aunt Eunice.'

'Oh I don't know, there are lots of cheap packages. I'll just go to the cupboard.' Eunice went.

'And when she got there,' murmured Tasha, 'the cupboard was far from bare . . .'

'What's that, Tasha?'

'Nothing, Aunt Eunice.'

Eunice found two brochures and, while Tasha struggled through a purl row, they sat close together in front of the electric coil of heat and Eunice read Venetian details aloud. *Romantic corners, magnificent palazzos, quiet canals . . .*

'One day,' she said, staring out of the window. 'It'd be just the place for a honeymoon.'

'Aunt Eunice, why have you never married?'

Eunice shrugged. 'Never met Mr Right I suppose. Or at least not at the right time. Ha, ha.'

'Ah.' Tasha pulled her chair closer to her aunt's. 'So you have met him then? Tell me! Go on!'

'I might, I might not, that's all I'm saying.'

'Oh, say some more, Aunt Eunice! I shan't tell.' Tasha put a hand on her aunt's arm to restrain her from getting up. 'Is he still alive?'

'Of course. I'm not *that* old.'

'Does he love you?'

'I believe he does.'

'Why then –?'

'He's married to someone else.'

'The classic triangle then?'

'I don't know about that.' Feeling uncomfortable, feeling that she had already said too much, Eunice got up to make coffee. She set two chocolate snowballs on a plate. That was Saturday afternoon's treat.

'It's your birthday in a couple of weeks' time isn't it, Aunt Eunice?'

'Something like that.' She had been thinking about it as little as possible.

'Why don't we have a party? After all, it's a pretty special birthday – half a century!'

Eunice took a large bite out of her snowball and wished she'd bought them two apiece. It was great to be young and she hoped Tasha appreciated that. She probably didn't.

'We'll have Mum and Dad and Aunt Edmée . . . and shall we ask Liffey?'

'Suppose we could.'

'Don't you like him?'

Eunice glanced sideways at her niece but the girl's blue eyes seemed to be gazing at her innocently enough. Not that she was much of a judge of innocence, she realised, not after that evening when Tasha had surprised her by smoking and drinking in the pub. She said, off-handedly, 'He's all right.'

'Mum doesn't like him now. She used to though. She won't let him come into the house any more.'

'Oh. What do you make of that?'

'I think he made a pass at her.'

'A pass at your mother? *Liffey*?' Eunice knocked over her coffee cup and the greyish-brown liquid spread across the floor. 'I'm sure he wouldn't do a thing like that. You must be wrong, Tasha. *You must be!*'

Tasha looked at her.

'I hate spilling things,' said her aunt vehemently and went down on her knees with a fistful of tissues to blot up the mess.

142

Isabel made slow progress. The swelling in her leg subsided and the colours dimmed but it was agonising for her to put the foot to the ground. She found the settee more comfortable and was getting used to being idle. Funny how she'd always thought she'd never be able to thole it. It was all right for the fool of a doctor to tell her she could use her leg if she tried. It was her pain, not his.

'You'll have to encourage her,' the doctor told Thomas and Eunice. 'It'll be a bit sore, I grant you that, but sometimes it's necessary to be cruel to be kind.'

'You can do the encouraging, Tommy,' said Eunice. 'The old besom's digging in for the winter if you ask me.'

'I can't stay till spring,' said Thomas. 'Claire –'

'She's getting fed up, is she?'

'Well, it's not fair on her. Either we live together or we don't.'

Eunice went off to the shop where she had already dug in for winter with her supplies of brochures and instant coffee and packets of biscuits. She longed to put a bed, even an old camp bed, in the back shop, but thought the supervisor might not go for that.

Thomas, left to cope with the house and its patient, went with determination into the living room and said, 'Come on now, Mother, up you get! You can lean on me.' He took her hands in his and eased her up.

'Oh your head be it then, Tommy Peterson.'

'Now take my arm, put your weight on me. That's great, you're doing fine!'

'Cruel to be kind indeed!' muttered Isabel, whose ears had not been affected by her fall.

As they turned at the end of the room, she slipped on the linoleum surround and Thomas, while he was able to prevent her from falling to the ground, could not stop her twisting her ankle. Her bad one. God, the agony of it! It was like being pierced by ten thousand darning needles. She had never been one for making a fuss, had kept her mouth clamped tightly together even in the throes of childbirth, unlike some she could mention – Liffey's mother for example, who'd made so much racket she'd kept the street up all night – but this pain took her by surprise and before she could bite it back a long scream came

143

out of her. It was loud enough to bring Effie Finlay in from next door.

'I thought somebody's got murdered,' she said as she helped Thomas lift his mother back on to the settee. 'You should have known better, Isabel. Now you're back to square one.'

'I never did have much luck at snakes and ladders,' said Thomas.

Eunice's half-day came round again. Getting away on her own was one of the good things about her mother being anchored to the settee. She rode in to Edinburgh on the top of the bus in the front seat. It was a a lovely day, bright and sunny, more like spring. Made her think of spring holidays. She wouldn't mind a few days in the bulbfields of Holland. Variety was the spice of life after all.

The city was looking good, with all its spires and rooftops and the craggy castle itself, which made her think of fairy tales, standing out against the bright blue sky. The air seemed truly to sparkle. She strolled around the town, imagining she was a Yank tourist, seeing everything for the first time. She went along Princes Street admiring the flowers in the gardens and up the Mound to the castle esplanade where she gazed over to the ancient Kingdom of Fife then she descended from the hill into the less picturesque areas of Tollcross and Fountainbridge.

All along, though she might have seemed to have been wandering aimlessly, she had known where she was going. Oh yes indeed. *I know where I'm going*. The refrain ran through her head. *And I know who's going with me*. Fountainbridge: this was her destination.

'Okay, 007, I'm coming to get you!' she said softly. She smiled and a man passing looked oddly at her. Why shouldn't she smile if she felt like it? In Italy they wouldn't think you were bonkers if you smiled. Still smiling, she gazed at the grey stone tenements, examined the doors, read the names beside the bell pulls even though she knew of course that she wasn't going to find Connery, or if she did it would be the wrong one, unless it had been left over from a long time ago. It was always possible. Some of the old brass bells and nameplates were dull and greening with neglect and might have been there since the time *he* was a boy. They ought to put a plaque up, really they should. She might write to the *Edinburgh Evening News* and suggest it.

JAMES BOND LIVED HERE.

She stood back and saw the plate shining like pure gold.

A man lounging in a stair doorway was watching her.

She said to him, 'I don't suppose you'd know where Sean Connery lived would you? You know – James Bond?'

The man stared at her as if he did not quite understand what she was saying. How ignorant people were. She went on, 'He was born and brought up around here. Did you not know that? Amazing isn't it to think that someone like that . . .?' The man was still standing, in a very strange way, and it occurred to her that he might be on drugs. Half the city was on heroin if you could believe what you read in the papers. Which of course you couldn't. Half of those journalists didn't know fact from fiction, it was a fact. She cleared her throat, nodded at the man and continued with her tour, encircling every block, and with every step she took she thought that *he*, too, had once walked here. *In her master's steps she trod . . .* There was no snow to lie dinted, but some moisture had crept into the air and she realised that her head and shoulders were damp, which did not trouble her. Any woman in James Bond's life would have to be able to put up with a lot more than that. Hell and high water, if necessary.

Her 007 pilgrimage concluded, she went back up the hill to the Royal Mile and treated herself to a pub lunch and a couple of vodkas and then, with a feeling of well-being, made her way over to the courts. It was amazing how you got used to a place after three or four visits, felt almost at home. The security man on the door nodded and said, 'Good afternoon' to her.

'Anything interesting on today?'

'Attempted murder in Court Three. Couple of civils – divorces – that's about it.'

'Is Miss Armstrong on?'

'Don't think so. She's in, though. Want me to see if I can track her down?'

It was all right thanks, said Eunice, and proceeded along the corridor past the advocates' boxes, slowing to read MISS ARMSTRONG on the brass plate and see if she had any letters waiting for her, before sauntering over to the notice board which she read with interest. One day fairly soon, next month probably, Liffey's name would be up there. R. v. Finlay. He'd be in the dock. She shivered.

From there she went into the Grand Hall with its raftered ceiling, stained glass windows and gold-framed portraits, and sat down on one of the benches. A grand, curved affair it was, nothing like a park bench, and it had a high straight back. She rested her feet on the fender provided and watched the comings and goings of the men, and women – though there were not that many of them – in black.

The advocates came in and out with their gowns floating round them, formed clusters for a few minutes then detached themselves and were off again. Most of them looked pretty solemn, which is what she would have expected, but sometimes one of them would open his mouth and have a good laugh. She'd have liked to have known what they were laughing about.

She would come to the court for Liffey's trial, half-day or no half-day (she'd get Marilyn in to watch the shop) and when he was cleared – for there was no question that he would be – he'd come over to her afterwards and she'd smile at him.

Congratulations, Liffey.

Thanks, Eunice.

I always knew you were innocent. I had faith in you.

I appreciate that, Eunie. I knew I had your support . . .

She blinked, for coming towards her, just a yard or so away, was Thomas's fancy woman and Liffey's defending counsel.

She stopped in front of Eunice and said, 'Hello, Miss Peterson, can I help you in any way?'

Eunice felt that stupid old heatwave come swelling up out of nowhere again and put a hand round the base of her neck to try to cover its effects. She couldn't seem to get a word out, it was as though her throat had sandpaper stuffed down it.

'How's your mother's leg doing?'

'Taking its time,' said Eunice in a voice which sounded like a frog's and then she suffered a violent attack of coughing which made her splutter and her eyes stream.

'Are you all right, Miss Peterson? Can I get you a glass of water?'

'I'm fine thanks,' said Eunice and without looking in Claire's direction scrambled awkwardly down from the bench and hurried across the Great Hall and along the corridor, dodging loiterers and passing the security man with only a quick wave, and at last emerged into the fresh air of Parliament Square. A cloud of pigeons flew up in front of her.

It was only then that she stopped coughing. She found a Polo mint in her pocket and thrust it into her mouth. What a fool she'd been to let that stuck-up little bitch with the fancy voice and the cool grey eyes throw her like that.

She went into a pancake place nearby to get over it and had two large pancakes with hot chocolate sauce and two cups of coffee. Tommy *was* an idiot to give up Sarah for that girl. He'd live to regret it. She looked at her watch. There was plenty of time to fit in a visit to Sarah. Tommy could get on and cook their mother's tea since he was always bumming about what a good cook he was.

'I've just sold the house,' said Sarah.

Eunice couldn't believe it. It gave her a shock to hear that it was actually done, she had kept hoping that at the last minute Sarah – and Tommy – might have come to their senses. With the house gone, she and her mother might even lose Sarah out of their lives.

'Yes, it's done,' said Sarah. 'That property developer put in an offer this morning – a good one – so I rang Tom and we took it.'

'So it'll be made into flats?'

'I know, it's a pity, but it can't be helped.'

'You're free now, Sarah,' said Aunt Edmée who was there stretched out on the settee wearing purple velvet trousers and smoking one of those funny flat cigarettes of hers through a long holder.

'There's still Tasha.'

'But she'll be sixteen soon. And then –?' Edmée waved the long cigarette holder about.

'She can hardly be abandoned at sixteen,' said Sarah.

'She certainly could not!' said Eunice, who had gone out to work at fourteen. But then that had been different. 'Where will you go, Sarah?'

'I'll buy a flat, somewhere in the district.'

A flat would be an awful come down after this house, said Eunice, but Sarah did not seem to be bothered. It was as if she were already gone from the house in spirit.

'And think of it this way,' said Edmée, 'a flat is a lot easier to lock up than a house.'

Eunice stirred uneasily.

'Travel *is* a great renewer,' Edmée continued. 'It gives one different concepts of time and space. Wouldn't you agree, Eunice?'

Eunice nodded. She had a brand new batch of brochures in her bag. China, Japan, Thailand. All the pleasures of the Orient. She'd only had time for a quick look but she fancied a holiday in Japan, at cherry blossom time.

'*You* need a new concept of time and space, Sarah,' said Edmée, 'before you make any decisions about the next stage in your life. You have been too long confined.'

Thomas moved around his mother's living room, not exactly pacing up and down, since there was not enough room around the settee and the two fireside chairs, the television set and the card table, the sideboard and the china cabinet, for pacing, but dithering rather, knocking into things, rearranging antimacassars which he had disarranged. He ignored his mother's injunctions to sit down or else go for a walk and stretch his legs properly.

'I really *should* go into Edinburgh this evening.'

'But it's Eunice's birthday. She's fifty. It's not every day that you're fifty.'

'But it's Claire's parents' anniversary. They're having a party.'

'So are we. I don't suppose ours'll be as grand as theirs, of course –'

'It's got nothing to do with being grand. It was just that I promised –'

'But you promised Tasha. The party was her idea after all.'

'I know.' He rumpled the back of his hair the way he had done as a boy. 'I'd forgotten the date, you see.'

No, she didn't see; she only knew where his duty lay.

148

Tasha kept the shop while Eunice went to get her hair streaked.

'Going somewhere special tonight then?' asked the hairdresser, pulling a painfully tight pink rubber hat down over Eunice's head.

'Having a party,' said Eunice, wondering if the blood was going to stop circulating in her head. Her bald head stared back at her from the mirror. She looked as if she were about to swim the Channel.

'A party eh?' said the hairdresser, taking a long implement like a crochet hook and yanking strands of hair through the tiny holes in the cap. 'That's nice.'

'Yes,' said Eunice, wincing with the pain. Her eyes began to water. 'Go on, Aunt Eunice,' Tasha had said, 'be a devil!'

'It's my birthday.'

'Fancy that!' The hairdresser began to attack the back of Eunice's head with greater vigour. She had large heavy fingers which reminded Eunice of uncooked pork sausages. 'Many happy returns!'

'Thanks. I thought I might as well treat myself today. You only live twice after all.'

'I thought it was once.'

'But James Bond – don't you see?'

'I get it. It was a great film, wasn't it?'

Eunice declared her preference for Sean Connery over the other James Bond impersonators. 'Well, I mean, he *is* Bond, isn't he?'

'He lives in Spain these days. So a woman was telling me.'

'Spain?' said Eunice thoughtfully. 'I suppose you wouldn't know which part? The Costa del Sol, or the Costa Brava, or the Costa Blanca?'

The girl thought. 'Might have been Blanca.'

'Blanca,' repeated Eunice and regarded herself in the mirror. Strands of hair were sticking out from her head like young sprouts; now they were to be coated with a strong-smelling blue solution which made her eyes smart even more, then her head was put under a steamer. To bring the colour up, said the hairdresser. 'And now I'll leave you to have a nice read.'

Eunice had some new brochures in her bag, on Switzerland and Austria. She had thought they would make a nice change from some of those other hot places, but now she'd have to get some brochures on Spain. It was a long time since she had taken any on Spain – well, everybody went there, it was kind of common, say what you like. Imagine Sean living there. Of course where he lived wouldn't be common, you could be sure of that. He'd be in some classy part far from the cries of the Bingo callers or the smell of fish and chips. She opened a brochure and took a look at Austria and Switzerland. They looked pretty classy; a different type of person would go there from Benidorm and Tenerife. They looked like fairy-tale countries with their castles and icing sugar mountains. Settling back to enjoy them, she reflected that maybe it wasn't so bad being fifty after all. Wakening that morning, putting her foot on the cold hot water bottle, hearing her mother snore through the wall, she had felt right down in the dumps. But that mood had gone and she was determined to have a good time, while the going was good.

'Interesting, is it?' asked the hairdresser, peering over Eunice's shoulder.

'Fascinating. The mountains are magnificent and the scenery is unforgettable.'

'I'm not sure if I'd fancy all that snow.'

'One can always go in springtime, when the mountain flowers are blooming and the air is soft and sweetly scented. The villages are simply charming and the people warm-hearted and hospitable.'

'Could do with a few warm hearts round here.' The girl gazed out into the street. 'Could do with a bit more business.'

'Same goes for us all,' said Eunice.

She read on until the colour of her hair turned. The effect had been worth suffering for, as the hairdresser had promised.

'Takes years off you. It does really. I'm not just saying it.'

Eunice examined herself in the mirror. 'I think I'll wear that red dress my sister-in-law gave me. Might as well be a red devil eh?' They laughed together and Eunice gave the girl a larger tip than she had intended.

Feeling ten years younger, she hurried back to the shop which she had been away from for much longer than she had expected. She waved at Jean Finlay, who looked as if she had not been to the hairdresser's since last Christmas. 'See you later,' she cried.

150

Opening the shop door, she saw Tasha sitting with the area supervisor behind the counter. They were drinking coffee and eating jam doughnuts. The supervisor, who had never been known (by Eunice) to eat sweet buns before, was licking sugar off her red-tipped fingers. Eunice stared for a moment then quickly began to apologise. 'It's the first time I've ever –'

But the supervisor interrupted saying, 'That's all right, Eunice, don't worry, your niece has been doing splendidly.' She smiled and waved the lurid fingernails about and the gold bracelets clunked around her wrist. Eunice had never seen her so cheery.

'Tasha tells me you're having a party tonight?'

'Just a few folk in. Neighbours mostly.'

Tasha provided a description of the food which she had shopped for yesterday in Edinburgh. 'And Mum's baking a cake – an orange one – and Dad's buying the wine.'

'Sounds super,' said the supervisor, snapping open her gold cigarette case and offering it to Eunice. 'Cigarette?'

Eunice took one feeling a little uneasy. It was the first time her boss had ever given her a cigarette.

'Your hair looks really dishy, Eunice. It suits you.'

'Thanks. Do you want to have a look at the books now?'

Plenty of time, said the supervisor, and went on to tell them about her recent holiday in Minorca. The sun had shone, the wine flowed free, and the men, she hinted, had been delicious. Eventually she said,

'Tasha, could you leave us alone for a few minutes now, dear, so that your aunt and I can talk business?'

Tasha said she'd run home and see how her father was getting on with his side of the arrangements.

'Charming girl,' said the supervisor when Tasha had gone, and offered Eunice another cigarette.

Eunice said no thank you.

'She's clever too I would think?'

'We're hoping she'll go on to university.'

The supervisor nodded. 'The better qualified you are these days the better chance you have of a job.'

'I suppose it's always been like that.'

'Yes, there's nothing to beat a good education.'

Eunice waited. The supervisor frowned as if she were in a

little pain and lifted a hand to her temple making the bracelets ring.

'I'm afraid I have some rather disappointing news for you, Eunice.' She sighed. 'Well, times *are* difficult, aren't they? And it's happening to everybody.'

'What's happening?' cried Eunice.

'Redundancy. Eunice, I'm afraid we're going to have to close this branch after all.'

Happy birthday to you, happy birthday to you, happy birthday, dear Eunice, so sang her mother and brother and niece and Sarah and Sarah's Aunt Edmée and Mrs Finlay who was downing the sherry as fast as she could get her glass refilled and Marilyn whose husband was minding the baby so that she could have an evening out and Jean who was the only one (apart from Eunice's mother) who was watching that she didn't drink too much and Liffey who had arrived with a carrier bag clinking with bottles and was in great form.

'Hip, hip!' he cried. 'Three cheers for the birthday girl!'

They cheered and Eunice's cheeks flamed until they almost matched her dress. She had already blown out her candles. One for each decade. As Sarah had said to her mother-in-law, fifty would have made the cake top too crowded and not given Eunice much chance to extinguish them all at once. Eunice had huffed and she had puffed and she had blown the five candles down. And everyone had clapped and Edmée shouted, 'Bravo!'

'You'll get your wish now,' said Tasha, for before Eunice had bent low over the cake, she had closed her eyes and made a wish. 'Don't tell what you wished or it won't come true!'

But Eunice had no thought of telling. She looked round the room and said, 'Thanks, everybody. It's nice having you all here.'

Earlier, Thomas had made a long telephone call to Edinburgh and since the phone was in the hall, and the walls thin, his mother, sister and daughter had had no difficulty hearing what he had said.

Of course I want to be with you, Claire. Of course I want to go to your parents' dinner party. Yes, I do know it's their anniversary and that they asked me specially. I'm sorry it's put the numbers out.

'Numbers out,' Eunice had snorted. 'It's put her nose out of joint if you ask me.'

'Doesn't say much for her, does it?' said Isabel. 'Trying to take him away from his family.'

But the family was united now. From her seat on the settee, Isabel Peterson looked on contentedly. There were Thomas and Sarah drinking together, talking together, with no sign of any spite showing between them, and sitting at their feet, looking happy in the way a fifteen-year-old should look, was their daughter. She transferred her gaze to her own daughter.

Eunice was drinking too much again. She tried to catch her eye but Eunice was not for letting her eye be caught this evening. She had been into the pub on her way home from work, had had a drink or two there to start with; her mother had smelt it on her when she came in.

'It's my birthday, isn't it?' Eunice had said. 'If I can't do what I want today when can I?'

Liffey, who also had a fair skinful of drink inside him, had the vodka bottle in his hand and was facing Eunice.

'You're looking great, Eunie. Can I fill you up?'

'Make it a large one. I'm needing it.'

'That the way your birthday affects you?'

'I'm going to have a good time tonight.' She raised her glass. 'Never say never again!' she said and laughed and he laughed and they both drank deep, their eyes on one another over the rims of their glasses.

Isabel saw that Jean was watching them too and shifted uncomfortably. Eunice would have to watch herself, see that she didn't go over the score, though sometimes she wondered if Eunice knew what the score was. She turned to her daughter-in-law whom you could always rely on to behave perfectly in company and not give you a red face. She praised Sarah's cake. 'You're a grand baker so you are, Sarah. Now that you've got those women off your back you'll have more time for baking again.'

Sarah smiled. Thomas, finishing his piece of cake, declaring it to be excellent, surreptitiously eased back his cuff to take a look at his watch. Both his wife and mother noticed the movement.

153

Tasha put a record on. 'Come on,' she cried, 'dance, everybody dance!' She leapt towards her father and pulled him to his feet. Sarah got up with Marilyn. And Eunice held out her hand to Liffey.

'Are you dancing?'

'Are you asking?' He bowed. 'It'd be a pleasure, mam.'

'Dance!' cried Tasha again. 'Come on, everybody, dance!'

'Fair going their dinger, aren't they?' said Mrs Finlay, helping herself from the sherry bottle. 'Och well, they're only young once.'

Isabel, Mrs Finlay and Jean remained side by side on the settee. Mrs Finlay tapped her foot and swung her shoulders in time to the music. Isabel and Jean sat quite still.

When the record came to an end they heard the doorbell ringing.

'I'll go,' said Tasha and dived into the hall singing at the top of her voice.

'I hope it's not the polis,' said Mrs Finlay cheerfully.

The door re-opened and Tasha came back, saying, 'Guess who?' With a flourish she ushered in Peter Finlay.

'Peter!' His mother got to her feet. 'I wasn't expecting you till tomorrow.'

'Thought I'd surprise you. The kids said you were here. Happy birthday, Eunice.'

'Hi, son!' Liffey came forward to slap him rather heavily on the shoulder and their eyes engaged for a moment; but without warmth, noticed Eunice.

Peter's mother and grandmother were fussing round him asking if he'd had anything to eat and declaring he must be tired after that long journey. You'd think he'd come from the moon. They piled a plate high with sausage rolls and cake and crisps. 'I'm sure you could be doing with a square meal though, son,' said his grandmother. This would do fine: he nodded at the plate, but ate only a few crisps. He took the attention of his women folk comfortably, as one who has been accustomed to it from an early age. He was good looking, he was successful, he was sure of himself. Eunice, watching, drained her glass and wished he had waited until tomorrow to come home. She was the only one who seemed not to like him (apart perhaps from Liffey); most people went for his easy ways and ready smile. His arrival had cut right through the mood of the party, changed its course, and now they were all standing around waiting to hear about Peter's life in London. Some people got things so easily!

She looked over at her brother who got things easily and lost them easily too and who was watching Peter while pretending not to. She read his look. 'Like looking into a glass of water,' she muttered but nobody heard. She went to the sideboard to refill her glass.

'Don't you think you've had enough, Eunice?' said her mother.

'No, I don't. I'll never have had enough.'

Midnight struck and Sarah and Edmée said they must go. 'It's been a lovely party, Eunice.' Sarah kissed Eunice's cheek, a habit which Eunice found awkward even after twenty years or more of knowing Sarah. Edmée, too, followed suit.

Now came Marilyn to say her goodbyes, though she did not go in for kissing. Nor did Jean who was saying they must be making a move, Peter would be needing his bed. Peter protested, but his mother and grandmother were already on their way out to the hall to collect their coats.

'Looks like it's time to go,' said Liffey. 'When the Boss calls . . . It's been a great party, Eunice, simply great.'

He did not go in for kissing either, not tonight. He backed away.

'Everyone's going at once,' said Eunice.

'That's the way parties usually end,' said Thomas.

They helped their mother up to bed. Her leg had gone stiff on her and she had to take her time, holding on to them both and pausing for short rests. She talked about Sarah's orange cake all the way up the stairs. Tasha was asleep in the spare room before they got their mother's light out.

Back downstairs, they surveyed the dirty plates, empty glasses and bottles and full ashtrays.

'Fifty,' said Eunice.

'It comes to us all in time.'

'It's all right for you to talk.'

'I'm glad you think so.'

She looked over at the sideboard where Thomas as Gala King sat crowned and robed with his Gala Queen.

'He's doing well – Peter – isn't he?'

'Seems to be.' Thomas started to collect the glasses.

'You can't imagine him being made redundant.'

'Oh I dunno. These days –'

'I'm sick of these days,' cried Eunice.

'Why don't you go to bed? I'll finish up here.'

'I don't want to go to bed. I want another drink.' She up-ended the vodka bottle into a dirty glass. There were only a few drops left. 'Well, here's to my early retirement.'

'What did you say?'

'My early retirement. The shop's not doing too well so they're closing it down. They're closing me down and all. Amazing isn't it, how easy they can do it to you?'

Thomas looked stunned.

'One thing, Tommy – Peter'll be smarter than you and me. He's got what it takes, you can tell. He's not going to be pushed around. You must be proud of him?'

Thomas stopped still. 'Why should I be proud of him?'

'Come on now, you don't have to pretend to me. Don't you think I haven't guessed, all these years?'

PART FOUR

Thomas Himself

Pushing down on the pedals, raising himself high over the handlebars, Thomas put on a spurt and left his mother's house behind. He felt as if he had been there for months, for years. He felt as if he were leaving home for the first time all over again. His stay had been extended far beyond his earlier imaginings. Claire had gone skiing in Austria with an old school friend over the Christmas holidays; it had been arranged in the summer, when he was still living with Sarah. 'How did I know then that you would leave her?'

Stay in the flat if you want to, Claire had said to Thomas but he had found it like a deserted theatre when she was not there and had come home to his mother's house, not having any other to go to. Tasha had been there too, for much of the time, and Sarah had come out to see the New Year in with them. 'It's been a good Christmas and New Year,' his mother said when she kissed him goodbye. 'Like old times.' He felt her eyes on his back until he turned the corner. When he was clear of the straggling village and out on the main road he would lower his head, bringing his body almost into a straight line and go skimming into Edinburgh like a well-fired arrow.

He had ridden a bicycle until he married Sarah whose father bought them an old second-hand car. His grandfather had given him his first bicycle. Thomas had come down on the morning of his ninth birthday to see the machine standing in the living room on a spread-out newspaper. In the background his mother hovered, anxious about something that belonged out-of-doors being indoors as if it might bring in not only drips of oil but bad luck. The chrome flashed in the sunshine, the paintwork gleamed. His grandfather spun one of the pedals and laughed. 'Your freedom machine,' he said and Thomas's mother backed out to the kitchen to begin cooking the break-

fast. 'It will enable you to fly. Everyone needs to be able to fly.'
Not Thomas's mother of course, she liked to have her feet on
the ground, and her own four walls about her, and probably
not Eunice either for all she seemed to be interested in at that
time was covering herself with lipstick and frizzing her hair
and hanging about on street corners with a gaggle of other girls
whistling at boys and making herself look cheap; but everyone
like *them*. 'Now you can travel . . .' His grandfather's blue eyes
shone, like the bicycle.

It had a three-speed gear and was brand new, unlike Liffey's
which had been bought third-hand in the street and had no
gears at all. Thomas could now go steaming up hills leaving
Liffey panting far behind, croaking that it wasn't fair, until
Thomas would dismount and wait for Liffey to catch up. 'Give
us a shot,' he was forever demanding and sometimes Thomas
did, in the street, running alongside him, his hands stretched
out ready to stop him from toppling and bringing the machine
crashing down on to the rough road. Once he acceded to the
request at the top of a steep hill out in the country and Liffey
had whizzed downwards waving his arms like the wings of a
dove and shouting, 'See no hands!' He hit a bank at the bottom
and was thrown in an arc over the hedge to land in a patch of
long grass, unmarked but for a few scratches on his hands and
knees. The bicycle had lain upside down, the beautiful leather
saddle resting on the road, one wheel spinning, the other
buckled, the shiny racing-green paint no longer shiny but
chipped and scored as if someone had taken a corkscrew to it.

'I always told you he would bring you bad luck,' said
Thomas's grandfather. 'He is not a good friend.'

Thomas slowed as a lorry lumbered past belching exhaust
fumes. He thought of the prig he must have been when he was
nine years old, taking all that care over his possessions,
'sticking in' at his lessons so that he could 'get on'. He had
enjoyed it though: none of it had been a penance, it hadn't been
a case of slaving over his books and listening enviously to the
cries of children playing outside. When he was lost in a book he
heard nothing, not even his mother calling him to tea. And he
had done his share of playing.

He put on another spurt and urged his freedom machine
forward. He smiled with pleasure at his self-propelled

movement. It was the only mode of transportation he had now, at the age of forty-five, as at the age of nine. But he was happier with his feet on the pedals and his head in the open air than he would have been in a smogged-up bus or even closeted inside a car, which was something his mother would not be able to understand, nor would he expect her to. She liked lives to go forward in straight lines and refused to recognise that most stood still after a certain point; one, like his own, which did a few zigzags and loops and even back-bends confounded her.

He had swept past the woman with the bowed shoulders carrying the bulging carrier bags before he registered that it was Jean; without a closer look she was indistinguishable from the other women trudging up and down to the shops, but during that swift second when they had passed like trains going in opposite directions he had seen an expression on her face which was beseeching him to stop. It was an expression that he had seen gathering for some time. Ever since Liffey had been arrested and charged. Reluctantly, Thomas squeezed the brake and came to such an abrupt halt that the tyres squealed. He did an about-turn and wheeled his bicycle back to meet her.

'Tommy, I'd like to talk to you.'

'What about a cup of coffee?'

They went to the Café in the main street, next door to the hairdresser's. He pushed his bicycle in the gutter, she walked beside him, carrying her shopping. Remembering his mother's rejection, he made no offer to suspend it from the handlebars. The girl who worked in the hairdresser's rapped on the window with the teeth of a comb and waved to them. Jean waved back.

The café had formica-topped tables and a juke box which was silent at that time of the morning. It was not much different from when they'd been teenagers. They'd spent hours in here, drinking Coke, holding hands under the table, not talking very much, not having much to say, the sound of Elvis Presley holding silence at bay. There'd been nowhere else to go except up the back lanes which was where they'd go later, under cover of darkness.

They took a table in the corner and put their backs to the room.

161

Jean had never wasted time over preambles; she said, 'Tommy, I want to tell Peter the truth.'

'I thought you might.'

'It's with Liffey's case coming up.'

Thomas nodded.

'I won't unless you agree.'

'I agree.'

It scarcely mattered any more, he might have added, but did not for she might have interpreted it the wrong way. So much was open to misinterpretation.

'What about Liffey?'

She shrugged. 'I don't think he'll care. They've not got on for years.'

'I'm sorry, Jean,' said Thomas, as he had done twenty-seven years before.

'It's all right,' said Jean, as she had done then, too, for she was not one to rant about the unfairnesses of life. She got on with things, made the best of them, which in its way was admirable, though it had made her into a resigned, rather dull woman. He felt guilty at letting himself attribute the epithets to her and offered another coffee.

'No, thanks, I must be getting along. I've got to get the lunch on.'

Thomas cooked an extra special meal – pheasant in red wine – to celebrate his return to civilisation. By that thought he meant not to censure his family for their lack of appreciation of Schubert's Trout Quintet (which he was listening to whilst cooking), or of the Georgian architecture of the New Town (which he had to admit pleased him more than between-the-wars council housing), or of pheasant in red wine (which his mother and sister might appreciate given the chance), but to censure himself rather for the state of barbarism into which he descended when he returned home. He bickered with Eunice in a manner which he found offensive but, once caught up in, could not seem to escape from; and he felt sullen and resentful towards his mother for her demands upon him. And then he would feel guilty for being resentful! In that narrow house he felt caged, not only physically, but by the restrictions and echoes of the past, whereas Sarah, lacking them, enjoyed his mother's living room and found it soothing. When alone in it with his mother, whose eyes rested on him with thoughts he could read only too well, he found it difficult to sit still and would get up and down to go to the window to look at the street where nothing would have changed since he had last looked out.

'You're aye restless,' his mother would say, increasing his restlessness. The one person from his past with whom he had felt in tune was long dead. Not that he would any longer agree with his grandfather on most things, and the old man would certainly not have taken Claire to his bosom.

Thomas browned the bird and sealed in its juices, according to the instructions of the propped-up French cookery book. He enjoyed cooking. Perhaps he should open a small bistro, with just a few tables . . . He smiled. His grandfather would have had a collapse at the very idea.

When he heard the flat door opening, he called out Claire's name.

The bagman from the court answered. He had his own key. 'It's only me, sir, delivering Miss Armstrong's bag.'

Thomas went into the hall. 'Is there much?'

'Looks like she's going to have a busy evening,' said the man cheerfully. 'Nice smell,' he observed before departing.

Thomas rushed back in time to save the bird from scorching. He added the wine and then the telephone rang.

Tasha wanted to know if she could see him that evening. She *needed* to see him. It was about something important, she hinted, but would not be more specific. Thomas said firmly that it would have to wait, he was spending the evening with Claire, he had seen very little of her recently. 'It's about Mother,' said Tasha. 'I think she's planning something.' 'I'm sorry,' said Thomas. Now that he felt less guilty about deserting Sarah he was finding it easier to resist Tasha's demands. He knew that Claire was right when she said it wouldn't do Tasha any good in the long run if he gave in to her all the time. Claire was rational and very often right about relationships. She was used to standing back, from divorces, tugs-of-war between children, rapes, and – without passing judgement – weighing up the pros and cons and seeing the picture from every side, whereas he could only see his own situation from his own point of view. And how limited that was. But it was enough for him: to see any more would be intolerable, except in small bursts. Since last night he had been seeing life from Eunice's eye view and only the energetic cycle-run into town had managed to disperse the feeling of claustrophobia which had settled on him when she had told him of her impending redundancy. What was it about them that they should both become functionless in the active years of their lives?

'You're not interested are you?' said Tasha.

'I'm cooking, love. I'll see you soon.'

He had everything ready, held at a simmer, and the wine uncorked, when Claire came in. She was pleased to see him, of course she was, she said in response to his question, which he had earlier determined not to ask. You doubt yourself too much, his grandfather used to say: you are as good as the next person, better! Learn to trust yourself!

Claire sniffed and commented on the smell. Pheasant in red wine, said Thomas, displaying the glossy picture in the book. 'I thought we should have a celebration.'

'I've got work to do I'm afraid.'

'You've always got work.'

'Just as well, isn't it?'

'Since I haven't?'

'I didn't mean it like that.'

'Didn't you?'

'Forget it!' she said.

How could he forget it? Why did they have to get off on the wrong foot when he had planned everything so carefully? He wanted to fling the rice into the sink, then his shoulders slumped. 'I'm sorry, Claire love.' He would not have said that to Sarah. With her, the argument would have continued. He was aware that, with Claire, he trod carefully, so as not to put his foot through the delicate shell beneath their feet. The very knowledge of its delicacy increased the pleasure he found with her. He held out his arms to·her and she moved into them saying she was sorry too. He stroked her glossy hair.

'I've missed you,' he said.

'Have you?' She looked up at him and smiled but did not say

that she had missed him too. The omission registered in his head like an amount rung up on a till, although, he told himself, chidingly, the fact that she had not said she had missed him did not mean that she had not. She may have meant him to take it for granted that she had. But he could not be certain about that.

'I'm starving,' she said and they separated so that he could put the final touches to the meal. As he put the rice into a dish, the doorbell rang.

'Expecting someone?' he asked.

'As a matter of fact I'm not,' said Claire, her voice cool.

The bell rang again.

'Somebody seems to be in a hurry,' said Thomas and made for the door, forestalling Claire who was also moving towards it. He had a vision of Donald standing on the landing mat with his feet planted wide apart and that silly grin on his face. If the bell-ringer should be Donald, thought Thomas, he would send him packing.

'If it's friend Liffey don't let him in!' Claire called after him.

With that possibility in mind, Thomas opened the door only a few inches.

On the mat stood Peter Finlay. And he was not smiling.

'Peter,' said Thomas. 'You'd better come in.'

'I suppose I should apologise.' Thomas smiled ruefully but no corresponding flicker crossed Peter's face which looked as if it were carved from stone. 'I seem to have spent my life apologising.'

'If you'd done the right thing in the first place you wouldn't have had to, would you?'

He is young, of course, thought Thomas, though maybe not *that* young, to be talking of doing the 'right' thing, as if anyone could know what that might be. Peter meant that Thomas should have married his mother. Thomas remembered the ferocity of his grandfather's rage when he had told him he intended to. 'Don't be such a bloody fool! You'd be bored after a few months. You can't spent your life in bed. What would you say to her day after day? What would she say to you? Can you imagine your life?' Thomas had been able to, only too

165

well, and had known that he did not want to live in a council house in the village of his birth and come home from a job in the pit or some miserable clerking job in the city to a waiting wife and baby. 'You have your whole life ahead of you,' his grandfather had said. 'University, the wide world waiting . . . You can't give up everything you have worked for, everything *we* have worked for.'

'It wouldn't have worked, Peter,' said Thomas.

'And do you think it's worked with Liffey?'

'He wanted to marry her.'

'So she was just a pawn to be pushed about between the two of you?'

'But what is Jean to do?' Thomas had asked his grandfather. The old man had believed there was a woman in the next street . . .

'*Have an abortion*?' said Jean. 'Do you know what you're asking?' Of course Thomas had not. 'She's an old witch that woman you want me to go to. She sticks knitting needles into women and wire coat hangers. Effie McGraw nearly bled to death.' Thomas shuddered. 'You musn't go to her then, Jean, you musn't!' 'But what am I to do?' 'I'll marry you.'

That night he had not slept. He lay awake thinking about walking on eggshells and how dodgy life was. One false move and you were through that thin shell, down there floundering amongst the slippery stuff. Before sunrise he rose and cycled far out into the country. Riding slowly and rhythmically, he watched the first pale streaks of light seeping into the eastern sky and the flocks of seagulls swooping down on to the dark brown fields and the mist dispersing from the coarse blond grasses of the moors. On the horizon, the Pentland Hills sprawled, looking splendid and pure, powdered with fresh snow, the first of winter. In the middle of the moors he pushed down harder on the pedals, until the wheels beneath him spun faster and faster and his heart hammered and he had the sensation of flying. Everything then – birds, hedges, trees, cottages, smoke rising – passed in a blur. He wanted to go on pedalling and never come back.

He went home to tell his grandfather he would have to marry Jean after all.

'Does this girl mean more to you than I do?'

'Of course not!'

'Then you must *not* marry her.' His grandfather took out his handkerchief and wiped the sweat from his face. He had been ailing for months, though was not to die for several years, not until after he had seen his grandson graduate and make a suitable marriage. A creaking gate, that knew how to keep its hinges oiled, was what his daughter-in-law called him. 'It will kill me, Thomas.'

His blood pressure had risen to an alarming level, they had to call the doctor who gave him stronger pills and advised total rest and no excitement. Thomas had not been able to take on the responsibility of killing his grandfather.

'I can understand you not wanting to get married at eighteen,' said Peter. 'But I despise you for abandoning my mother.'

His eyes met Thomas's. They radiated coolness rather than anger. Thomas could have coped better with anger; he was used to it in his own family, all of whom in their temperaments – except for his mother – were inclined to vent rather than restrain their passions.

The door opened and the two men turned, both welcoming the arrival of Claire who had come to announce the imminent disintegration of the pheasant.

'I don't think you've met Peter, have you, Claire?'

'Liffey's son?' She regarded him with interest. 'No, I haven't.'

'Listen, love –' said Thomas. 'I have something to tell you.'

Claire needed a drink, as they themselves did, and time to get used to the idea. She stared at Thomas and then at Peter.

They dined off the remains of the pheasant and overdone vegetables made palatable by a couple of bottles of good red Burgundy. Afterwards, they drank coffee and a great deal of brandy and Peter sat slumped in the armchair beside the fire with his feet spread across the rug. It was strange, he said, when one had completely to rethink the past and see it in another perspective.

'It's difficult to come to terms with the knowledge that for the first twenty-six years of your life you've lived with a major lie. I would call being told that your father is someone who he is not a major lie, wouldn't you?'

Thomas assented, not wishing to get involved in a discussion as to whether the withholding of the truth was the same as outright lying. That was a topic into which Claire, too, might have entered, with her professional experience. He did not want to prolong any of Peter's discourses. He would have enough to say as it was. And Thomas himself wanted to say as little as possible. He felt burnt out.

Peter talked on about the past, recalling incidents from his childhood, which now, in retrospect, took on a new significance. Liffey calling him a bastard after an especially bitter row. Liffey singing to him the refrain, '*And loudly sings cuckoo!*' And laughing. 'I knew there was something I didn't understand because it upset my mother so. Once I was old enough to realise what her life was really like with him, I hated him.' Peter looked across at Thomas. 'I liked you when I was a kid, though.'

'I liked you too.'

'Funny – I even used to wish you were my father.'

'I used to wish I could acknowledge you were my son.'

'Why didn't you then?' demanded Peter, fierce for a moment, before subsiding again.

When, eventually, he heaved himself up on to his feet saying it was time he went, Claire said why not stay? He had had rather a lot to drink and he shouldn't really be driving and the spare bed was there doing nothing. 'After all, you're family, aren't you?'

Peter turned to Thomas.

'You might as well stay.'

Getting undressed, Claire said to Thomas, 'Why didn't you tell me before?'

'We had sworn, Liffey and Jean and I –'

'But that was years ago, and you could have trusted me. It would have explained Liffey's hold over you too. At least you'll have him off your back now.'

'Yes, I suppose I will,' said Thomas slowly. He had not yet taken in that aspect of it.

'You told Sarah presumably?'

After a short hesitation, he said, 'Yes.'

Before turning over to go to sleep Claire said, 'It's a wonder they didn't all see it years ago – he may not *be* very like you, but he looks like your son.'

'So how do you feel about him now?' asked Sarah. They were on their knees, she and Thomas, on the living room floor amongst piles of papers, letters and photographs. He had come to help her pack up the house.

Sarah was always wanting to know how people felt though, at the same time, she believed that they should keep those feelings in check. Reasonable check, that was, but not totally smothered. 'She seems like a nice well-balanced girl,' his mother had said approvingly after their first meeting. Just what you need, Thomas had known she was thinking.

He sighed, not knowing what he felt about Peter. Not much at the moment. Less than he'd ever felt before in a strange sort of way.

'He hates me anyway, that's for sure.'

'That'll lessen in time. Most emotions do.'

'I don't know – some must deepen.'

'Like hatred? Unless of course it finds release in revenge.'

'Ah well,' said Thomas and looked down at the clutter surrounding them. 'What a mountain of stuff!'

'Possessions. Anchors. Without them, we are either set free or cast adrift, whatever way you see it. No, it's all right, I'm not going to *start* anything.' Sarah picked up a heap of photographs, some black and white, some coloured, and let them rain down from her fingers on to the floor where they lay, in disorder, the one overlapping the other, forming a collage of their married life together. Tasha, aged twelve, in white blouse and striped tie and navy skirt, hair shining, eyes shining for the school photographer; almost obscured Tasha, aged three, digging on the sands, knees bent, bottom in the air; and she in turn was half masked by her mother, robed in white, holding a bunch of tea roses, and her father looking like a penguin in a long-tailed coat and clutching a top hat under his arm.

Sarah laughed until the tears streamed. 'You look so po-faced!'

'I had a hangover.' He had gone drinking the night before

with Liffey who wouldn't take no for an answer. He'd come for him at his mother's house. 'You've got to have a last night out before you're shackled, Tommy.' The women supported him. 'It's customary,' said Thomas's mother. 'Any man worth his salt has a stag night out,' said his sister.

Sarah dried her eyes.

'You look as if the thorns were sticking into your fingers from the roses,' said Thomas.

'My dress was too tight. I couldn't breathe.'

Afterwards, lying in bed in a cottage on the Hebridean island of Barra (there were photographs of that too – white sand, clear green water, women cutting peat), they had laughed about Thomas's hangover and Sarah's tight dress and the pompous speeches and the icing on the cake which had set so hard that it had had to be cracked open with a hammer in the kitchen.

They sobered, said they'd better not start getting sentimental. It *was* the past after all. And here they were now faced with its leftovers. Thomas shovelled half the photographs into a plastic carrier bag, Sarah stuffed her share away in a box. The books posed more of a problem. Ninety per cent of them were Thomas's – he'd started haunting the second-hand bookshops in Edinburgh when he was twelve years old, used to cycle in on a Saturday morning, returning home at teatime with the back end of his bicycle wobbling – and as yet he had nowhere to put them.

'Claire's spare room?' suggested Sarah.

Peter had slept in the spare bed for the past three nights. He found life in his own house difficult now that he knew that Liffey was no longer his father. And now that Liffey knew that he knew. Besides, there were no spare beds in the Finlays' house so he would have had to have slept on the settee which was not quite long enough for him. He might as well stay with them, Claire had said, and it would be handy for him to be in town for Liffey's case. It was coming up the following week.

'I don't mind Peter being here,' she said to Thomas. 'He's easy to have around.'

Thomas spent hours packing books into cardboard cartons which he begged and stole from grocers, greengrocers and wine shops. They jammed the hall of the Portobello house, occupied all the available floor space in the dining room, encroached on the sitting room. How would he ever get them moved?

'Hasn't Peter got a car?' said Sarah.

Peter was obliging, regardless of what he was feeling about Thomas, and didn't mind either making repeated trips in and out of Edinburgh or carrying boxes that felt (to Thomas) as though they were laden with stones. Peter carried them up the stairs as if they were filled with feathers. Behind him came Thomas, puffing a little, though not too much, he reflected, for a man of his age. But he felt the age gap between them – as any man would with a son. On the return visits to Portobello, Peter and Sarah chatted easily over cups of coffee which she provided to refresh them. Thomas drank his coffee quickly, wanting to get Peter away before Sarah would give him the opportunity to start recalling the past again. In the evenings, at Claire's, he had enough of it. Peter seemed to have a Proustian memory. *I remember you bringing me a dump truck for my birthday . . . It was red, with yellow wheels. I remember the look on my mother's face. I remember how Liffey kicked it out of his way afterwards and scuffed the paint and I cried . . .*

The boxes of Thomas's books, piled one upon the other, covered all the available floor space in Claire's spare room. The bed lay like a turquoise-blue island amongst a fawn-coloured cardboard jungle. There was just enough room for Peter to climb over the boxes and crawl in.

'This will be a classic case,' said Claire. 'Was she willing or was she not?' She finished her breakfast coffee and rose to go. 'It's going to be difficult to know who is telling the truth.'

Thomas and Peter walked up to Parliament House together.

Peter's mother and grandmother were waiting outside the court room behind four unknown women in felt hats who smelt of boiled sweets and whose powdered cheeks bulged as if abscessed. 'They're empanelling the jury,' said one, turning to the two men. Regular visitors to the court, obviously. Peter's female relatives were saying nothing. They stood with their eyes cast down. Peter touched his mother on the shoulder and she nodded gratefully.

The court room door opened and men and women began to

stream out, obliging the group in the corridor to stand to one side. 'Rejected jurors,' said the informer. 'I was once a juror,' said one of her friends. 'Murder.' She shifted a black and white striped ball from one cheek to the other. When the way was clear the informer moved out in front and led them into the court.

The sweet-suckers ensconced themselves in the middle of the front row, the two Mrs Finlays took a pew half way down and Peter and Thomas went into the row behind them. Peter immediately leant forward to have a quiet word with his mother, on the side away from his grandmother.

Claire was sitting at the table below the judge's bench talking to Donald. She had looked up when they came into the court and smiled and Donald, too, had lifted his head and then his hand in salutation. Thomas watched Claire's face. She appeared unfamiliar to him in her black gown and short wig, unreal almost, like a character in a courtroom drama.

'You don't have to stay in the whole time,' Thomas overheard Peter say to his mother. 'He's my husband.' 'He's never let that stand in his way.' 'Hush, Peter.'

Thomas thought of his freedom machine and wished he were riding across the moors. You always run away when things are difficult. Was Eunice right? He did not think so, not always, anyway, for he might often be tempted – as surely most people were? – but he only occasionally ran and sometimes flight *was* better than staying put.

Voices in the corridor, hushed yet penetrating, telegraphed the approach of Eunice and her mother. They were asking the policeman if they'd got the right door. 'R v. Finlay?' said Eunice. Her woollen hat bobbed into sight. She waved and turned to tell her mother that the others were already there. The four women in felt hats twisted their thick necks to examine the new arrivals who were carrying bags provisioned for the day's outing. The elder women walked with the aid of a stick which caused some difficulty as she struggled up the steps, the younger seemed impatient for her to hurry along more quickly.

They established themselves eventually in the pew beside Thomas and Peter. Eunice removed her hat, her mother did not. Both got out their knitting.

'It helps to have something to do with your hands,' said Isabel.

'I wonder if Sarah will come,' said Eunice, craning her neck.

'Looks a bit like a playpen, I always think.' Isabel nodded towards the dock.

The entry of Liffey sandwiched between two white-gloved policemen silenced them. Eunice put her hand over her mouth. 'Not bad looking,' said one of the four sweet-suckers. Liffey was led into the pen where he sat upright and still, looking like an overfed insurance salesman in a tight-fitting navy-blue suit. His hair had been cut, he wore a collar and tie. He, too, was like a character playing a rôle.

The macer appeared on the bench shouting, 'Court!' They all rose, the judge in scarlet and white, emblazoned with crosses, entered, the lawyers bowed, and the drama began to unfold.

'I reckon we have a fifty–fifty chance,' Claire had said before leaving the flat. 'A lot will depend on the jury.'

Thomas watched the faces of the seven women and eight men as they were sworn in. They looked unremarkable. Claire had told them that the women, particularly those who were married and/or not young, were often harder on the victim than the men: they thought she should be above reproach if she had children, that she should not drink in pubs, allow herself to be escorted home by a man other than her husband, and if she had no husband then she was that faintly suspect person known as a 'single parent' who ought to be conserving her money and not leaving the children on their own but giving them even more of her attention as compensation for the lack of a father. Claire expected the verdict to be a majority one, considered it unlikely that fifteen people would be able to come to an unanimous decision in a case which was as open as this. And a majority of women in the jury might favour the defence.

As the council for the prosecution, the Advocate Depute, rose to open the case for the crown, Sarah slipped in and sat at the back.

The first witness, the police photographer, was called and gave evidence and then the court was cleared so that the victim could take the stand.

Isabel and Eunice had a fuss getting out again. 'We've only

just sat down,' said Eunice. Knitting needles were dropped, as Thomas knew they would be, and Eunice's hat and gloves. His mother's stick fell sideways, and her leg had stiffened up so that her limp was more pronounced and her walk slower. The Advocate Depute waited without showing a twitch of impatience. Claire gazed down at her notes. Donald watched the decampment with interest. All the other participants in the case remained in their places without moving, like players frozen into statues.

'I don't see why they couldn't have let us stay in,' said Isabel, on reaching the corridor. 'It's not as if she was a young lassie. It'd take a lot to embarrass *her*!'

'How are you supposed to follow what's going on?' asked Eunice, getting out the thermos flask.

'Use your imagination,' said Thomas.

They lined up on a red leatherette bench: Sarah, Isabel, Eunice, Thomas and Peter. Jean and Mrs Finlay would not sit, they wandered off down the corridor. The women on the bench drank tea from the thermos flask and ate half-coated digestive biscuits, the men sat with their arms folded.

'I suppose she'll be raking up all that old stuff about Liffey and Jinty Smith,' said Eunice.

'She's got to,' said Thomas.

'There was never much in it, of course. She did all the running.' Suddenly remembering Peter's presence, Eunice flushed and became confused. She started to apologise.

'It's all right,' said Peter and got up to join his mother and grandmother.

'You should watch your tongue, Eunice,' said her mother. 'I mean it is his father after all.'

'I wasn't saying nothing against Liffey.'

'I guess he knows what Liffey's like,' said Sarah.

'What *is* he like?' demanded Eunice, looking across her mother at her sister-in-law.

Sarah shrugged, would not be drawn.

'Oh well, we all know Liffey's fond of the girls,' said Isabel.

'That doesn't mean he'd rape a woman,' said Eunice.

'No one's said it did,' said Thomas wearily. Eunice was jumping about like a hen on a hot griddle, spilling crumbs and slops of tea and every few minutes she complained about not being able to smoke.

'We all know that Jinty Smith's fond of the men,' she said.

Thomas half-turned his back on the group to look up the corridor where Peter was talking earnestly to his mother. Was he saying, 'You don't owe him anything. Just because he married you when you were in trouble.'

'Why should he want to marry me?' Jean had asked when Thomas had told her of Liffey's offer.

'Liffey's always – well – liked you, you know that. And he's earning quite good money,' went on Thomas desperately.

'Got yourself into trouble eh, Tommy?' Liffey had said. 'Would never have thought it, a nice straight guy like you.' Thomas had told him to cut the cackle, it was no joke. They'd gone to the pub to drink to the end of Thomas's prospects of a glorious career (using his grant money) and as the evening progressed Thomas grew more and more depressed envisaging himself sitting on a high stool in some dingy office and bringing home a turkey for Christmas dinner (if he was lucky) and Liffey grew more and more cheerful until, when the barman called for last drinks, he slapped Thomas on the back and said he wouldn't mind marrying Jean himself, to help an old pal out. 'That's what mates are for isn't it? You'd help me out sometime wouldn't you, Tommy?' 'Sure,' said Thomas, who did not at that point believe that Liffey meant what he said. He liked to shoot his mouth off. And to tantalise. 'Any road, I've always fancied Jean.' Thomas knew that. And it had always been so, Liffey coveting whatever he had, whether it was a glass marble, a three-speed bicycle, or a girlfriend. 'I mean it, Tommy.'

'Would you like to marry Liffey?' Thomas had asked Jean.

'If you think it's for the best.'

'It's what you think too!'

He had wanted to take her by the shoulders, shake her, shout, tell her to hit him, swear at him, tell him to marry her, for if she told him he might find the resolve to do it. To do the 'decent' thing. He had been brought up by his mother and grandfather to think of himself as someone who would always do the decent thing and now his grandfather was imploring – demanding – that he do the indecent thing and act dishonourably, he who liked to talk of honour.

175

He wanted to take Jean by the shoulders *now*, shake her, tell her to tell Liffey to go to hell, not to be so bloody bowed! But could he when he was one of the ones who'd helped bend her?

Liffey did not move as they filed back in to the court and resettled themselves.

'It'd be a bit of a lark, wouldn't it,' Liffey had said after he'd made his offer, 'to have *your* bun in *my* oven?' He was picking his teeth with a match-stick and smiling. Thomas saw that Liffey wanted to marry Jean *because* she was pregnant with *his* child. He wanted to punch him in the mouth and knock the hand and the match-stick flying. But he didn't. He couldn't afford to, not now. And another realisation hit him at that moment: he would not have carried on the relationship with Jean for so long had it not been for the fact that Liffey fancied her.

Jinty Smith, who had by now described, in minute detail, how Laurence Ian Fyffe Finlay, on the night of September 13th last, had, in a lane off Barns Road, assaulted her, grabbed her by the throat, dragged her to the ground, forcibly removed her clothing, lain on top of her, forced her legs apart, and raped her, glanced round to see who was coming into the public gallery. She seemed cheerful, Thomas thought, too cheerful. He could not judge from the expression on Claire's face how she felt about her cross-examination. She was going to have attacked Jinty's reputation and stressed the bitterness she had felt when Liffey had terminated their affair. ('I *have* to attack her reputation. Okay, so a lot of this isn't going to be very nice.') Later, that evening, she told Thomas and Peter that Jinty had denied any former sexual relationship with Liffey, quite categorically, and had insisted that the first time she had had sex with him had been on the night of the alleged rape, in the lane, when he'd forced her.

The Advocate Depute was standing to the left of the jury with one hand in his pocket. He, too, looked cheerful. He called the next witness, Mrs Black, Jinty's neighbour on her left-hand side.

Mrs. Black told the court that on the night in question she had heard a noise in the street which sounded like a woman

176

crying out. She had just been getting ready for bed so it would have been about eleven o'clock. Give or take a minute or two. The counsel nodded encouragingly, asked if she had looked out and, if so, what had she seen?

'A man and woman scuffling near the entrance to the lane.'

'When you say scuffling, what do you mean exactly? Was the woman trying to fend the man off?'

'I object to that question, My Lord.' Claire was on her feet quickly. 'That is a leading question.'

The judge turned to the counsel for the prosecution who bowed his head in submission and rephrased the question. 'Would you please tell us, Mrs Black, what the man and woman were doing?'

'The woman was trying to fend the man off, like you said.' Claire frowned with annoyance.

'You are sure of that?' asked the counsel.

'Oh yes. I saw her give him a push and then he pulled her into the lane.'

'Pulled? You are quite sure – pulled?'

'Quite sure, sir,' said Mrs Black, who had never had so many eyes turned upon her. She stood in the witness box with her handbag clasped in front of her stomach and when she said, 'Quite sure, sir,' which she did quite often, she glanced around the court to make sure that everyone was aware of her certainty. Claire was listening intently and every now and then she bent her head to make a note. Beside Thomas, Eunice huffed and her fingers flew more frantically along the knitting needles. The ball of purple wool bounced off her knee and rolled under Thomas's feet.

'What did you do then, Mrs Black?'

'Well, I didne know what to do. I was in by myself – my husband was on the night shift and we havne a phone and I'm right nervous of going out in the dark, I suffer with my nerves, you see, and the woman up the back from us got cut –'

The counsel had had enough on that tack. He said sympathetically that he understood. He restated her evidence: she had been worried about the woman but was unable to go to her assistance because of her nerves? Did she attend the doctor for her nerves?

'I do, sir.' Mrs Black was delighted to acknowledge the fact publicly. She went on to tell the court how she had kept up her vigil until the couple reappeared from the lane. 'The woman broke away from the man and came running along the pavement. I saw then it was Jinty Smith.'

'What did Mrs Smith do then?'

'She went into her own house.'

And the man – could she identify him? – and if she saw him in the court would she please point him out?

All eyes but Mrs Black's went to the dock. She allowed hers to rove around the court initially, as if the man might be lurking anywhere; they passed over the rows of faces in the public benches and then those in the jury box. For a moment it looked as if she might point to a juror. But no, she smiled and shook her head. Finally, suggesting that the thought had only just occurred to her, she swung round to face the dock. 'That's him, sir,' she announced and thrust a finger in the direction of the accused.

'The man between the two policemen?'

'Yes, sir.'

Mrs Black then recounted the arrival of Jinty Smith at her back door in a terrible state with her clothing torn and blood on her face.

Claire rose to cross-examine.

'Mrs Black, you thought a woman was being attacked by a man–'

'Yes, miss.'

'Yet you did nothing?'

'I've already told the gentleman.'

'I heard what you told him. I am asking you if you thought a woman was in serious danger and did nothing?'

'Yes, miss. My nerves –'

'Even with your nervous condition you could have run out quickly to a neighbour, could you not? You could have gone next door to Mrs Smith's for that matter?'

'But she was in the lane.' Mrs Black was triumphant.

'You didn't know that at that time though, did you? You said you recognised her only after she came out of the lane.'

Mrs Black looked confused. 'I suppose I didne.'

'Did you or did you not know?' No answer. 'Are you sure of what you saw outside on that night?' The witness hesitated. 'I put it to you that you are not?'

'I'm sure.' Mrs Black was sullen.

'You said that Mrs Smith went into her house and came out after a couple of minutes? Are you certain that there was a gap of only two minutes?' Mrs Black was becoming less certain of anything by the second. Perhaps five minutes, she conceded, but would go no further. No, she hadn't timed it. Her hands tightened over the handbag and she looked appealingly at the counsel for the prosecution who had been so much nicer to her, a real gentleman. (He was studying his notes.)

Claire went on relentlessly, peppering her with questions.

'Mrs Black, when Mrs Smith came running along the pavement were her clothes torn? Was there blood on her face?'

'I didn't notice. It was dark.'

'There were street lights were there not?'

'They're no that bright.'

'Mrs Black, is it not the case that you did nothing that night to raise the alarm because you saw and heard nothing that alarmed you?'

'No, it is not.' Mrs Black was stubborn.

'Liar!' said Eunice and jerked the wool so violently that the ball bounded from Thomas's feet to Peter's.

'Are you a friend of Mrs Smith's, Mrs Black?'

Mrs Black looked sideways at Jinty. Claire repeated the question. 'We're neighbours,' said Mrs Black. Claire pushed her until she had an admission of friendship.

'I put it to you, Mrs Black, that you have been lying in the witness box here today in order to help your friend Mrs Smith?'

'That's not true.' Mrs Black was outraged. 'I wouldne lie for anybody.'

At four o'clock the court was adjourned for the day and Liffey was led away to the cells where he would spend the night. Jinty went off arm in arm with Mrs Black. Eunice, protesting loudly about Liffey being locked up, went home on the bus with her mother and Jean and Mrs Finlay.

Thomas and Peter walked down the Mound with Claire

between them.

'Well, there's one thing we can be certain of,' said Claire, 'and that's that Mrs Smith and Mrs Black are lying, to some degree or other. The question is – to what degree?'

'They may not even know themselves,' said Thomas.

'It's going to be a case of establishing that there is reasonable doubt.'

'And there is,' said Thomas.

'Oh yes. But the jury could be swayed one way or the other.'

'You're swaying *me* anyway,' said Peter.

'Thank you,' said Claire, turning to him, and smiled.

After dinner, which he had cooked, Thomas cycled down to Portobello. Helen, Sarah and Tasha were drinking fizzy wine in the kitchen.

'Helen's got a job,' said Sarah. 'Housemother, in a children's home. Living in.'

He drank a glass of wine with them to celebrate, then said to Tasha, 'Come for a walk.'

When they were outside she said, 'So it's just going to be Mother and me left now. The last of the green bottles. "*Ten green bottles . . .*"' She began to sing. 'It's all right – I'm not drunk!' She tucked her hand into the crook of his arm.

They went down to the sea and walked along the sands, which under the light of a half-moon looked whiter and cleaner than they did by day.

'There is something that I think you should know,' said Thomas.

Tasha listened while he talked, staying close to him, putting in the occasional question. 'Well!' she said, when he had finished. 'Imagine – Peter Finlay is my half-brother! I don't even know that I like him all that much.'

'You don't have to.' Then Thomas asked, 'Do you think I should have married Jean?'

'Certainly not! It would have been a disaster. You don't think you should have, do you?' Tasha sounded scandalised that he might.

'I don't know.' They would be better suited, Liffey and Jean, his grandfather had said, and it might even be the making of

Liffey. 'Her marriage to Liffey's been pretty much of a disaster.'

But Tasha did not care about Jean and Liffey, she was for *him*, her own father, totally. 'I'm certainly glad you didn't. I wouldn't have been here, would I? And you'd rather have me than Peter, wouldn't you?'

'Well, I don't know about that!'

They laughed.

He put his arm round her shoulders and they went down to the edge of the sand where they stopped to listen to the soft swish of the waves and watch the white froth come curling out of the darkness to break close to their feet. How reassuring the sound of the sea was, thought Thomas. Whatever else happened, this would remain.

'Dad, what happened between you and Mother? I can remember you laughing together.'

'We were laughing only the other day, over some old photographs.' He tried to explain that over the years relationships shift – 'Nothing in the universe is static after all' – and some resettle in a comfortable, acceptable way, but others slide, causing cracks too wide to be papered over, and if they are, the paper ruptures under the slightest pressure. 'Tasha, disenchantment is no easier to explain than enchantment. Oh not that I expect to be enchanted *all* my life – I'm not that immature, or at least I don't think I am!' But she would not let herself be even a little amused. She was gazing down at the dark sand and kicking it up with the heel of her shoe. 'I still feel great affection for your mother,' he said. 'And great regard.'

Now Tasha lifted her face up to his. 'Won't that do?' she cried. 'At your age?'

Claire called the accused. The four hatted women stopped rummaging for black and white striped candy balls. Eunice dropped a knitting needle and did not notice. The members of the jury who had been asleep roused themselves.

Raising his right arm, swearing most solemnly and soberly by Almighty God whose name he only normally took in vain, Liffey stood up to his full height of six feet two inches in the witness box. At thirteen, he had topped six feet, had been a full

181

head taller than Thomas who was slower to grow and never did catch up. The women jurors seemed to be warming to Liffey, thought Thomas, all except the elderly one in the middle of the front row who looked as if she would not warm to anybody.

Claire began by asking about Liffey's previous relationship with the complainer.

'Complainer's the right word for her,' muttered Eunice and leant forward to rest her arms on the pew in front.

'We went around for a while,' said Liffey.

'What do you mean by "went around"?' asked Claire. 'Were you lovers?'

'Yes.'

'Who broke off the relationship?'

'I did.'

'How did Mrs Smith take it?'

'She wasn't pleased.'

'So she had a grudge against you? Would it be fair to put it that way?'

'That is the way I would put it.'

'We'll have to fall out, won't we?' Liffey had said. 'At least kid on we have. Otherwise nobody's going to believe the baby's mine. If we have a set-to they'll think we were fighting because I've taken your bird away from you and managed to shag her when you didn't.' He grinned. He put up his fists and began to jog around on the balls of his feet. 'After it's born we can make up again and you can come round and see him. As long as you don't let on to him. That's part of the deal, isn't it? You'll be his Uncle Tommy. Come on, Uncle Tommy, put your mits up!'

Thomas lunged at Liffey landing him a jab on the edge of the chin. Liffey laughed, did another little dance and came back with a blow that sent Thomas staggering about. The earth spun. Liffey had been a junior welterweight boxing champion. Thomas shook his head, sucked in a lungful of air and charged. They closed on one another, their grips locked, they grunted and they bellowed and they struggled, using hands, heads, feet. They fell to the ground, they rolled over and over, and then Thomas, with an immense effort, pushed Liffey's shoulders back, and straddled him. Liffey's chest heaved, blood spouted from his nose. It was the first time Thomas had ever felled Liffey. He sat recovering his breath letting his racing heart subside. I could kill him now if I wanted to, he thought. He put his thumbs tentatively against Liffey's throat, saw Liffey's eyes dilate. Then he got up on to his feet and walked unsteadily away.

He left home on his bicycle, with a rucksack on his back and his left eye closed. His grandfather had withdrawn his savings from the post office. 'It's not much, but take it, go into town, rent a room and study there in peace until things blow over.' At a roundabout, on the way into Edinburgh, Thomas was knocked down by a car approaching on his blind side and spent the next month in hospital with multiple injuries. For two days he was in intensive care. His mother and grandfather sat at his bedside. Jean sent a Get Well Card. He never wanted to go back to the place of his birth again as long as he lived.

By the time he came out of hospital Jean and Liffey were married. And by the time he did go back home on a visit, to see his grandfather, who was ailing, dying, it was thought, there were as many versions circulating about his break-up with Jean and his fight with Liffey as it was possible to think up.

'You are quite certain,' asked Claire, 'that *she* approached *you* in the pub.'

'Quite certain. She came over and offered to buy me a drink and said, "We might as well let bygones be bygones."'

'Were those her exact words?'

'Her exact words,' confirmed Liffey.

Those had been his words to Thomas when they had met again two years after his marriage. They met by accident. Liffey put out his hand to Thomas and after a second's hesitation, Thomas took it. They went for a drink in the pub. 'Like old times, eh, Tommy?' And they almost quarrelled, again.

'I fancied Jean before you did,' said Liffey. 'That was why you asked her out in the first place, wasn't it – *because* I did?'

Thomas, who was now in love with Sarah and could scarcely remember feeling any desire for Jean, denied it.

'Come off it, Tommy, you know I fancied her first! I

remember telling you I had my eye on her and that I was going to ask her out for a date. And you jumped in first, put a spoke in my wheel. But it's all right – I forgive you!' Liffey slapped him so heavily on the back that he lurched forward against the table edge and spilled his beer. 'Sorry, pal!' Liffey mopped up the beer with his handkerchief and Thomas, wanting to lay the matter to rest, had accepted forgiveness for a sin which he did not believe he had committed.

Liffey, in the witness box, was talking now about his relationship with a different woman, describing how, when they had left the pub together, she had taken his arm – and oh yes, he was sure of that too, even remembering the way she'd gripped his elbow – and they had walked up to the top of the housing scheme to the back lane where they used to go when they were lovers.

Thomas looked at the back of Jean's head and wondered what she was thinking of.

'Oh no, she made no objection when I kissed her,' said Liffey, in response to Claire's questioning. 'So then we lay down on the grass and had sex together. She was all for it, just the way she used to be.'

Eunice was shaking with rage. Thomas, fearing she was about to rise and shout aloud, laid a restraining hand on her arm.

'So Mrs Smith made no objection whatsoever?'

'None. She was a willing party, same as me.'

The Advocate Depute spoke smoothly and unaggressively. There was nothing of the bully in his demeanour. He observed that Liffey was a married man with four children, yet he seemed to lead the life of a Don Juan? A lady killer, he explained to the jury, in case there should be any misunderstanding. He put it to the accused that he was a man of fairly loose morals? Liffey was indignant. That was not true. And he certainly didn't go round raping women.

'The truth of that is what we are here to establish. Now we have heard that it had been raining earlier on that night and the lane was muddy. You are telling us, Mr Finlay, that a woman would be so eager to have sex with you that she would consent to lie down in the mud. She was wearing a new jacket, she told us. She supports her children on social security so that getting a new jacket is not an everyday occurrence. Do you expect us to believe that she was so carried away that she didn't care about that?'

'She'd had a few drinks.'

'As you had yourself. Again, when clothes are difficult to come by, do you really think it likely that she would have ripped them apart.'

'I think she could have done it out of spite.'

'And scratched her own face?'

'Yes.'

'You would have us believe, Mr Finlay, that she was prepared to go to great lengths?'

'I think she was.'

'I put it to you, Mr Finlay, that you are not used to taking no for an answer from a woman and, when Mrs Smith refused you, became angry and forced her against her will to have sex with you?'

'That's not true, sir. I did not force her. It happened like I said.'

Mrs MacAteer, Jinty Smith's neighbour on the right-hand side, had a different story to tell from Mrs Black. Her manner from the start was vituperative, and therefore worrying for Claire who had to try to tone her down. Mrs MacAteer had seen Jinty Smith coming along the pavement at a quarter past eleven on the night in question; she had no need to give or take a minute or two, she had known the time exactly for she had been watching at the window for her daughter coming home. Mrs Smith had looked just her usual, she said, as if she'd been out for a good time and had had a drink or two. 'She's in the pub two or three nights a week, leaves those bairns on their own, it's a right disgrace . . .' Mrs MacAteer might have waited years for this opportunity.

Claire cut in quickly to ask if Mrs Smith had been distressed or crying.

'Crying? Her? I've never seen that one in tears.'

Mrs MacAteer testified that she had seen her neighbour stop

185

to pick up a toy on the path on her way into her house, that she had seemed in no great hurry and that she had remained indoors for fifteen minutes and then come out again to go into her neighbour Mrs Black's, and shortly afterwards the two of them had gone off down the road together arm-in-arm. 'Quite the thing they were. As if they were off for a night out.' Mrs MacAteer concluded her evidence cheerfully.

Claire sat down, not looking too happy, and the counsel for the prosecution rose with a little smile.

Mrs MacAteer appeared to be very aware of the passing of time? he observed. She agreed. He asked if her watch kept good time? She half-raised her wrist, let it fall again. It was at the mender's, she said. In a kindly voice he continued his inquiry. Did Mrs MacAteer go to the pub two or three nights a week herself?

'Certainly not.'

'So your evidence in that respect is based on hearsay?'

She was reluctant to answer. He pressed her and she supposed that it was. He also pressed her to admit that she and Mrs Smith were not friends, that they had had a difference of opinion a year or so previously, something to do with their children, and since then they had not been on speaking terms.

'*Were* you on bad terms, Mrs MacAteer?'

'Sort of.'

'I put it to you that you had a grudge against your neighbour and that in this court this morning you have been lying in order to damage Mrs Smith?'

'That's not true. I told the truth.'

'Thank you, Mrs MacAteer.'

Jean sighed, almost imperceptibly, but enough for it to be audible to Thomas and Peter in the row behind. Peter leant forward yet again to touch his mother's shoulder. Thomas thought of cycling across the moors and of Liffey behind bars.

Claire rose to try and repair the damage. Mrs MacAteer looked grateful to be back with this interrogator who was on her side; she answered in a quiet, pained voice. She had no wish to harm anyone, she had always been sorry for Mrs Smith ever since her husband had walked out on her and left her on her own with the three children. 'I tried to help her but she didn't seem to want help. And I was just telling the truth,' she insisted. 'That's what I came here for.'

'I am here to put to you the case for the crown,' said the Advocate Depute conversationally, sliding his hand back into his pocket. In the other he held his notes thrust forward so that the front row of jurors might have read them had they wished. They didn't look as if they would wish. They gazed at him expressionlessly. Some of them appeared to have sunk back down into slumber, thought Thomas, who wished it was possible to open a window. The room was beginning to feel like a steam bath. He eased off his jacket. 'It is your job to decide, ladies and gentlemen, which witnesses you believe and which you do not believe . . .'

The knitting needles lay inert on the yellow varnished seat. Eunice had her hands knotted together in front of her, as if in supplication. Did she believe in God? wondered Thomas, who was not sure whether he did himself or not. Even in those frames of mind when he disbelieved he had doubts about his disbelief. It was not a matter he and Eunice would ever discuss. Her lips were moving slightly. Hurry up, Thomas was saying inside his own head, get on with your summing up, enough has been said. Between the two policemen Liffey still sat upright, intent on making a good impression to the last.

'. . . and so you should consider the state of her clothing, her injuries, and the evidence of her neighbour Mrs Black. You have also heard the evidence of Mrs MacAteer which conflicts to some degree with that of Mrs Black, but I will leave it to you to decide which version is the more credible . . .'

Claire's voice had a clear bell-like quality which carried into every corner of the court; she made no attempt to be either conversational in style or openly persuasive. This is what I believe, she seemed to be saying, and I believe it to be the truth, and I believe therefore that you should believe it also.

'I'd like to start off by stressing the seriousness of the case. The charge of rape is one of the most serious that a man can face. I wish to remind you that you must be satisfied beyond reasonable doubt – I repeat *beyond reasonable doubt* – and that it is up to the crown to prove the charge and not the accused to prove his innocence . . .'

Her speech was simple and direct. She pinpointed factors which should give pause for thought and stressed that consideration must be given to the reliability and credibility of the complainer. It was a case in which undoubtedly lies had been told, it was a case in which evidence conflicted, it was a case in which it was difficult to be *certain* about what had happened in the lane.

'We may never know the exact truth of what happened that night. Only two people know and each has given a different version. I put it to you that you should accept the version given by Mr Finlay that this was an act of intercourse previously agreed. If you are not prepared to accept his version, although I ask you to do so, I would put to you that there must be reasonable doubt in your minds as to Mrs Smith's version, and if so, I would ask you to give the benefit of the doubt to the accused.

'I ask you to bring in a verdict of not guilty or not proven.'

They patrolled the perimeter of the Great Hall pausing every few steps to examine the portraits of the old men of the law. Anything to pass the time. It crawled forward minute by minute. Claire had said the jury could be out for anything from a quarter of an hour to three hours. She had gone off with Donald after saying that she couldn't say what Liffey's chances were. Fifty-fifty perhaps. Which was what they were at the beginning. She sounded subdued. Mrs MacAteer of course had turned out to be a rotten witness, whereas on paper she had seemed to stand up. But she had been so obviously out to do Jinty Smith down that her evidence was bound to be suspect. 'You don't think they're going to send Liffey to jail?' said Eunice. 'If they find him guilty they will.' 'But they couldn't find him guilty.' 'They could.'

'Anyone with half an eye could see that Jinty Smith was lying,' Eunice was saying for at least the tenth time. 'Couldn't they, Sarah?' she demanded of her sister-in-law, for the others had stopped to examine a sculpture of Sir Walter Scott.

'All this business of telling lies or the truth is difficult,' murmured Isabel. 'Looks almost real, doesn't it?' she said, nodding at the statue. 'Very lifelike. You feel as if you could talk to him. Quite a different sort of man from the one sitting up in his monument in Princes Street all cold and distant like.'

Thomas regarded his mother with surprise. 'I always thought you thought that truth was cut and dried?' He remembered when she'd told him not to believe everything his grandfather said. 'He's an old phoney, Tommy, you must see him for what he is. He's got a fine imagination, that's the best way I can put it. He hasn't done the half of it. He was never shipwrecked in his life nor has he set foot on the Steppes of Russia nor seen a wolf. He was only ever in a ship the once and was so seasick on the crossing that when he stepped ashore at Leith he vowed he'd never lift his foot from dry land again. Your grandmother told me. He begged her to take him home.' Thomas had said, 'That doesn't matter.' Couldn't she see? It wasn't what his grandfather had done that was important but what he had to tell. Too much imagination could land you in trouble though, his mother had cautioned. And too little, he had rejoined. He had been fourteen then, had reached the age when he could think up smart rejoinders to his mother's – and sister's – remarks.

'I've never thought that, Tommy,' said Isabel Peterson, as she gazed at the face of Sir Walter. 'Not cut and dried. Only a fool could think that.'

The court bell rang when the jury had been out for almost two hours. They hurried back to their pews. Thomas longed for a long cool pint of beer to slake his dry throat.

Liffey did not glance at them as he came in. His head was slightly bowed now. The effort of remaining upright was beginning to tell. Being held in custody for two days was beginning to tell. Thomas thought of being locked up for four or five years. Then he thought of the open moors and the winter wind rippling through the coarse bleached grass. Eunice's adam's apple was moving rapidly up and down as if she was trying not to retch. Her mother patted her hand. In the Great Hall Isabel had said to Thomas that she thought the excitement was too much for Eunice. She had always tended to be excitable, ever since she was a young child. Thomas's mother had confided to him also that she was worried about Eunice altogether. What would she do when her job folded next month? They would have a hard time financially though Isabel felt confident about managing – hadn't she always? – but on top of that Eunice would be at a loose end. Hanging about. On holiday, for ever and ever, with no place to go to, but the pub.

The jury filed back in. Watch their faces, Claire had said. Their expressions seemed non-committal. Some of the jurors fiddled with objects, handbags, newspapers, others examined the judge's bench, only one or two looked at the accused.

'Ladies and gentlemen of the jury,' said the clerk of the court, 'who speaks for you?'

A woman rose. 'I do.'

'Have you reached a verdict?'

'We have.'

'What is your verdict?'

'Not guilty, my Lord.'

'He was lucky,' said Claire to Thomas. She was gathering up her notes from the table. 'I thought at best it was going to be not proven.'

'You cast lots of doubt, Claire,' said Donald. 'You reasoned well.'

Her guess was that it had been a close shave, a majority verdict of probably eight to seven; later she found that she had been right.

'Nothing wrong with a close shave,' said Donald, fingering his neck. 'One only needs to win by a point, isn't that right, Thomas? Victory is the thing! So, it's all over bar the shouting.'

There was quite a bit of noise, some of it almost akin to shouting, in the High Street pub where Liffey and friends gathered to celebrate. Thomas did not ask Claire and Donald to join them, assuming that Claire would rather not, so that when he saw them coming in, he hesitated, giving them time to retreat if they wished. Or if Claire wished. Thomas knew that Donald would enjoy the opportunity. But while they hesitated, Peter was already up on his feet and making his way over to them to invite them to join the party with Liffey following close on his heels.

'Come on and have a drink,' cried Liffey. 'You've earned it.'

Claire looked inquiringly at Thomas who raised his shoulders in a slight shrug. Beside him Eunice sniffed and said it was a pity Sarah couldn't have joined them.

'Go on over and meet the folks,' said Liffey and went to the bar. Peter shepherded Claire and Donald across to their table and Thomas rose to introduce his mother and his sister and Liffey's mother and Liffey's wife.

'It's a pleasure to meet you.' Donald leant over to shake the hands of Thomas's mother. 'I've heard a great deal about you.' He would prove to be to her liking, Thomas knew that. Every inch a gentleman. No side about him.

'You'll be pleased then?' Mrs Finlay eyed Claire.

'Oh yes. Are you?'

'Well of course! Mind you, we always kent our Laurence was innocent. Wouldn't hurt a fly would Laurence. Isn't that right, Tommy?'

Hurriedly, Jean cut in to thank Claire. Peter told her he thought she had been fantastic.

'I'll say!' Liffey had arrived with a trayful of drinks. Doubles for Claire and Donald for saving his life. 'When you think I might have been in the cooler for the next four years!' Eunice protested volubly. There had never been any chance of that! 'Well, here's to me,' said Liffey, 'the free man!'

'The free man,' said Eunice and drank deeply.

Thomas drank too but did not repeat the toast. When the two white-gloved policemen had stepped back from Liffey in the court and allowed him to go free, he had remembered Claire's words on the night she had learned the truth about Peter: at least you'll have Liffey off your back now. He did feel free from Liffey now, relatively anyway, in so far as one could ever disentangle oneself totally from the past. The past makes you what you are, his grandfather used to say. This was the premise on which he had reared Thomas. The real or imagined past, he might have added, but Thomas knew that the dividing line had blurred in the old man's mind long before he died. He *had* lived through a shipwreck, he *had* trembled when describing the ship juddering against the rocks and the green water pouring in, engulfing them, sucking them under; he *had* seen a pack of wolves, heard them baying and snapping, as they came towards him.

And it was not his grandfather's fault either that he had not married Jean: that was a white lie he had sheltered behind. From the moment she had told him she was pregnant he had resolved to get out of it. *I can't, I can't* . . . The words had hammered through his head. He had felt as if he were in a dark tunnel that could only get narrower and narrower the further he went in, and he knew that when he reached the end he would find the exit bricked up. He had gone to the old man knowing what he would say; he passed the buck. That was what he had done, and perhaps it was feeble of him, but he had been young and inadequate. A poor excuse, but all he had, and he did not even feel the need for an excuse any more. It was one of his multitude of sins that no longer pricked him.

He drank his beer and watched his son talking to Claire. He was a man who seemed determined to chart his own destiny, yet was caught up in the past too. And there was Liffey drawing his chair up close to Claire's on the other side and vying for her attention, still playing the game he and Thomas had started a long time ago.

I withdraw, said Thomas to himself. For him the game was ended.

He was first to notice Jinty's arrival. She entered on the arm of her friend and neighbour Mrs Black. She saw them at once and breaking from her friend so that she could navigate a path between the tables more easily, moved in on them like a sailing ship with all its sails billowing. Thomas leant forward to touch Liffey's arm and give him warning.

'Having a wee celebration, are you?' asked Jinty in her slow voice. She looked around the circle and let her gaze settle on Claire. 'You should be ashamed of yourself.'

'Look here!' said Donald, springing up.

'No, I won't look anywhere.' Jinty's voice was sharper now. She addressed the group again. 'I hope she's pleased with what she's done – getting a rapist off and her a woman herself!'

'You bloody bitch!' Liffey leapt to his feet and Thomas

followed, telling them both to cool it.

'Cool it, he says!' Jinty's eyes blazed. 'How would you like it if he was to rape your woman, Tommy Peterson?'

Liffey surged forward as if to seize her by the throat, Eunice let out a small scream. Thomas placed himself in front of Jinty. Donald told Liffey to sit down, he would handle this.

'You lawyers think you can handle anything,' said Jinty. 'You're all a bunch of crooks.'

Claire rose. 'I can take care of myself, Donald.' She faced Jinty. 'It was a fair trial.'

'With him lying?'

'Did you tell the truth? The whole truth?'

'You wouldn't believe me even if I did.'

'I can't believe you *just* because you're a woman.'

'You're only interested in getting paid, aren't you? You don't give a damn.'

'I think we should go,' said Donald, putting his hand under Claire's elbow.

'Come on, Jinty, please.' Mrs Black took Jinty's arm. 'Let's go somewhere else. There's plenty other pubs.'

'He was guilty I tell you,' Jinty called back as she allowed her friend to lead her away. 'Guilty.'

'Well,' said Liffey, 'I think we could all use another drink.'

But Claire was preparing to go, pulling on her coat, looking for her gloves. She was tired, she said, she wanted to go home. No wonder, said Donald; he would escort her. All the men were circling around her making similar offers. She said she would prefer them to stay and finish their party.

'I *have* to go,' said Donald, buttoning his overcoat. 'It's Amanda's Baroque night.'

'I'll walk with you too,' said Peter. 'I could do with some air.'

'It's time we were getting home and all, Eunice,' said Isabel.

'Us too,' said Jean, whose face was the colour of putty. 'The kids'll be home.'

'Don't everybody leave me,' wailed Liffey. 'Christ, I've just got my freedom. Tommy, you can't go. You can't run out on a mate . . .'

Thomas stayed.

'What *did* happen, Liffey?'

Liffey laughed. 'Look, I've already been through the third degree. Okay, so maybe I did more or less force her at the end but, hell, she was asking for it. She led me on deliberately, I tell you. She was out to pay me back. She let me kiss her and then when I was all worked up and raring to go she gave me a push and said, cool as a cucumber, "That's all you're getting!" I said, "Wait a minute now," and she started to scream blue murder and then I saw red. . . So, am I guilty or not, Professor?'

Frost sparkled on the fields, the sun was trying to emerge through the mist. Thomas did not hurtle the machine forward on this journey; he pedalled rhythmically, enjoying the cool air about his head, letting himself adjust to the morning. They had stayed up late last night, he and Claire and Peter, and drunk a lot of red wine. Peter had been talking of applying for a job in Scotland, he liked London well enough, he said, but when he came back across the border he felt a different sort of life come into him.

There was not much life about in the village as Thomas approached. Behind the half-steamed up café windows the tables were empty; the hairdresser was reading a magazine. Thomas rode on past to the wool shop. He dismounted and chained up his bicycle.

Marilyn was sitting behind the counter. She had the baby on her lap and a bruise on one cheek. She looked up when Thomas came in and said, 'Eunice has just gone out for a message. She'll not be long.'

He pulled up a chair and put out his finger for the baby to play with. The small fingers closed round his. He restrained himself from telling Marilyn that the child would grow up only too quickly, while he listened and nodded sympathetically to her lamenting broken nights and broken days. She was desperate for Gary to reach the next stage. The crying was getting on Billy's nerves. She touched her cheek.

'Having trouble again?'

'I should have listened to Sarah. I don't suppose – Well, I was wondering if she'd have me back?'

'She's sold the house. She's moving into a flat next week.'

'Would there be room there for us?'

Thomas said he would ask Sarah. He withdrew his finger and looked around the shop. The shelves were half empty, knitting patterns and travel brochures stood in stacks on the floor. Marilyn's gaze followed his.

'It's terrible, isn't it? It's going to break Eunice's heart when she has to give this place up. You could almost say it's her home.'

Thomas nodded. 'Being homeless is no fun.'

'Are you still stopping at your girlfriend's?'

The door jangled open, Eunice was back, bearing a carton of milk and a white paper bag. She went at once to fill the kettle, Marilyn got up. No, she wouldn't stay, Gary was becoming restless and would be due a feed shortly.

'Poor girl,' said Eunice, infusing the tea. 'There's nothing worse than a bad marriage. The things I could tell you that go on about here! I get it all over the counter.'

'Don't tell me,' said Thomas.

Eunice sighed. 'It's a pity about you and Sarah, Tommy.'

He said he had nothing more to say on that subject.

'You're aye looking for something over the rainbow, aren't you?'

'The curse of the Petersons.'

'Speak for yourself!'

'You dream too though don't you, Eunice?'

She turned away, embarrassed, to pour out the tea.

Thomas took a cup but shook his head at the vanilla slices. He was not hungry. He had come to talk to her and he must say what he had come to say before he lost his resolution.

'You know we've sold the house? We get the money next week. I want to give you my half.'

'Give me –?' Eunice's cup rattled in the saucer. She pushed it aside. 'Don't talk daft. Why should you?'

'It would be only fair. You had to sacrifice a lot for me. You didn't even have the choice.'

'That was years ago.'

'I want you to set yourself up in your own business, either here or in town. I *want* to give you the money, Eunice.'

Eunice got up and walked about the shop. She touched some of the balls of wool as if needing to reassure herself that this was not a daydream. She turned back to Thomas.

'But what about yourself? What would you do?'

He would manage. He might sell second-hand books by mail order from home; he could start by selling his own books, or most of them. 'I've got dozens I never even look at any more, they just sit collecting dust.'

'But would she want you cluttering up her place with them?'

'I'll take a room somewhere. Eunice, I mean it. I might even look for a job doing something entirely different. I like cooking.'

'Cooking? You couldn't –'

'I could. So what do you say?'

'A place of my own?' She picked up a ball of fluffy wool and squeezed it between her fingers. 'I could call it Miss Moneypenny's Boutique,' she said softly.

'You could call it anything you liked.'

And then her shoulders drooped and she let fall the flattened woollen ball. She reached for her cigarettes.

'It's no use, Tommy. Mother'd never let me.'

'It's got nothing to do with her. It's between you and me. I've had plenty of chances. I want to give you one.'

What price freedom? Oh well, it had had to be done. 'It's so good of you, Tommy,' Eunice had kept saying and he had kept denying it. 'It's not good of me at all. The money's yours. You helped pay for my education.'

He felt liberated though, as he cycled across the moors. Another burden had dropped off his back. He moved his shoulders up and down feeling the muscles ripple. He knew the price of this particular freedom of course, had ruminated long on it before making his offer to Eunice: it meant the curtailment of another, his freedom of choice when taking the next step in his life. It would soon be time to take that step, to make a fresh start, but not yet, not this morning.

The sun had come properly out, the mist had dispersed and the landscape stretched wide and open before him.

It was darkening as he returned to the city. The lights glistened in the filmy grey mist reminding him of the frost sparkling in

196

the mist in the morning. That early ride now seemed far away, on the other side of a divide. Then he hadn't known if he could do it – give away almost every penny he had.

He had cycled a long way during the day, along narrow roads that twisted and turned and plunged and rose, round the edges of placid reservoirs fringed with dark green trees, over dun-coloured moors where no trees grew. Carrying his machine up the steep stone steps, he felt tired, but agreeably so, in the way that one expected to be after fresh air and hard exercise. And after paying off a major debt.

On putting his key in the lock and pushing open the door, he sensed, rather than heard, what was going on. When he had closed the door he stayed still and listened.

The murmur of voices came from behind Claire's bedroom door. Thomas walked noisily into the sitting room and with hands that shook poured himself a brandy in a dirty glass. The glasses lay as they had been left the night before.

He stood at the window and drank and stared at the gardens across the street where Tasha used to come and keep her mournful watch. She was settling down now, adjusting, he supposed it would be called, giving weight to the view that human beings were infinitely adaptable.

'Thomas?'

He turned.

Claire was in the doorway, bare-footed, her body wrapped in a kimono of brilliant turquoise and orange which she held together with one hand.

'How long have you been in?'

'Does it matter?'

She sighed. 'I'm sorry.'

'You can hardly claim to have been caught unawares?'

She came into the room, poured herself a drink.

'So Peter's paying off old scores?' said Thomas.

'I don't believe so.' Her voice was sharp.

'He's a better age for you of course. A little young, though not much. But at least he's not middle-aged and clapped out. He's got prospects and a whole life ahead of him.'

'I've never given a thought to his prospects.'

'Why should you? You have your own.'

'Don't be bitter. Look, I know you must be feeling –'

'Surely I can be allowed a little bitterness? And I don't want your sympathy. Or understanding. It would choke me.' Thomas put down his empty glass. 'If you ask him to vacate your room for a few minutes I'll pack my stuff. I'll have to leave the books till later. I don't think there's much to be gained from him and me "talking things over". Or making efforts to be civilised. Whatever that's supposed to mean. Making no fuss perhaps. Well, I'm not going to make a fuss. There'd be nothing to be gained from it, would there?' As Claire went towards the door he said, 'I'd have gone if you asked me, I've always realised I was here on short-stay terms. You didn't have to do it this way.'

'I'm sorry,' she said again.

He stayed that night with an old friend from university days and in the morning rode out to Portobello. The contents of the house stood about as if they were lined up for an auction sale, a downmarket one. It was amazing how tacky the stuff was. Most of it had come out of sale rooms, before Tasha was born.

Thomas and Sarah drank coffee in the kitchen, the room which had retained the most semblance to normality. It was the room they had lived in when they had first moved in. Once Sarah said she wondered if she needed anything more than a kitchen and a bed recess.

Thomas told her about Claire and Peter. 'I can't say it was a total surprise. Maybe I even helped it along.' Sarah raised an eyebrow. He said, 'I did leave them on their own rather a lot.'

'I hope you weren't punishing yourself?'

'Who knows?' He didn't want to talk about it any more, he had sat up half the night boring his university friend into a stupor chewing over everybody's motives. 'What about you? What are you going to do?'

'Ah,' she said, 'I do have plans.'

'Tell me.'

'They involve you.' She got up to fetch the coffee pot and refill their mugs. 'Before I take up normal life again – whatever that is, or whatever I decide it's going to be – I am going to go on an extended journey with Aunt Edmée. I've kept back part of my house money, taken out a bigger mortgage. We're going to go half-way round the world, overland, that kind of thing, carrying water bags and tins of corned beef and pressed dates and we shall sleep in the Land Rover and live in villages, friendly ones of course. We might even write a book when we come back. We plan to be away for a year.'

'But what about Tasha?'

'That's where you come in. I feel I've done my bit . . .'

When he left Sarah he walked along the promenade pushing his bicycle. Another couple of years, and Tasha wouldn't need either of them, as Sarah had said, not full-time anyway, but for two years she would need at least one of them.

Thomas mounted his bicycle and, putting his back to the sea, rode off to meet his daughter coming out of school.